SECRET RAGE

SECRET
RAGE

BRENT PILKEY

ECW PRESS

Published by ECW Press
2120 Queen Street East, Suite 200, Toronto, Ontario, Canada M4E 1E2
416-694-3348 / info@ecwpress.com

LIBRARY AND ARCHIVES CANADA CATALOGUING IN PUBLICATION

Pilkey, Brent
Secret rage / Brent Pilkey.

ISBN 978-1-55022-965-3
also issued as: 978-1-77090-247-3 (PDF); 978-1-77090-248-0 (ePub)

I. Title.

PS8631.I479S42 2012   C813'.6   C2012-902701-4

Cover and text design: Tania Craan
Cover images: apartment building © Tania Craan; falling woman © Masterfile
Author photo: Andrew Hay
Printing: Trigraphik   1   2   3   4   5

The publication of *Secret Rage* has been generously supported by the Canada Council
for the Arts which last year invested $20.1 million in writing and publishing throughout
Canada, and by the Ontario Arts Council, an agency of the Government of Ontario. We
also acknowledge the financial support of the Government of Canada through the Canada
Book Fund for our publishing activities, and the contribution of the Government of
Ontario through the Ontario Book Publishing Tax Credit. The marketing of this book was
made possible with the support of the Ontario Media Development Corporation.

Printed and bound in Canada

For Mary, my love

*With you, I'm becoming the man
I've always wanted to be.*

I spent my fair share of time in old clothes down in 51 Division and provided backup on the odd hooker sweep. But to get the first hand experience of posing as a 51 hooker, I turned to two wonderful ladies and amazing cops. Thank you Trish and Julia for your stories and insights. I hope Jenny does you proud.

A man is three things:
what he thinks he is
what others think he is
what he really is
— ancient Druid triad

The heat hung lifeless in the night air, a soggy mass refusing to relinquish its oppressive grip on the city. Star Logan stood on her usual corner at Church Street and Gerrard Street East, praying for a cool breeze. The passing cars left the air oily with exhaust fumes and she stared enviously at the people comfortable in their air-conditioned havens.

She glanced at her watch. Not even midnight. Too early and too slow a night to call it quits. But damn, it was hot. Even in a halter and miniskirt, it was hot.

"Hey, Star. How you doing, girl?"

Star looked up and smiled. "I'm doing okay, Casey, but not much business tonight."

Casey Joanes, a veteran of the downtown Toronto streets, smiled back. "I hear that, sweetness. Hang in there a little longer. The bars'll be closing soon and there's always some poor white boy who needs to get laid."

Star laughed. Casey could always cheer her up, was always there to help. Star had met her almost a year ago, after taking her first working steps on the streets. The tall black working girl had taken the young blonde runaway under her wing and taught her how to survive. They worked the corner together, watching each other's back, enduring a life neither of them had chosen.

Star was checking the cars coming north on Church and spotted the cop car. "Casey, cops on the way. Better take off."

"Thanks, sweetness." Casey sauntered away, never glancing over her shoulder at the approaching cruiser. Star admired her nerve, doubting she herself could be so cool under the same circumstances, but Casey had taught her early on about the cops. If there was a warrant out for you or if you were breaking bail conditions, the last thing you wanted to do when the cops were around was give them the old nervous glance, no matter how casually you walked away. Might as well hold up a sign saying, "Wanted. Come and Arrest Me."

Star kept an eye on the cop car. The street lights kept reflecting off the windshield, stopping her from getting a look at the cops inside. It didn't take long to learn faces, to know which cops were only passing by for a free look and which ones were apt to check you out. She was clean right now, no wants, no bail conditions, so she didn't have to hide.

As the cop car drew closer, she turned and slowly walked up the sidewalk, swaying her hips provocatively. She had a good ass and knew it. The longer she could keep the cops' attention on her ass, the more time it gave Casey to duck out of sight.

From the corner of her eye she saw the cruiser slide up to the curb and stop. Oh well, time for name, date of birth and address.

"Excuse me, miss. Could I talk to you for a moment?"

The cop in the passenger seat had to be a rookie. He was young, probably not much older than Star herself, and she couldn't remember the last time a cop had said "Excuse me, miss" to her.

She took her time walking over to the car, a bemused smile on her lips as she watched the rookie try not to look at her legs below her short — very short — miniskirt. She squatted by the door and let her eyes slide shut as she luxuriated in the cold air spilling out of the open window.

"Hey, Star, how's business?"

Oh, shit. She forcibly fixed the smile on her face before opening her eyes.

The driver slouched in his seat, a hungry leer on his fat face. He was a slob in uniform whose gut had grown out to touch the steering wheel. He was a regular in the area, always cruising by the girls, asking for free flashes, and he could be quite the shit if he didn't get what he wanted. It was hard to do business with a police car sitting at your corner.

It could be worse, though. Star had never heard of him demanding free hand or blow jobs. She figured he had a small dick and didn't want the girls laughing at him behind his back. At least, no more than they did already.

"Business ain't too good, Sean." That was another thing. He insisted on the girls calling him by name. Star had asked Casey about that once and the older sex worker had laughed and replied, "So he knows what it's like to have a woman say his name, sweetness."

"You gotta show more skin, baby doll, if you want the tricks."

"I'm not likely to get any business with you sitting here." The clammy heat was making her irritable and she almost added *Boris* but pulled it back in time. Other, less lecherous cops had told the girls in the area that Boris was Sean's nickname but warned them against using it to his face; he hated it and was likely to go apeshit all over them.

Boris brayed an ugly laugh. "Hey, Star, show the rookie why you're called Star."

"That's all right, miss. You don't have to." The young cop shifted uncomfortably in his seat, his eyes darting nervously between her face and his hands entwined in his lap. She felt sorry for him, having to ride with a pig like Boris, but also wondered how he figured he was going to make it as a cop if he didn't have the balls to look a prostitute in the eyes.

Boris whacked the rookie in the shoulder. "Of course she has to. You ain't a fag, are you, Artie?" He hawked and spat on the car floor between his legs — Star was amazed he could still hit the floor past his belly — then wiped the spittle from his lips with a meaty hand. He glared at Star. "C'mon, Star. Show him. Or I might have to drink my coffee here. And every night after — I'm working in 52 now, baby doll, so you're in my division. You're going to be seeing a lot more of me." He had ugly little eyes. The kind of eyes that told Star if he was a trick he could be cruel.

She glanced at the rookie once more to see if he had the backbone to speak up, but he sat silently, a small boy playing at being a policeman. Disgusted by the pair of them, she stood up and turned her back to them. She obediently hiked her skirt up to her waist to reveal the shooting star tattooed on her left cheek.

"Now that's an ass! Nice thong! See ya, Star." Boris peeled away from the curb.

"Asshole." She adjusted her skirt and watched as the police car made a fast right without stopping for the red. She imagined she could hear the fat slob braying like a donkey as cars braked to avoid the cruiser.

That's it. I'm going home.

She slung her small purse over her shoulder and, cursing the fool who had made stiletto heels — it had to be a man — headed home. She and Casey shared an apartment up on Maitland, a quick walk from their corner. She wondered if Casey had seen Boris's cruiser as a warning and decided to pack it in for the night. If she was home they could share some wine and the weed Star had taken as payment for a quick hand job.

She had made it less than a block when an old Honda eased up beside her. She glanced at the car and thought about ignoring the open passenger window but decided against it. It had been a slow night and she could use the cash one more trick would bring. She fluffed her shoulder-length blond hair and strolled over.

"Hi. Looking for a date?" Leaning into the open window, she gave the driver an eyeful of cleavage while she checked him out.

The first rule of survival Casey had taught Star was never — never! — get into a john's car without examining the situation first. Look for weapons, look for people hiding in the back seat, learn to read people and if anything didn't feel right, walk away. Fuck the money and walk away. Tricks are like streetcars, Casey said. Another one will be along in a few minutes.

Star had gotten good at reading johns and had only a few bad dates in her time. Nothing serious. One look at this guy and she knew his story. He was young, her age, and he wore a shapeless T-shirt, but his forearms were thick with muscle. His hair was a dull brown and it looked like he had cut it himself, hacked short and uneven. Not bad looking but his jaw was too heavy for her liking. Not that it mattered; she wasn't going to be jerking off his chin.

She figured him for a jock, maybe a university kid who couldn't get a date for the night or had one but she didn't put out. *Young and with a bad case of blue balls.* She'd be on her way home in five minutes.

The guy opened his mouth to answer her but choked on his words. Star smiled. Probably his first time with a working girl. She opened the door and slid into the passenger seat.

"How much you got, honey?"

"A hundred," he managed, his voice barely above a whisper. He glanced at her and then away. His hands anxiously gripped the steering wheel.

"Well, hon, a hundred'll get you the best blow job you've ever had." She put a hand on his thigh and he jumped. "Relax, hon. You interested?" He swallowed and jerked his head in a frantic nod. "Then turn up the AC, hon, and let's get going."

Star had a hotel room where she normally took her tricks but this one looked like he'd come before she got his zipper down so she opted to stay in the car. Rolling up the window to take full advantage of the AC, she directed him to a laneway off Gerrard and had him park close to the street but out of sight.

"Business before pleasure, hon. You'll enjoy it more if we get the money out of the way first."

Rule number two: always get the money first.

He reached into his jeans with a trembling hand and pulled out two crumpled fifties. The bills disappeared professionally into Star's purse. He was back to gripping the wheel and staring out the windshield. Poor guy. Some cocktease of a bitch had probably stuck him for dinner and a movie and left him hanging.

"What's your name?" She hardly ever asked a john his name but this one was so pathetically nervous she felt sorry for him.

"T — ah, Tim. Why?" He looked startled she had asked but at least he was looking at her.

Star smiled. If he didn't want to use his real name, Tim was fine by her. "I like you, Tim. I want to give you a little extra." Whether it was the long, slow night or a bad feeling left over from Boris's visit, she couldn't say, but she wanted this john to really enjoy himself and maybe she could have a bit of fun herself.

She popped the clasp on her halter and let it slip down her arms. Her nipples puckered in the car's cold air. She shook her breasts at him and smiled. "Do you like them?"

He could only stare and nod. Despite the cold air blowing through the vents, sweat beaded his brow.

Star snuggled into him. She could feel the muscles in his arm where her breasts pressed up against it. She slid her hand across his chest and he flinched. Hard muscle, not huge like a bodybuilder but definitely a jock. Her hand slid lower. She could feel his stomach muscles quivering under her touch.

"Relax, hon. Lie back and let Star take care of you." Her fingers expertly popped the button on his jeans and inched the zipper down. "You got something in there for me, Tim? Something big and hard?"

His elbow smashed into her jaw, rocking her back in the seat. Pain exploded in her mouth and she tasted blood. The thought that Casey would be very disappointed in her judgement flashed through her mind before the john rammed his fist into her nose. She felt and heard her nose break. All thoughts of Casey vanished in a wild surge of panic.

Oh my God, he's going to kill me!

She opened her mouth to scream but he was on her, a powerful hand clamping shut her throat, cutting off her voice and air. He dragged her close, close enough to kiss.

"You're a fucking whore," he snarled at her and she could hear the hate in his words as he spat his anger in her face.

She went for his eyes, gouging flesh. He roared and shoved her away. Her head smacked against the passenger window, shattering stars across her vision. Dazed, half-blinded by pain, she groped for the door handle. If she could get out she could run, reach the street and people. Safety was there. All she had to do was open the door.

Her fingers found the handle. Pulled. The door jerked open just as strong fingers dug into her hair, dragging her back. She tried to turn, to go for his eyes again, but he smashed her head against the dash. Again. And again.

He flung her back into the seat, her consciousness all but gone.

"Fucking whore."

She barely heard his words through the drumming in her ears. And the pain, so much pain. Better yet to just let go, sink into the darkness, away from the pain. Escape. But a part of her wouldn't let her escape, the part that stayed free while johns used her body, distanced her from the daily filth, forced her to stay awake. To survive.

She knew if she continued to fight back she would die so she sagged in the seat, feigning an unconsciousness that was so tantalizingly close. She lay there as rough hands pushed at her skirt. She did nothing as they ripped her underwear. She survived as fresh pain tore through her.

Dimly, she heard someone crying.

Thursday, 19 July
1200 hours

The tennis ball hit the ground with a loud *thwump* and rebounded high into the air. The young German shepherd leapt and deftly snatched the ball on the fly before landing as nimbly as a cat. A seventy-pound cat.

"Good catch, Justice! Bring the ball here."

Justice darted across the freshly mown grass of the hydro field, apparently oblivious to the heat. Jack Warren watched his dog sprinting beneath the cloudless sky and shook his head in quiet disbelief.

That dog would stay in a sauna if it meant playing with tennis balls.

"Good boy," Jack praised as Justice skidded to a halt in front of him. "Drop the ball."

Justice obediently spat the ball out and backed up a few steps, tail wagging ferociously. He barked impatiently as if to say, *Well, hit the damn thing already!*

It was Jack's turn to obey and he let the ball fly, putting as much muscle into the swing of the tennis racket as he could. Justice was off like a bullet, unerringly chasing down the arc of the ball. For a second Jack thought the dog would overshoot, but Justice knew what he was doing and neatly snagged the ball before it hit the ground, like a talented receiver plucking a perfectly placed football over his shoulder.

"That's a good idea, using the tennis racket."

Jack found an older gentleman standing next to him with an equally elderly and rather pot-bellied beagle sitting patiently in the man's shadow.

"Had no choice," Jack admitted. "My arm got tired from throwing the balls before he did. Case in point." Justice was back and eager to fly. Jack fired off another high-arcing lob.

"My Jasper could only dream of ever running that fast." The man bent down and gave Jasper an affectionate pat as if to forgive him for his lack of speed. "How old is your dog?"

"Eighteen months, two years. Somewhere around there. Not really sure. I only got him a few months ago and he was so malnourished and dehydrated that my vet had a hard time estimating his age."

"Well, he seems to have recovered splendidly."

"He sure has." Jack knelt to retrieve the ball Justice had just dropped and paused to run his hand over the glossy black and tan coat. It was almost impossible to believe that this was the same dog he had pulled off the streets back in March. Malnourished was an understatement. Justice had been emaciated, every rib showing painfully through his matted, filthy fur. Now, not quite four months later, he was a tennis-ball- and squirrel-chasing speed demon. And Jack's best friend.

"I sincerely hope whoever had him prior to you was appropriately reprimanded for mistreating him," Jasper's owner stated as he watched Justice snag the ball again. Jasper himself was less than impressed and had gone to sleep in his master's shade.

"I believe he was," Jack assured the man, thinking back to the beating he and Justice had laid on Joey Horner down in Moss Park. "I doubt he'll ever own a dog again." *If he values his life, he won't.*

"Well, it's time for Jasper and I to seek shelter from this heat. Come on, old man, wake up."

Jack watched Jasper waddle away with his owner, a happy grin playing about his lips. The close bond between them was evident as the man automatically shortened his steps to accommodate Jasper's squat legs and swaying belly. Jack smiled down at Justice who, despite heavy panting and a drooling tongue, was eager to keep playing.

"C'mon, buddy. Time for your dad to go to work."

Connor Lee was bored.

"Bored, boring, all fucking a-bored."

At least he had a scout car to sit in, although the labouring air conditioner was barely keeping ahead of the sauna effect the summer sun was having on the car. He had the dial cranked to Max and the output was cool at best.

"Fuck, I've gotten better chills from ex-girlfriends."

Guarding a crime scene — *homicide, my ass* — when the rest of the platoon was out chasing criminals and getting up to shit was not what Connor had pictured himself doing when he had transferred into 51 Division. His old division, 53, shared the radio band with its neighbouring division to the south and for years Connor had listened to the 51 coppers racing around, responding to gun calls, fights, foot pursuits. All the fun, exciting stuff everyone had in mind when they first put on the uniform.

So here he sat, out front of 285 Shuter Street, to make sure no one was stupid enough to walk under the yellow police tape and over any possible evidence that might be lying on the ground.

"This is a waste of time," he told himself, not for the first time. "If there's any evidence it's up in the apartment where the fall started. Not down here where it ended."

The police tape with its stern *POLICE LINE DO NOT CROSS* stretched across the north side of the apartment building and took up a good chunk of the parking lot. Connor had to hand it to whoever on day shift had taped off the scene: he had certainly gone for big is better. The supposed crime scene went the length of the building from the front doors to the west end and sprawled across an easy fifty feet of parking lot, the plastic tape looped around trees and light poles, sagging in the heat.

Connor would have gone smaller; the only things of interest down here were the dark blotches left behind on the sidewalk when the body had been hauled away.

Probably had to use a spatula. Connor sipped on his iced coffee. Seven floors wasn't all that high, but it was most certainly high enough when landing on concrete. *Besides, it isn't the fall that kills you, it's the sudden stop at the end.*

Why they were wasting all this time on a simple suicide was beyond him. And a crack whore to boot. So what if some neighbour thought he might have heard an argument just before the girl went splat.

"Probably jumped 'cause her AC quit." Connor took another sip of his drink.

Only four more hours before he was relieved at the shift's midway point. "Fuuuuck me," he groaned. Why did he leave 53? If he had been guarding a scene up there, there would have at least been some scenery.

"Scenery at the scene," he chuckled, congratulating himself on his wit. As far as Connor could tell, the attractive people lived in 53, the average ones filled out the rest of the city and the butt-ugly ones lived in 51. No wonder the division was called Toronto's toilet.

"And here comes one now."

A local was strolling over to the cop car on bow-legged limbs. Connor estimated his age somewhere between a bad-looking fifty and a good-looking ninety.

Keep going, keep going, Connor chanted silently, but the man had that fixed look in his eyes that all cops learned to loathe, the "I have a theory" look, the look of vast knowledge accumulated via hours of watching CSI. Sure enough, the man stopped beside Connor's window.

Connor considered not rolling down the window but figured the old fart would just stand there until he had an opportunity to solve the crime. Sighing, Connor lowered the window.

"Help you, sir?" he asked, purposely stressing the lack of enthusiasm. *Get the hint, go away.*

"What happened here, officer?" The man's voice was a gravelly mix of beer and cigarettes.

Keeping his tone flat, Connor simply said, "Homicide."

"Homicide. Hm." The man surveyed the scene with a critical, knowing eye. "So," he asked. "Anyone get hurt?"

"No, ma'am," Jack patiently explained for the fifth time, shifting the phone to his other ear. "I understand the store delivered your new fridge with the door hinged on the wrong side but that's not a police matter."

He stared wistfully past the police station's front desk as the woman on the line insisted, yet again, that having a defective appliance forced upon her was indeed a police matter. A matter of utter urgency.

Jack sighed. If he sat up straight in his chair and craned his neck, he could peer down the short flight of steps leading to the front doors and catch a small glimpse of daylight.

Only another four hours to go. Fuck me.

A shadow fell across Jack's desk. He looked up at a cop who was vaguely familiar and had an amused grin on his face.

"Ma'am, I have to go," Jack interrupted, cutting off the woman's rambling tirade. "All I can say is that in the future don't let the delivery men leave without first inspecting whatever it is they're delivering. Call the store and complain to them." He hung up and let his head droop tiredly, pausing to enjoy the blessed silence.

"Don't you just love dealing with the public?"

"Is there a full moon tonight? It feels like I'm drowning in nuts today." Jack sighed again and leaned back in his chair, gesturing at the phone. "Last month she called 911 because her toilet was clogged. Unfortunately, the idiot copper who attended made the mistake of unclogging it instead of getting her to call the superintendent and now she calls all the time." Jack squinted up at the cop. "It wasn't you, was it? If it was, I'm giving her your cell phone number."

"Do I look like the kind of guy who'd root around in some dirty toilet?" The cop laughed, professing his innocence with his hands splayed across his chest. He extended a hand. "You're Warren, right? Connor Lee, nice to meet you." They shook and Connor propped a hip on Jack's desk.

Connor looked to be about Jack's age, pushing the big 3-0, with a trim build and wavy black hair that was just long enough to get him in trouble if he ran across the wrong sergeant. He had an infectious smile and a slight Asian cast to his tanned features that Jack figured his wife would describe as "prettily handsome."

"You just transferred in, didn't you?" Jack had seen him around the station last week on day shift but had never had the opportunity to introduce himself.

Connor bobbed his head. "Yup. Came in from 53. Thought I was going to spend most of today guarding that stupid jumper scene but they closed it up early."

"Lucky you. What brought you to our fair lands?" 51 was notorious as the Service's penalty box and other divisions frequently used it as a dumping ground for their problem officers. The irony was, Jack had yet to meet a copper sent to 51 against his or her will who didn't end up loving it in the city's smallest yet busiest division.

"Just needed a change of scenery," Connor explained rather vaguely.

Dumped in the penalty box, you mean. Jack could relate.

"So, when are they going to let you back on the road?"

"Fucked if I know," Jack said, shaking his head. "I've been riding this desk since the end of March. The siu is being its usually thorough and slow-moving self."

But things could have been a lot worse. He could have been suspended, going stir-crazy at home while the Special Investigations Unit tried to decide whether to charge him with murder for throwing Randall Kayne off a bridge. Well, only technically speaking. Was it Jack's fault the boarding on the bridge gave way when he threw Kayne against it?

I'm sure they think so. Now they just have to find a way to prove it.

Randall Kayne had been a crackhead maniac running around the division carving big Ks in people's foreheads with a piece of slate. He wanted to prove he was the baddest fucker in town and thought slicing up a cop would cement his rep. Unfortunately for Kayne, he ended up splattered all over the Rosedale Valley Road. Since then, Jack had been riding a desk, waiting to see if he was going to jail or not.

Stress? Juuuuust a little bit.

"They've probably got it in for you ever since they couldn't do you for shooting that guy in your house."

"Who knows? I'd just like to go a year without having them in my life."

Connor laughed. "Well, it'll be good to have the Reaper back out on the road."

Did I hear that right? "The what?"

"That's what they're calling you."

"Who's calling me what?"

"The Reaper," Connor repeated. "The assholes on the streets are calling you that 'cause everyone who goes up against you ends up dead."

"Oh, great." The criminals, like their badge-wearing counterparts, loved nicknames. Again like cops, some handles were given in honour, some in disrespect. Jack wasn't sure which one this was. "Let's see if we can keep that from the SIU, shall we?"

A timid voice spoke up from the front counter. "Excuse me, I need some help."

A bespectacled man barely tall enough to see over the counter was peering pathetically at the officers.

Jack made to get up but Connor waved him back to his seat. "I've got this." He walked briskly to the counter. "How can I help you, sir?"

Connor was standing off to the side, so Jack was able to see the little man's eyes darting about nervously. Jack was reminded of a squirrel twitching at the side of a road as it tried to find the courage to plunge into traffic. Behind the glasses, dark, heavy bags sagged below the man's eyes. His hair was a rumpled mess and even though Jack couldn't see the man's hands, he was sure they were anxiously knotting themselves together.

Jack's curiosity was piqued and he joined Connor.

"How can I help you, sir?" Connor repeated.

The man checked behind himself then leaned in to whisper,

"Is it safe to talk here?"

Connor nodded seriously. "Absolutely. We sweep for bugs every day."

The man looked at Connor, confusion clear on his face. "I don't mind bugs. I have them in my apartment. But bugs aren't the problem," he assured the officers as both of them instinctively shifted back, putting a bit more space between them and this decidedly odd walk-in.

"I'm glad you're happy with the bugs, sir," Connor told him. "So what's the problem, then?"

Another glance over the shoulder, then, "I've been cursed."

"Cursed?" Connor echoed.

"As in someone's put a curse on you?" Jack asked, trying to clarify.

"Exactly. Exactly that," the man confirmed, yet there was a hesitant expression on his face, as if he had confessed this before and his plea for help had been rejected.

Well, that's a new one.

"Are you sure it's a curse and not a hex?" Connor wanted to know.

A struggle of emotions ran across the man's features. Elated relief at being believed and simple puzzlement. Bafflement won out. "What's the difference?"

"It's a matter of severity, really," Connor explained patiently. "A curse is much stronger than a hex and therefore much more difficult to cast. A curse requires a very talented and powerful practitioner of black magic and they're incredibly expensive. Hexes, on the other hand, are much simpler and cheaper. It's like the difference between the common cold and lung cancer. My guess is that you've been hexed, not cursed."

"How can I be sure?" the small man inquired breathlessly, eyes fixated on his newest saviour.

Jack was staring as well, awed by Connor's seriousness.

"Well, I'm not feeling a cursed emanation off you and

anyone who's been cursed, it hangs off them like a neon sign."

Jack surreptitiously slid a hand over his mouth to stifle a giggle.

But Connor wasn't finished. "Has anyone taken some of your blood lately? And not just a little bit with a needle. I mean like draining a bucketful from you."

"No, never."

"Do you get a pain behind your eyes when you pee?"

This time the giggle couldn't be contained and Jack had to turn away.

Peeing obviously didn't give the man a headache as Connor announced, "Then you're in luck, my friend. You have a hex, not a curse."

"How do I get rid of it?" A very serious question.

"You need to find someone who practices white magic and they can break the hex in no time."

"Can you do it?" The question was asked hopefully.

"Oh, no, not me. I'm not a practitioner. I just have some experience in the field."

Jack bit down on the inside of his lips to keep from laughing.

And still, Connor wasn't done. "But if you head over to the Church and Wellesley area and ask around, I'm sure you'll find someone who can help you out."

"Thank you!" From the sound of it, the man all but flew out of the station.

Jack wiped a tear from his eye. "You know a lot about magic, do you?"

"Not a fucking thing," Connor admitted cheerfully. "I may be new to 51, but I know where Gaytown is. Hey, if you can't have fun with the nuts, what's the use of being a cop?"

He sat up in bed, squinting against the bright afternoon sunlight. The AC unit chugged asthmatically in the window, sucking electricity but doing little for the heat in the bedroom. He scrubbed his face and winced, the knuckles of his left hand protesting the movement.

"Son of a bitch," he swore as he inspected the hand. The knuckles weren't bruised but when compared to his other hand, they were slightly swollen. "Son of a bitch," he repeated. "Should've slept with an ice pack on it."

He remembered little of last night. He could recall stopping for the whore and parking in the alley. After that, his recollection became fuzzy, blurred by a haze of red. How badly had he beaten her? Judging from the tenderness of his hand, pretty bad, but it didn't matter. He'd only given her what she deserved, what they all deserved.

"Lying, useless whores. If not for them, my . . ." He hesitated, forcing his thoughts back into place. "My sister would still be alive," he finished.

Other than his hand — and it was nothing a few Tylenol with codeine couldn't fix — he was feeling pretty good. A decent sleep could do wonders. Yeah, he felt a little groggy from the pills but after a night like yesterday he needed the drugs to keep the dreams away. And he always dreamed after . . .

After what?

"After losing my cool, that's all." He swung his legs out of bed and stretched, luxuriating in the crack of his spine. "Besides, it wasn't my fault. If Sherry hadn't —" He stopped again, his arms held out like he was accepting applause. Or waiting to be crucified.

If Sherry hadn't what?

If you leave me, I'll tell!

He clamped his eyes shut. "It was her fault, her fault, her fault," he intoned, a mantra to protect him from the memories. "If she'd just left me alone. I tried to tell her it wouldn't work, couldn't work, but she just kept pushing.

"Fuck this," he declared. He jumped to his feet and headed for the bathroom. He inspected his reflection approvingly. True, his cheeks were looking somewhat sunken but that was to be expected if he kept his body-fat level low. He clenched his teeth, liking his heavy, strong jawline. That was good. Twisting, he examined his profile, fingering the bones of his cheeks and brow. No problem there. Even the scratches near his one eye were fading. The whore hadn't raked him as deeply as he feared.

"Looking good."

He stepped back from the mirror and flexed his arms. He had to lean side to side in the cramped bathroom to view each arm. His biceps knotted up dramatically, looking like hardballs implanted under the layer of skin.

Satisfied, he selected a vial and new syringe from his dwindling supply. *Almost time to restock.* Using a nail file, he scored the glass around the vial's thin neck then snapped the top off. He dipped the needle into the thick, gold-tinged fluid and patiently drew it into the syringe.

He shook out his arm to loosen the shoulder muscles then positioned the needle over the thickest part of his deltoid. Damn, he hated this part. He knew guys who could jam a needle in themselves as easily as clicking a pen, but he never could.

You'd think it'd get easier after all this time.

He averted his eyes as he began to exert a slow, building pressure on the needle. There was a moment's resistance then a quick ripping sensation as the tip jabbed through the skin. He sank the needle in until its mounting butted up against his flesh. He depressed the plunger and imagined — he knew this was all in his head but, damn, how he loved it — new strength and vigour coursing through his muscles.

Once it was empty, he withdrew the needle. *Always easier coming out than going in.* He capped the syringe and stored it with the other used ones to be properly disposed of later. The vial went into the garbage.

He checked his watch. Plenty of time to return Greg's car

and for his workout before heading to the club. Damn, he was feeling good. Now, if only his knuckles would stop hurting.

The phone rang impatiently, demanding attention.

"Can't you be quiet for just a few minutes?" Jack pleaded. Anyone who thought working the front desk at a police station was an easy go had never been part of the inside crew at 51 in the summer. Besides handling the phones and any complaints that walked in the front door — it seemed everyone and his family had decided it was a nice day for a stroll to the cop shop — Jack had also been helping out in the booking hall and print room due to the high numbers of arrests coming in. Drunks, crackheads, drunks, dealers and more crackheads, drunks, the occasional wife beater and the usual assortment of criminal low-lifes had poured in through the booking hall in a seemingly endless flood. And still more drunks. It was summertime in the shithole of the city and business was up.

Jack answered the phone. "51 Division, Constable Warren."

"Dude, you sound like shit."

"Nice to talk to you, too, fuckhead," Jack said with a smile.

Manny laughed. "I've been listening to 51 and it sounds like it's going nuts, man."

"And that's just inside the station," Jack confirmed. "How you doing, Manny? Or did you just call to rub in the fact that you actually have time to make a personal call?"

"Hey, man, we move at a much slower yet meticulous pace up here at Ident."

"It's 'we,' is it? You're one of them now?"

"Dude, it's awesome up here!"

Not quite six months ago, B platoon had lost its long-time leader to retirement and a six-figure position at a bank's fraud department. Rourke had been an easygoing staff sergeant who always looked after his officers and when he pulled the plug, the shift had lost a good friend. And in return, they had received

Staff Sergeant Greene, a colossal prick with an equally offen-sive handlebar moustache. Waxed, of course. It reminded Jack of Dustin Hoffman in *Hook*.

Greene was the type of person who didn't get along with people all that well and he had immediately set his sights on Jack's friend and partner. William "Manny" Armsman was the kind of copper who spoke his mind, even when he shouldn't, and that had not sat well with the new staff, whose idea of com-promise was . . . Well, Jack wasn't sure what it was, or even if Greene knew the meaning of the word.

Greene had threatened Manny with a six-month lateral to Forensic Identification Services, figuring the patience and concentration required for the exacting, detail-oriented work would drive Manny — whom Jack often described as a puppy with ADD — insane. Two weeks ago, the sword dangling over Manny's head had finally fallen and he had found himself the newest member of FIS.

"It's awesome?" Jack asked, not sure he had heard Manny correctly. Manny, who had been scared shitless of going to Ident, loving it?

"Dude, the things they can do! You know how I always bitched about how long it took for them to clear a homicide scene?"

"Don't we all."

"But now I understand why it takes them so long. Jack, these are the guys that solve the crimes. It's so freaking cool."

Jack had to laugh. Manny, an Ident geek. "So, you thinking of staying?"

"Maybe," he said seriously. "Right now they've got me doing the smaller stuff like I did back in the division but sometimes they let me tag along on the big scenes. We're working that machete homicide over in 52 right now. If I want to stay when I'm done my lateral, they'll send me to Ottawa for the Ident course. You should come over, Jack. It's cool."

"No thanks," Jack said quickly, not needing time to think about it. He'd seen and waited through what Manny used to do as a Scenes of Crime Officer — or SOCO for short — and dusting for fingerprints wasn't high on Jack's job list. Unless, of course, everything got analyzed and solved as quickly as it did on CSI.

"You should see the apartment we're in. Someone took a machete to this guy's head and hacked it apart. I can't believe the amount of blood. It looks like someone tried to paint the room red. It's so cool."

"You called to brighten up my day with that?"

"Nah, dude. We're taking a break and I thought I'd call to say congratulations."

Perplexed, Jack asked, "Congratulations? For what?"

"'Cause the SIU cleared you, dude. What else?"

"What are you talking about, Manny? I haven't been cleared yet."

"Yes, you have," Manny argued, and the gravity of his voice told Jack this was no joke. "Hang on, it's in the paper." Static-like paper rustling filled the phone, then, "Here it is. 'SIU clears officer in bridge death,'" Manny quoted.

"Get the fuck out," Jack breathed. "Don't be joking, Manny, not about that."

"Dude, I'm serious." Paper flapped in Jack's ear again, and he could picture Manny snapping the paper straight in his hands. "'The Director of the SIU,'" he read, "'said, "In my view, there are no reasonable grounds to believe that the subject officer"' — that's you, dude — "'committed a criminal offence in relation to the death of Mr. Kayne. Mr. Kayne fell to his death while struggling with the subject officer, who was attempting to arrest him. At this time, no criminal charges will be laid."' See, dude? You're free!"

"I like how he tacks on the 'at this time' bit. Nice."

"Whatever, dude. It's over. Congratulations."

Jack was stunned, speechless. It was over?

"Didn't anyone call you? Dude, I'm not the first, am I?"

"You're the first, Manny. Thanks, but I'm going to let you go; I want to call the Association and my lawyer. Just to be sure."

"No problem, dude. Do what you have to do. I'll head back to my homicide. Congratulations again, buddy."

Jack hung up, smiling. Only Manny could sound like a kid on Christmas morning when he was heading back to a decapitated body. Jack paused in the middle of punching in his lawyer's number — after months of dealing with the SIU, he had the number memorized — thinking he should phone and tell Karen. His wife should be the first he shared the news with. But then again, it was almost nine, and he'd be off duty soon.

I'll tell Karen in person. It'll be the first bit of good news in a long while.

Keeping an eye on the clock, Jack dialed his lawyer.

Jack slid open the kitchen door and stepped out onto the deck. Justice bounded up the stairs from the lower level to head-butt Jack in the groin.

"Thanks, big guy." Jack scratched behind Justice's ears then nudged him aside with a knee. "Downstairs," he commanded and the shepherd dutifully trotted down the steps with Jack following.

The deck, a sprawling two-tier construct, was Jack's pride. The lower level boasted an enclosed hot tub and enough space for a half dozen people to lie out in the sun. Right now, with the sun gone and the first stars of the night sprinkled across the darkening sky, Karen and Justice had the deck to themselves. The dog flopped down next to where she was stretched out on a lounger and propped his chin on the chair next to her leg. She paid him no attention.

Jack paused at the top of the stairs to admire the picture before him. Karen was wearing denim cut-offs, leaving her shapely runner's legs bare to the warm night air. Her long blond hair trailed lazily over an old T-shirt.

God, she's beautiful; his heart did its usual pleasant little stagger-step. He could never comprehend how a front-line grunt wound up married to such an amazing woman. All the tension and unspoken pain that had haunted the house for the last four months dwindled away to nothing at the sight of his wife lying out in the gentle moonlight.

He tramped down the stairs. "Hi, hon."

"Hi."

That sounded kind of frosty. "Anything wrong?"

"How was your day? Anything happen at work?" she asked in lieu of answering.

Something is definitely wrong. He dragged over a chair to sit next to her, Justice between them. Sitting down, he wracked his brains trying to figure out what could be the source of this icy greeting. Everything had seemed fine when he left for work this afternoon, or as fine as it could be.

"Um, nothing out of the ordinary." Now was probably not a good time to attempt to lighten the mood by relating the tale of the cursed complainant. "I did get some good news, though. Very good, in fact."

"And?" She cocked an eyebrow at him, her eyes as chilled as her tone.

What the fuck? "I found out the SIU cleared me," he bluntly said. He'd planned on telling her the whole story of Manny calling, but if she wanted to be terse then he'd give it right back.

"I know."

"I guess —" *congratulations aren't forthcoming, then*, he almost said but bit off the words in time. It seemed Karen was spoiling for a fight, but it wasn't in him tonight; there'd been too many arguments, too many harsh words lately.

"You guess what?" She shifted onto her side to face him directly, arms crossed angrily beneath her breasts. The motion pushed her breasts up tight against the shirt. Braless, her nipples were clearly visible beneath the thin material. She knew where he was looking and glared at him, snapping, "You guess what?"

He dropped his eyes, feeling like a schoolboy caught sneaking a peek, as if he hadn't seen her breasts, held and stroked them thousands of times before. Jack felt his own anger stirring, rising in response to Karen's confrontational attitude. He pushed it down but not without effort.

"Nothing," he muttered. With his anger on leash, for now — *Please, God, don't let me lose my temper* — he felt crushed, deflated at Karen's hostility. The elation he'd been riding since his lawyer had confirmed the SIU's announcement was dead. Nothing but squashed roadkill. *Fuck.*

"When did you find out?" he asked, still staring at his hands.

"Mom called me just after you left for work. She read it in the paper." His eyes cut to her. "You knew all afternoon and didn't call me?"

She jerked back at his hard tone then visibly steeled herself. "I was wondering when you were going to bother calling me. But I guess calling your wife comes a distant fucking second to sharing the news with all your cop buddies."

Justice whined beneath the exchange of bitter words and sat up between their chairs, his ears flicking nervously.

"Actually," he informed her, "I didn't find out until —" he glanced at his watch "— a little over an hour ago. Manny called to congratulate me. It would've been nice to hear it earlier; I could've buggered off early and we could've gone out for a celebratory dinner." *And the way this is going, I should have taken up the shift's offer of wings.*

"To celebrate what, Jack?"

"Celebrate what?" he asked, perplexed. "How about the SIU not charging me with murder or manslaughter."

"You mean celebrate going back on the road."

Ah, now I see. "That's why you're mad? Because I'm going to get out from behind the front desk?"

"And what's going to happen this time, Jack? Another dead partner?"

Jack flinched. Karen had cut him with that one. "Karen, that's —"

She pushed on, ignoring his words, shoving the knife ever deeper. "How many more scars, Jack? How long do you expect me to sit here and wait for someone to come and tell me you're dead? Or you've killed someone else? That asshole broke into our house because of you and you shot him in my home! In my home!"

Your home? "What do you want me to do, Karen? Quit? Is that what you and your mother want, for me to quit? In case you forgot, I was a cop when we met and I was still a cop when we got married. It's what I do. It's who I am. And no amount of conniving and manipulating by you or your mother is going to change that. I'm happy as a cop. Don't you want me to be happy, Karen?"

"I want you to be alive!" she screamed.

"I'm not going to die. I have a greater chance of being killed driving to work than I do on the road."

"That's bullshit and you know it." She jabbed an angry finger at his shoulder, eyebrow and neck. "Any of those could have killed you."

The skin of his neck was clear, but the other two bore nasty, permanent testimonials to how bad things could get in a copper's life. He was lucky the cut to his neck hadn't been deep enough to scar, but then, if it had been any deeper, he probably wouldn't be sitting here and Karen would have gotten that solemn visit she feared so much.

"But they didn't, Kare," he said, softening his tone and reaching for her hands. She snatched them out of his reach and crossed her arms once again, practically clutching herself, shutting him out completely.

"It doesn't matter; you're dying anyway. That place is killing you, a little bit every day."

"Come on, Karen. That's ridiculous."

"Is it? You've got a temper now, Jack. You never used to. You work out all the time. You're obsessed with getting bigger. You swear, you're moody, you spend more time with other cops than you do with me."

If this is what I have to look forward to at home, who'd blame me?

"You're not the man I married."

Justice whined again, louder this time. He nudged Jack's fingers with his nose, trying to flip the hand onto his head. Jack stroked Justice's head and strong neck, letting the feel of the velvety fur soften his anger.

But Karen had no outlet other than Jack and she wasn't finished. "And *that dog.* I can't believe you brought it home. Neither can my mother."

"I really don't care what your mother thinks, Karen. If I hadn't rescued him, he'd be dead and after the hell he went through, there was no way I was going to dump him off at a shelter."

"When you're not here, he follows me around the house," she complained.

"He knows you don't like him and he's trying to win you over."

"You didn't even ask me if you could bring him home," she accused.

"Like you asked me about getting pregnant?" he countered.

She had no answer for that.

Jack rose to his feet. "I won't be a puppet, Karen. Not for you and especially not for your mother." He climbed the stairs, stopping at the kitchen door. "By the way, I'm back on the road tomorrow so I'll be starting at five, not one-thirty." He waited, not knowing what he was expecting or hoping for, but got frozen silence. He shook his head and went inside.

Justice walked to the stairs, pausing to look back at Karen, whining apprehensively. Faced with the same frigid stillness as his master, he darted up the stairs and disappeared into the house.

Friday, 20 July
1023 hours

Come on, Jack, up, up, up!

Jack clenched his teeth, fighting the barbell sitting on his shoulders like a dead weight. A three-hundred-and-forty-five-pound dead weight. He groaned out the last rep and took a shaky step forward. The barbell clanged onto the rack and he sagged beneath it, hands on knees, drawing deep breaths.

Good set, he congratulated himself.

One of the definite advantages of shift work was being off when the rest of the world was working. This time of day, the gym was all but deserted, just a few other mid-morning regulars, and Jack had the squat racks to himself.

He straightened up and loosened his weight belt. Normally, he'd be in the small, cramped gym in the station's basement training with Manny, but because the inside crew always started earlier than the road coppers, their training time together had suffered since Jack had been on restricted duty.

But now I'm back on the road and he got his ass transferred to Ident. Oh well, Manny always hated training legs. Just wish they had a power cage here.

Jack preferred doing his squats in the rack with the adjustable safety bars. The gym near his home only had the type with the fixed rack angling slightly away from the mid-thigh-high supports. Not the best if you ran out of gas at the bottom of a squat.

Not much chance of that happening today.

Jack now knew that anger was amazing workout fuel. He and Karen had gone to bed last night with a minefield of unresolved issues separating them. The king-size bed had felt a mile wide and the new day had done nothing to reduce the distance. Karen was a fourth-grade teacher currently enjoying summer break and Jack had learned that a downside to shift work was both of them being home when neither of them especially wanted to see the other.

Jack's anger had simmered in the silence and instead of sharing a leg workout with Karen, he'd found himself alone in the gym.

Fine by me, he told himself and quickly stamped down any thoughts that dared to say otherwise. If Karen wanted to be mad because he was going back on the road, that was her problem, not his. He was a cop when they met and if she had harboured a secret plan to change that, well, too bad. And the more Karen and her mother plotted behind his back, the more he wanted to dig his heels in. There was no scheme that could get him to quit the job he loved.

Especially getting pregnant.

That's when the trouble really started. Not when I threw Kayne off the bridge, not when I brought Justice home, but when Karen and her mother decided a baby was the leverage they needed to get me to quit. Well, fuck you, Evelyn. I won't be a puppet for you or your daughter.

Jack's anger was boiling up again so instead of adding twenty pounds to the bar, he slapped on thirty pounds of plates.

Fuck it. It's my heavy set anyway.

He cinched up his weight belt and ducked under the bar. Letting the thick trapezius muscle act as a cushion, he hoisted the barbell and stepped back from the rack. The ends of the bar bounced ever so slightly as he settled his stance. Jack grinned at himself in the mirror. Nothing like lifting heavy.

He squatted until his thighs were parallel with the floor then powered up, the weight fighting him all the way. Standing straight, he sucked in a couple of deep breaths then dropped into the next rep, then the third. On the fourth squat his quads were screaming and the weight had tripled on his shoulders but he squeezed out the rep.

Come on, Jack, one more rep. Fuck Evelyn and her plans.

He hit the bottom of the rep and immediately knew he was in trouble. He was driving up with everything he had but sinking lower into the squat. The weight was compressing him. His ass was almost on the floor and his chest was being driven into his thighs.

Fuck me!

Jack was about to let go of the bar and pray it didn't do a number on his spine as it rolled off his shoulders when it finally thunked down onto the safety rack. He squirted out from under the bar and collapsed to hands and knees. He grasped the rack to pull himself to his feet, then hurriedly scanned the gym to see if anyone had witnessed his blunder. No one was paying him any particular attention and he sighed in relief.

At least my dignity's intact.

Everything between his knees and shoulders felt like it had gone through an ironing press. He had an irrational fear about taking off the weight belt as it might be the only thing holding him in one piece. Whether he fell apart or not, one thing was certain: this workout was getting cut short.

Wearing the gun belt tonight is going to be a fucking treat.

"Sheee-it, buddy! That gotta hurt," Connor crowed, laughing.

"It did," Jack validated with an embarrassed grin tugging at his lips. "And that's why I'm not driving."

"And that's why I don't do heavy squats."

Jack actually wasn't feeling all that bad. His ribs were a little sore on one side — probably from being squished up against his thighs — but his lower back hadn't stiffened up like he had feared it would. In fact, it felt kind of loose, like he'd just had an amazing massage.

My own personal version of the medieval rack. I think I'll stick to my massage therapist.

But despite how unhurt he felt, there was no sense in pushing his luck. The gun belt and Kevlar vest were enough additional weight and restrictions; no sense throwing driving into the mix as well. Jack knew he was damned lucky to have escaped serious injury. So, he'd gladly accept the sore ribs and a wounded ego and consider himself fortunate.

And even if the barbell had permanently folded him in half, he still would have hobbled in to work. After four months of sitting behind a desk, there was no way he was going to miss out on getting back in the cars. His only disappointment was in being paired up with Connor Lee, Mr. White Magic, instead of Jenny.

Connor must have been reading Jack's mind. "Thought you'd be working with Jenny, bud."

"She's taking off early tonight. Got a bachelorette party or something to go to." Jack hooked an arm out the passenger window. It was another hot, humid evening but neither Connor nor Jack was in the mood for air conditioning.

"Bachelorette party, eh? Those can get pretty wild, bud." Connor whistled appreciatively. "Damn, I'd give my left nut to see that Jenny get all nasty. You don't have any naked pictures of her, do you?"

Jack turned from watching the pedestrians on Sherbourne Street to look unbelievingly at Connor. "What?"

"Hey, bud, no offence," Connor said with a smile. "I heard you two were pretty tight. Thought you might have taken a few candid pics, that's all."

Jack laughed. There was no sense getting mad; Connor wasn't the first copper to ask about photos. Hell, Jack had once told Jenny he could retire if he had nude pictures of her to sell. Tall and lean with just enough muscle to give her curves under the uniform — even better in civvies — with waist-length, raven-black hair and crystal blue eyes, Jennifer Alton was a magnet for every horny copper and firefighter in the division. When Jack had first met her, she'd been wearing a fake wedding band to discourage come-ons, but apparently a gold ring meant little to men in uniform.

"Sorry, no photos. You've been here two weeks and you're already getting up to date on the station gossip?"

"You bet, bud. Gotta keep my ear to the ground and you two are a pretty hot topic. From the sounds of it, you're banging her in the scout car whenever you work together."

Jack burst out laughing, then bit it off as pain flared in his ribs. "Every time we work together, huh?" he asked when his ribs had settled down to a dull ache. "That's funny, considering we've never worked together a single day."

"No shit?"

"No shit. She only came to the shift after I got shot. After that, I was in 53. When I finally got back down here, I did one day shift then ended up riding the front desk after I threw that mumblee off the bridge. You should know the gossip in a police station is like the gossip back in high school."

"Damn," Connor swore, shaking his head. "I was hoping you could tell me what she's like. Damn."

"Sorry, man. You'll just have to use your imagination."

"That's cool; I've got a good imagination." After a moment's silence, he went on. "Hope you don't mind working with me, bud. I mean, I'm okay working with you 'cause I know if I get killed, you'll avenge my death."

"What?" Connor was developing a habit of confusing Jack.

"You'll avenge me," he repeated. "I'm working with the Reaper."

Jack had no answer for that and luckily the dispatcher gave him an excuse not to look for one.

"5103, in 2's area. The Keg Mansion at 515 Jarvis Street. See the manager. Looks like it started as a dispute with a couple of customers when they tried to leave without paying. Now the complainant's saying they assaulted him when he called police."

Jack hooked the mike as Connor swung the car onto

Wellesley Street. "10-4, dispatch. We're just around the corner. We'll be there in a few seconds."

The Keg sat on the northeast corner of Wellesley and Jarvis streets. A fancy steakhouse restaurant inside an old Victorian mansion. Jack liked eating there; it gave dinner a Gothic atmosphere. Connor wheeled into the parking lot and their complainant trotted down the front steps to meet them as they got out of the car.

Jack stretched as Connor spoke with the manager. God, it was good to be back on the road.

"They just got up and left without paying," the manager, a thin man in a stiffly starched white shirt, explained as Jack sauntered over. "Their waitress, Sally, told me and I caught up with them here in the parking lot. I wasn't about to let them walk out on a three-hundred-dollar bill."

"Three hundred for two guys?" Jack didn't know if he should be impressed or disgusted.

"They could eat a lot."

"They assaulted you?" Connor asked.

"Absolutely. One of them, the shorter one, knocked my cell phone out of my hand and stomped on it." The manager gestured to a woeful smear of plastic and electronics on the asphalt.

"Anything else?"

"The other one shoved me." The poor guy turned around and the back of his stiff white shirt was anything but.

Connor pulled out his memo book. "Can you tell me what these guys look like?"

"Actually," the manager mused, scanning the streets, "I might be able to show them to you. They went into that convenience store over there then, just before you got here, they started walking up Jarvis. They didn't seem to be in much of a hurry." He stepped out onto the sidewalk and looked north. "Yup. There they are."

The two men the manager pointed at were strolling up Jarvis

Street and were definitely not in any hurry. Judging from their size, Jack wondered if they could hurry.

Oh, fuck me.

"Should we take the car?"

Jack shook his head. "I think we can catch up to them and besides, I don't think they'll fit in the back of the car."

"How's your back feeling, Jack?"

"Let's hope we don't have to find out." Jack pulled out his mitre — he'd never found anyone, not even an old timer, who could tell him why the portable radios were called mitres — as he and Connor started hoofing it after their suspects. "5103, call radio."

"5103, go ahead."

"The suspects from this dine-and-dash and assault are walking northbound on Jarvis. Looks like they're almost at Earl. We're going to catch up with them and have a chat."

"10-4, 5103. Let me know when you're with them. Would you like another car to drop by?" The dispatcher was following a basic rule of policing: when possible, the number of coppers should be greater than the number of assholes.

"You read my mind, dispatch."

The dispatcher voiced out for another unit while Jack and Connor jogged after their delinquent diners.

A scout car pulled up alongside Jack and the passenger window whirred down. "Don't you know it's easier to chase someone in a car than on foot?"

"Hey, Jenny. Yeah, I know," Jack admitted. "Do us a favour and cut those two guys off. It's too fucking hot to run."

"You mean the walking roadblock?"

"That would be them. 5103 to radio," he called as Jenny accelerated away. "Enforcement 51 is on scene and we'll be speaking with the suspects at the corner of Jarvis and Earl."

Earl Street was a little side road running east off Jarvis Street with a small patch of grass amid all the concrete and asphalt on the southeast corner. The white scout car, its blue and red striping looking as worn and tired in the heat as Jack felt, came to a quick stop, blocking the sidewalk. Jenny waited in the car, letting Jack and Connor approach the suspects. If the suspects ran — Jack doubted they would be good for anything beyond a short sprint — she'd be ready to chase them down the sensible way.

But the suspects didn't run. They simply stood and waited for the police to come to them.

"Guys," Jack hailed as he and Connor caught up to the suspects. Jack surreptitiously slipped his can of pepper spray into his left hand. "We need you to come back with us to the Keg. There are some allegations that need to be cleared up."

As Jack spoke with them, Connor slid off behind the suspects' line of sight while Jenny exited the car to flank them from the other side.

Great, we've got them trapped, but I bet they still outweigh us by a couple hundred pounds.

The two men were staring at Jack with either complete disinterest or mild contempt and, in Jack's opinion, with good reason. The tall one — he had to go six-three at least — was wearing a blue T-shirt so tight it might as well have been spray-painted onto his massive physique. Veins like garden hoses tracked the length of his arms, coiling about forearms the size of Jack's upper arms. Slap an Austrian accent on the guy and he could be Arnold's cousin. His bigger cousin.

Jack had been training at gyms for a long time and this guy was the largest bodybuilder he'd ever seen. And his eating buddy, who was shorter by a good nine inches, made him seem small.

Where Mr. Arnold was sculpted, his friend was a colossal block of human. His shoulders started just beneath his ears and the body below them, from chest to calves, was thick — impossibly thick — with muscle. He could be some sort of monster dwarf or troll out of a video game. A troll wearing a T-shirt that said SHUT UP AND FUCKING SQUAT. Jack figured the weight that had crushed him earlier would be a joke to either of these freaks.

It was no wonder these guys had packed away three hundred dollars' worth of food. Jack was willing to bet two-fifty of it had been cow.

"What kind of allegations?" Troll-man wanted to know. He went to cross his arms over his chest, couldn't reach, settled for hooking his thumbs in his jeans. Power-lifters weren't known for their flexibility.

"An unpaid bill, assault and a crushed cell phone."

Troll-man shook his head. "Naw, don't wanna."

Big fucking surprise there. "Listen, guys. We can't let you just walk away from this."

Troll-man looked to his buddy, cocking an eyebrow in question. Mr. Arnold turned to look at Connor then glanced over his shoulder at Jenny. Jack could see it in his eyes, Mr. Arnold had summed up the threat and dismissed it. He crossed his arms — barely — and sneered his opinion to Troll-man.

"Naw, we're going to a movie," Troll-man said, challenging Jack.

Out of the corner of his eye, Jack saw Jenny tilt her head to the radio microphone clipped to her shoulder. "Enforcement 51, we need some more units here."

"You come back with us or we arrest you, simple as that." Jack laid it out, throwing the challenge back.

Troll-man took a step toward Jack. "Then arrest me," he dared. "If you can."

Oh, fuck me. One day back on the road and I'm going to spend it in the hospital.

Jack had no illusions of escaping any fight with these two monsters unscathed. If either of them got hold of an arm, they could probably break it as easily as snapping a bread stick. But if Jack was going to the emergency room, then at least one of these guys was going to be there for an extended stay. He had little faith in pepper spray — it always seemed to work so much better on him than the assholes — but if things went bad, and he couldn't see them going any other way, he was going to shove the can up Troll-man's nose and empty it. Then he was going to take out his baton and aim for all the spots the defensive-tactics instructors told them not to hit: skull, throat, joints. Everything else had just too much padding on it.

If we can drop the first one fast and hard, maybe his buddy will think twice about acting up.

Jenny keyed her mike again. "Assist PC. Assist PC."

Good girl, Jenny. Call the troops.

In the distance, sirens began to wail and Jack had never heard a sweeter sound. When a copper called for help, everyone dropped what they were doing and hauled ass.

"You hear that?" Jack asked. "You got a choice. Turn around and put your hands behind your back or start the fight now before our backup gets here. Your choice."

"Tough guy, eh?" Troll-man scoffed. "Too chicken to fight fair?"

"We don't get paid to fight fair," Jack snarled. "We get paid to win." Anger stirred inside him. Freedom after four months of riding a desk and this asshole thought he could take it away? Fuck him. The anger was growing hotter and suddenly Jack *wanted* Troll-man to take a swing, to release the rage. "Go ahead and do it. I'm game."

Whether it was the approaching sirens or something in Jack's eyes, Troll-man's resolve wavered. His eyes shifted to Mr. Arnold, the brains — and that wasn't saying much — of the two. The big bodybuilder hesitated and Jack could see him weighing the odds. In the end, the approaching sirens tipped the scales and he shook his head.

And then the sirens faded away.

Mr. Arnold looked at Jack, smiling. "Fire trucks?"

It took Troll-man a few more seconds to figure out what diminishing sirens meant then he grinned as well. "Looks like you're on your own, chickenshit."

"Good," Jack growled and Troll-man's grin faltered. Jack

pulled out his collapsible baton and snapped it open. Fuck the pepper spray. "How well do you think you'll be able to train after I cave in the side of your skull?"

Troll-man's eyes flickered to the side.

"Don't look at him. Make up your own mind. And hurry up, I'm running out of patience."

The squat power-lifter paused, his gaze dropping to the baton in Jack's fist then back to Jack's face. Jack smiled. It was the deciding factor and Troll-man's nerve broke. He stepped away from Jack and turned around, hands waiting to be cuffed.

God damn it.

Jack took out his handcuffs.

"Fire trucks, bud. Fucking fire trucks."

Paul Townsend laughed hard enough he had to sit on the edge of a desk. When he came close to settling down, he glanced at Connor's grave expression and fell into another fit of giggles. Hearing a man Paul's size giggle was somewhat disconcerting. Paul was, up until meeting Mr. Arnold, the biggest man Jack knew. Huge, and "black as a midnight's stolen kiss" as he liked to say, Paul could stop a fight just by stepping into a room.

The two freakazoids had been processed and lodged — no surprise, they were already on charges for assault and intimidation — and now Jack, Connor and Jenny were just finishing their memo books up in the detective office. 51 station was an old, tired building, really too small to hold the division's uniformed officers and investigative units, and the CIB was no exception A big central island of metal desks and two smaller islands filled the Criminal Investigative Bureau.

Paul had come into the office looking for a quiet place to catch up on some paperwork and Connor had leapt at the chance to recount the tale. Connor was quite the storyteller and although he lacked Manny's flare for embellishment, he certainly didn't lack in fervour.

"I'm telling you, bud, I nearly shit when those sirens headed off another way. I thought for sure those guys were going to scrap with us. I mean, they looked at Jenny and me like we didn't exist. It was just Jack and this — what did you call him? A troll? — this troll going nose to nose. And the troll backed down. Man, it was beautiful."

"They were really that big?" Paul asked, doubt clear on his face.

"They were," Jenny confirmed.

"I know I'm not the biggest guy in the world," Jack admitted, "but I felt small next to them. Really small. The short one was so big he couldn't get his hands behind his back. We had to use two sets of cuffs linked together."

"Juicing?" Paul wondered.

Jack snorted. "I hope so. If they got that big naturally, I'd hate to see how big they'd get on 'roids."

Connor came up behind Jack, clapping his hands on Jack's shoulders. "But juice or no juice, my man the Reaper backed them down. That's why I like working with him. If I get killed on the job, I know my death will be avenged."

Jack groaned. Jenny shot him an amused smile. "Well, while the Reaper and his trusty sidekick gloat about their heroics, I have a party to get to." She headed for the door, pausing to lay a comforting hand on Paul's arm. "Don't worry, big fella. I don't care how big they were, you'll always be the big man in my dreams."

"Girl, if I wasn't married . . ." He made to wrap his arms around her but she skipped out of his reach.

"Promises, promises," she teased. "See ya, guys."

"You're not going to let that Reaper thing die, are you?" Jack asked Connor with an accusing glare.

"Nope." Connor's answering grin was very cheery and self-satisfied.

"Well, if I'm the Reaper," Jack surmised, standing up, "that makes you death's sidekick. Who would that be?"

"Pestilence?" Paul suggested.

Jack beamed. "I like it. Don't worry, Connor, I'm not going to call you pestilence," he assured when he saw the stricken look on his escort's face. "I'll call you Pest for short."

"You've never done steroids, have you?"

"What?" Jenny's question snapped Jack out of a pleasant daze. They were in the back parking lot, Jenny emptying out her car and Jack waiting for Connor, who had made a detour to the bathroom. Jack was leaning against the scout car next to hers and had been staring at her ass as she bent over to pull her duty bag out of the trunk and hadn't really heard her.

She straightened up. "You were looking at my butt, weren't you?"

"Absolutely," he declared.

She slammed the trunk. "You have no shame," she accused but with a smile.

"Not when it comes to your ass," he agreed. "Although, as good as it looks in uniform, I prefer it in jeans."

"Shameless," she repeated. "Seriously, you don't take steroids, do you?"

"Where did that come from?" he asked, then added, "no, I don't use 'roids. And no, I haven't used them in the past. Why?"

She smiled at him, embarrassed, and he felt that familiar flutter in his stomach. The same one he got whenever she smiled at him.

Man, I've got it bad.

"This is going to sound stupid, but . . ."

"But?"

"Well, you have gotten bigger since last summer, and when that troll guy was challenging you, you suddenly changed. Like you wanted him to fight, wanted to hurt him. And like Connor said, the guy backed down. He saw it in your eyes and he didn't want any part of it."

"And you were thinking 'roid rage, right?"

"I guess," she confessed.

"Well, don't worry, I'm clean." He tugged up the short sleeves of the black uniform shirt and held his arms out for inspection. "See? Some veins but no needle marks. No 'roid rage, just stress."

"Over what?" She put her duty bag down and set her butt against the car Jack was resting on.

"Don't you have a party to go to?"

"It can wait." She crossed her arms and Jack could tell from the tilt of her head there'd be no dissuading her.

Jack looked up at the darkening sky, drank in a deep breath. The excessive heat and humidity had fled with the sun and the evening air felt almost cool in comparison.

"The usual shit, I guess," he owned up. "Months of waiting to see if the SIU was going to charge me or not, then to find out through the news. When I got home last night, Karen and I had a fight about me going back on the road. Did I tell you she'd known I was cleared since the early afternoon? Yup, her mother read it in the paper and called her."

"She didn't call you at the station?" Jenny asked, shocked.

"Nope. Guess she and her mother were too busy planning their next move on how to get me to quit."

"I guess they've given up on the baby idea?" Jack had kept Jenny well informed on the tribulations in the Warren household. Sometimes she seemed the only thing that kept him sane.

"We're back to using condoms. Or we would be," he corrected, "but we haven't had sex since the whole Kayne thing."

"Ouch." She was silent for a minute, feeling his frustration. "Getting many headaches?"

Jack laughed without humour. "Only one, but it's lasted since Kayne hit the bottom of Rosedale Valley."

Jenny's eyes widened in alarm. "You're not serious, are you?"

He shook his head, forcing a smile. "No, but I get one so often now it seems like just one big headache."

"Migraines or headaches?"

"The odd migraine. Mostly tension headaches, though. Not surprising, I guess." Jack figured there was no need to worry Jenny with the truth, that the migraines, once a monthly occurrence, were now pretty much weekly. He was downing his prescription medication like it was candy.

"How's Justice?"

Jack immediately brightened. "He's doing great. You won't recognize him. He's put on weight, his coat looks good and he's growing like mad. I bet he puts on another ten or twenty pounds as he fills out. I'll tell you, Jenny, I'm so happy I found him. Sometimes, when things are really bad between Karen and me, he's the only reason I go home."

"You have to try and fix that. You know that, right?"

"Yeah, I know." He rubbed his face, suddenly tired. "I just don't know how."

"Well, I'm here for you. If you need an ear or a shoulder, let me know." She kissed his cheek and was it Jack's imagination or did her lips linger longer than a friendly smooch required?

"Aha!" Connor cried triumphantly. "I knew there was something between you two."

Jack groaned. "Jenny, you've met my sidekick, right? I call him Pest."

"The new dancer's pretty good, eh, Taylor?"

Taylor watched the woman on stage as she spun inverted on the stripper pole. "Sure," he replied noncommittally. "If you like blondes with long legs and nice tits."

Gregory laughed. "Yeah, and you don't." He slapped Taylor on the back.

The dancer finished her set to healthy applause. Filmore's was busy tonight. Taylor figured it had more to do with the air conditioning than the girls. He wasn't looking forward to trying to sleep with his shitty little window AC unit.

Give us a few months and we'll be bitching about the cold.

The two bouncers stood near the entrance, their black golf shirts meshing with the shadows and dim lighting, keeping them from the eyes and minds of the patrons. No one watching nude women liked having a hulking doorman looming close by, but the bouncers were always close enough for the times someone forgot about them entirely.

His colleague tapped Taylor on the shoulder. "I gotta take a leak," he told Taylor, leaning close to be heard over the music. "You got this?"

Taylor gave him a confident nod and the large bodybuilder ambled toward the back. Alone, Taylor felt bigger. At five-nine, he was by far the shortest man on the strip club's security force. Most of the other doormen could quiet rising trouble simply by stepping close, reminding patrons that there were rules even where there were no clothes. But in his three months at the club, Taylor had only resorted to force a handful of times despite his diminutive stature. Although short — by bouncer standards, at least — he carried enough muscle, clearly evident in the snug shirt, to give most troublemakers second thoughts and he had a way of speaking, when needed, that his co-workers called his "assassin voice." It was a tone that said, "If I have to fuck you up, I will, and I will do an extremely good job of it." More than one drunk had sobered up when Taylor had whispered in his ear.

But being the smallest was nothing new for him. Throughout high school he had been the small one, slender of build, and had to constantly prove himself to his teammates, the coaches, his father. Always his father.

You're not good enough, boy! You play like a girl. You're useless.

Taylor chased away his father's ghost as the new dancer, Chantelle — not her real name, of course; any dancer with half a brain used a stage name — wandered over, a red silk scarf wound interestingly about her lithe figure. Hired just a week ago, she no longer wobbled in her stilettos. With the four-inch spikes, she met him on eye level.

"Hey, Taylor, what did you think of my routine?"

"Real good, Sandra," he said, using her real name only after confirming no guests were close enough to hear. "You're working that pole like a gymnast."

She smiled and Taylor could tell it was genuine from the way her eyes lit up. A dancer's emotions rarely reached her eyes when she was smiling for a patron.

"Thanks." She gave his hand a quick squeeze before strolling away, her hips rolling seductively. She glanced over her shoulder to see if he was watching. He was.

"She's got the hots for you, man," Gregory said, back from his restroom break.

"I thought the dancers were off limits for us."

"Technically, they are, but the boss man don't care as long as you keep it off the floor and it doesn't get in the way of anyone working."

Taylor nodded, searching for Sandra, but the club had swallowed her from sight. "Thanks again for loaning me your car last night."

"Anytime, man. You sticking around for a drink after closing?" Gregory was an easygoing guy but he talked too much and asked way too many questions.

Taylor shook his head. "I'm gonna head home, try and get some sleep before the sun comes up."

"I hear that," Gregory said over the music then, miraculously, fell silent. Taylor took the opportunity to sidle away. He was feeling good tonight, calm, at ease with himself.

It pays to vent once in a while. Now if his knuckles would just stop aching.

"Are you saying you never go shopping in uniform?" Connor was flabbergasted.

"I'm not going to walk around a grocery store in uniform. Are you nuts?"

"Not grocery shopping, you moron." Connor shook his head at Jack's stupidity. "Electronics. Appliances. Cars. You've never shopped for anything like that while you're working?"

"Nope," Jack confessed, not bothered by Connor's animated disbelief. He swung the scout car onto Jarvis Street. Connor had gladly handed over the steering wheel when Jack had asked to drive. "This uniform attracts enough attention as it is. I don't need it while I'm shopping."

"And paying full price." He wagged his head sadly. "Jack, Jack, Jack. The uniform is an automatic discount in the right places. And a chick magnet." Connor looked at Jack, his eyes narrowed suspiciously. "You're not one of those, are you?"

"One of what? Gay? Come on, you're the one telling me I'm banging Jenny all the time."

"Ah, sweet, sweet Jenny." Connor crooned, smacking his lips.

"You sound like Taftmore," Jack observed.

"Who's that?"

"A guy up in Major Crime. He has the hots for Jenny, too. But —" Jack threw up a cautionary hand "— before you take any pointers from him, ask him how he ended up with a chair in his balls at a search warrant briefing."

Connor cringed. "Ouch. But I didn't mean a fag, dope, although that would be pretty fucking bad, too. Yuck." He shivered. "I meant one of those happily married suckers."

"Yeah, I am," Jack said defensively, then muttered, "most of the time."

"I heard that." Connor laughed self-righteously. "I don't know why guys get married but I'm glad they do. Wanna know why?"

"Not really," Jack sighed. "But I imagine you're going to tell me anyway."

"Bud, I only date married women. It's fucking awesome. Find a woman who's been married for a while. Hubby's packed on a few pounds, got the old beer gut going and pays more attention to football on TV than he does her. Bud, women like that are just dying for some loving and that's where I come in. I may not be as big as you or Townsend, but the ladies dig the six-pack." He patted his flat stomach through his Kevlar vest. "No strings, just fucking. Married women, bud. You gotta try it."

"No thanks. I've got enough trouble with one married woman right now."

"More for me, then." Pest sighed happily. "I tell you, bud, I was made for married women. If the uniform doesn't get them, the bod does, and with this complexion —" he appreciatively caressed his tanned cheek "— I can be anything from Asian to Latino or Hawaiian. I'm a walking fantasy factory."

"Latino? Really?"

"Hey, we're not talking rocket scientists, you know."

Finished gloating, Connor fell silent and Jack was willing to let the conversation rest. Connor was a decent guy and a good cop but he sure liked to talk, primarily about sex. Who he was having sex with, who he wanted to have sex with and what he liked to do when having sex. Jack wasn't really that keen on knowing the intimate details of Pest's latest conquest. They drove in silence until Jack turned off Jarvis Street onto Wellesley Street.

"Whoa!" Connor shouted, straightening up so fast he almost brained himself on the roof. "You're not going there, are you?"

"Where?" Jack glanced at Connor, puzzled.

"The fag coffee shop. We can't go there," he protested. "I heard they jerk off into the coffee."

"Listen," Jack explained patiently. "We almost got stomped into hamburger a little while ago and the night's just half over. The Second Cup is the only place I can get honey in my tea."

Connor drew back, eyeing Jack distrustfully. "You sure you ain't a fag?"

"Oh, for fuck's sake." Jack knew Pest was only teasing — at least he was pretty sure he was — but he was getting irritated nonetheless.

Connor pointed his crossed index fingers at Jack. "Back, foul beast."

"Bloody hell," he muttered.

The Second Cup at Church and Wellesley streets was a bit of an iconic institution in the heart of Gaytown, also called "the village." Manny had taken Jack there last summer and he'd been a regular customer since.

Jack pulled to the curb in front of the coffee shop. "What do you want?"

Connor crossed his arms defiantly. "I'm not going in there."

"Oh, for . . ." Jack rubbed his right eye. He could feel a migraine stirring behind it. "I'll go in. What do you want?"

"I don't want anything from there." Pest pouted and clamped his arms tighter around his chest. After a few moments of sulking, he turned to Jack. "Fine. I'll have a coffee."

"Finally."

As Jack got out of the car, Connor told him, "If you get raped in there, it's not my fault."

"I bloody don't believe it," Jack grumbled as he crossed behind the scout car.

The short climb of steps from the sidewalk to the front door was a local hangout sensibly known as The Steps, and on this sultry evening they were well occupied. As Jack mounted the steps three gentlemen, rather flamboyant in their shorts and mesh T-shirts, watched him warily. Police — especially 51 coppers — didn't have the greatest reputation in the village.

"He's afraid to go in there, isn't he?" one of them asked, gesturing to Connor, who was rigidly staring out the windshield.

Pest's window was down and Jack had the keys. "Yeah, he is," Jack confirmed. "Why don't you go down there and talk to him?"

A huge grin broke over the man's face. "Let's go, boys!" he cried and the small troop flounced down the steps to descend on a helpless Connor. There was nothing like a homophobic cop to bring out the gay in some people.

As he opened the coffee shop's door, Jack thought he heard Connor whimpering.

Saturday, 21 July
0145 hours

Sandra swayed off the stage to raucous applause. Last call had been announced prior to her set and soon would begin the task of ushering all the guests out the doors. Taylor wanted a quick look around for any potential problems: a table with a reserve of untouched drinks hoarded at last call, mean drunks itching for a brawl, or worse, the sober ones looking to scrap. All appeared calm, the most activity coming from the dancers as they escorted guests to the back for a final lap dance.

Taylor caught sight of Sandra as she weaved between the tables, stopping to chat and flirt, working the floor like a seasoned pro. She passed a table holding a lone drinker and the man grabbed her ass as she walked by. Sandra spun around and Taylor watched approvingly as she smothered the flare of anger in her eyes and slipped a smile onto her lips.

"Looking's free," she corrected the man. "Touching costs you a bit more."

The man lurched drunkenly to his feet, his hands pawing for the dancer. Sandra skittered out of reach just as Taylor slid in beside the man, grasping his wrist and neck. The drunk suddenly found himself face down in his own beer with his arm twisted up painfully behind his back.

Taylor leaned in to speak softly into the man's ear. "Calm down or I'll snap your arm," he informed the man pleasantly, giving the trapped arm an extra tug for emphasis. "It's time for you to leave now."

Taylor hauled the man upright and walked him to the door, Gregory and another bouncer silently falling in alongside.

Gregory opened the inner door for Taylor and his charge but Taylor opened the outer door with the man's face. Taylor shoved him onto the sidewalk with the simple warning, "Get going and stay gone."

The man was staggering erect as Taylor closed the door on him. "Idiot," Taylor muttered, taking up his position by the door once more. Gregory flanked Taylor on the opposite side of the door, and patrons passed between them on the beginning of their journeys home. When all but the stragglers were gone, Sandra cuddled up next to Taylor.

"Thanks again," she whispered. "That guy really frightened me."

"Just a drunk," Taylor dismissed. "Do you have a ride home? You know, just in case he's still hanging around outside."

She nodded. "I'm getting a lift with Amy and her boyfriend."

"Good." Taylor kept his eyes on the last of the guests as they shuffled out. "I'll wait with you till he gets here."

The air outside was thick, damp. It was hard to believe dawn was just a few hours away. Taylor, with a white tee in lieu of the club's black, stood on the sidewalk with Sandra and Amy, a leggy black girl, waiting for Amy's ride.

Amy was wearing a red miniskirt and matching halter, bought small to show off the breasts she had recently purchased. Sandra was more conservative with denim cut-offs and a T-shirt. Looking at them, Taylor had to fight to keep his face neutral.

Sandra caught him looking. "Do you think I should get a boob job? Amy gets more dances now."

Taylor shrugged uncomfortably. "I'm not much of a boob man."

Sandra giggled. "God, I hope you're not gay." Her hand flew to her mouth in embarrassment when Taylor's face went stony. "Oh my God, you are gay. I'm so sorry."

Taylor's stomach churned unpleasantly but before he had to answer, Amy broke in, laughing a high, edgy snicker. "Him, gay?

I don't think so, girl. No fag could take what he took from Rico."

"What's that?" Sandra asked, eying the tall dancer.

"Haven't you heard that story? It's crazy." Amy paused to light a cigarette. "It happened . . . what? Two, three months ago?" she asked Taylor as she tucked her lighter away into her tiny purse.

"Two," Taylor said unhappily, but Amy was already pushing ahead with the tale.

"It was one night after closing and a bunch of us were hanging around, you know, just having a couple of drinks before heading home." Amy dragged on her butt. Blowing smoke into the hot air, she dove into the story. "Taylor had just started working here and there was this other doorman, Rico, a real asshole. And he, Rico, says to Taylor . . . What did he say to you, hon?"

"I'm not sure anymore," Taylor murmured.

"I've got it!" Amy waved her cigarette triumphantly. "So Rico, he says . . ."

". . . that guy's got an ass cute enough to fuck." Rico was sitting at the bar, a greasy smile on his face. As greasy as the shit he had in his hair to keep it slicked back from his pimply forehead. No one at Filmore's knew if his bad complexion was from the oil trickling out of his hair or the 'roids he injected into his ass.

Rico was lounging on a bar stool, propped up on his elbows, a beer beside him and that nasty grin on his face. He'd been bouncing at the club for a year now and in that time the number of police visits had increased dramatically. Rico liked to hurt people and believed anyone who deserved to be tossed out also deserved a little something extra. Usually it was an extra shot to the face or ribs, bad enough that a lot of the ejected guests called police. So far he had escaped charges, mainly because the complainants were drunk and didn't make a good impression themselves. To date, all the incidents had been written off as vindictive drunks complaining about being tossed out.

But the other night, a guest's arm had ended up broken and the boss had to do a lot of negotiating to smooth things out. Rico was officially on probation. Deprived of his usual victims, it seemed Rico was turning his attention to the new guy.

Amy was sitting with a couple of the other dancers and they all watched as the new guy — *what was his name? Timmy, Tony?* — slowly stood up, a dark look hardening his face.

"What did you say?" the new guy asked in a low voice that carried in the suddenly quiet room.

Don't do it, guy, Amy silently pleaded. *It ain't worth it.*

"I said your ass is cute enough to fuck," Rico repeated, grinning happily. He slid off the bar stool. "You got a problem with that?"

The new guy strode over to Rico so that they were nose to nose, except Rico was about six inches taller so it was more like nose to chest. Rico smiled down at the smaller man. "Whatcha gonna do about it?"

Dancers and staff were hushed, waiting to see how the new guy would react. If he threw a punch over a mere taunt, he'd be seen as a hothead and it could cost him his job. But if he backed down . . . No one could afford to look cowardly when doing this job.

"If you're a fag, Rico, I don't give a fuck," the new guy snarled. "Just keep your fucking hands and comments to yourself."

Rico's nasty smile melted into an ugly sneer. "I'm gonna fuck you up." He reached for the smaller man, but the new guy ducked out of the way and smashed a hard fist into Rico's ribs, hunching him over. Everyone watching *oohed* as Rico took an elbow to the face.

Rico staggered back then shook his head to clear it. Droplets of blood, dark crimson in the low light, splattered the floor. The big bouncer gingerly touched his lip, wincing as his fingers came away bloody.

"You're fucking dead, asshole."

Rico stalked the smaller man, jabbing and throwing looping punches, but the new guy kept ducking and weaving, letting the bigger man's fists swing by. The staff cheered them on as if they were watching a professional boxing match. Every time Rico's fist missed its target the small audience roared its approval.

In the end, it was a chair that decided the fight. As he side-stepped another wild punch, the new guy hit a chair and, for a split second, took his eyes off his opponent. Rico may not have been the most skilled fighter — he was an untrained brawler who relied on size and strength — but he could capitalize on an advantage when it was presented. His next punch landed flush on the new guy's chin and knocked him sprawling over the chair.

Rico tossed the chair out of the way, hauled the smaller man to his feet and hurled him against the bar. The new guy's back hit the bar just below the shoulders and his head snapped back violently. His knees buckled and he sagged, only one hand clasping the bar keeping him from falling.

Rico hit him one more time, a sharp blow to the temple. The new guy hit the floor hard and Rico walked away, satisfied. The room was quiet as the big man lifted his beer and took a careful swig around his cut lip.

"We ain't finished."

The words were faint but clear and Rico turned to see the new guy back on his feet, a little unsteady but with his fists raised.

"Whatever you say, punk." Rico downed the last of his beer and advanced on his prey, rolling his shoulders. "I'm gonna enjoy this."

"Rico, leave him alone," Amy called out, a few others echoing her opinion.

Rico ignored them, his eyes fixed on the smaller man. This time it didn't take as long or a chair for Rico to land a blow; the new guy was still reeling from the last punch. Rico pummelled the smaller man to the floor then yanked him upright, his fists entwined in the new guy's shirt.

Rico stared at the man's battered face with curiosity. "Was it worth it, asshole? Maybe I should have just fucked your ass. It wouldn't have hurt as much." He opened his hands and the new guy dropped to the floor, as limp as a broken doll.

Rico wandered back to the bar, slowly flexing one of his hands. "Hey, Jimmy," he called to one of the bartenders. "You got any ice back there? I think I broke my fucking hand on his head."

"Never . . . again." Unbelievably, the new guy was pushing himself back to his feet. One eye was already swollen closed and blood from his nose and mouth smeared his chin. But as punished as his body was, his one eye blazed with an indomitable fury. "Never . . . fucking again."

"You gotta be kidding me." Rico stared in disbelief then shrugged as if to say *What can you do?* and pushed away from the bar.

"No. That's enough." Gregory and some others stepped between the combatants. "He's had enough, Rico."

"Fine by me." Rico didn't seem overly concerned that the fight was over; he was looking rather winded from the beating he had administered. "Just tell that punk to keep . . ."

". . . keep his mouth shut," Amy finished. "That's when we started calling him Rocky."

Sandra looked at the other stripper, puzzled. "I don't get it."

"He kept getting up," Amy explained. "Like that Rocky guy in the movies."

"Oh, I get it now." Sandra inspected Taylor's face. "You healed up pretty well."

"I'm a fast healer," Taylor offered, needing to say something with Sandra so uncomfortably close.

"You must be," she agreed, drawing her finger along his

strong jaw. "Rocky, huh?"

"Yeah, but I don't like it."

A car pulled to the curb and Amy squealed, "My baby's here, Sandra. Time to go," breaking the silence that had started to grow between Taylor and Sandra.

Sandra stepped back from the bouncer, smiling a secret little smile. "See you tomorrow, Taylor." She climbed into the car after Amy, waving good night.

Taylor lifted a hand in return then dropped it as the car accelerated down Dundas Street.

Don't go there, he reproached himself. *Don't you fucking dare.*

"You're an asshole. You know that, don't you?"

"Are you going to be this nice all night?" Jack asked as he tossed his duty bag and hat into the cruiser's trunk. He slammed the trunk and glared at Connor. "'Cause if you are, I'm warning you: I've got a headache, my ribs still hurt like a fucking bitch and my wife gave me the silent treatment all day."

Connor pouted at Jack over the roof of the car. "Big deal. I had nightmares because of you."

Jack slid into the passenger seat and powered up the workstation. "You're dreaming about me now?"

Connor's face screwed up. "Yuck. You wish. No, asshole, because you sicced those fags on me yesterday, that's why. You know you had the keys so I couldn't roll my window up?"

Jack snickered. "Yeah, I guess I did have them. Sorry, force of habit."

"Yeah, right." Connor started up the car, muttering, "Asshole."

Jack almost smiled. Karen had ignored him when he got up and while he was showering she had left to meet her parents for brunch. And she hadn't returned by the time he left for work.

"Jenny wasn't on parade," Connor commented as he fiddled with the AC vents. "That must have been one hell of a bachelorette party."

"I guess." Jack had been disappointed to see Jenny's usual seat vacant during parade. *But then again, maybe working with the woman my wife hates isn't such a great idea.*

"5106, just signed on," the dispatcher called to them. *"Are you still at the station?"*

"Just leaving the lot. What can we do for you?" Jack released the mike key. "Saturday night in July. Bet we're gonna be busy."

"Let me see . . ." the dispatcher dithered, most likely scanning a lengthy list of pending calls. *"5106, in your area, Moss Park. See the complainant by the baseball diamond. Threatening to overdose, no further details.* CIT *attending. Time, 1747."*

"And awaaaay we go!" Connor chimed. He turned onto Shuter Street and goosed the car through the yellow light at Parliament Street.

Moss Park was a neighbourhood stretching from Parliament Street in the east to its western boundary of Jarvis Street with apartment buildings, the Salvation Army hostel and stores occupying the east end. The actual park was in the west half, unfurled between the community centre and the Canadian Forces armoury building. Not surprisingly, the police didn't get many calls at the armoury.

A white Crown Victoria was parked on Shuter Street by the baseball diamond. Instead of parking next to the unmarked police car, Connor bounced the scout car over the curb and sidewalk to park by the bleachers. A small group of three people watched as the uniformed officers stepped out into the heat. Jack recognized two of them.

Sue Dennis, a PW with vibrant crimson hair tied back in a loose ponytail, was dressed in the Crisis Intervention Team's semi-plainclothes uniform: police T-shirt and gun belt, jeans and running shoes. She was standing off to the side, a bored expression on her sulking face.

The Crisis Intervention Team, a relatively recent addition to the division, paired a copper with a mental-health nurse from St.

Michael's Hospital to respond to calls involving the mentally ill. The modified uniform was to alleviate any anxiety or stress with the team's "clients."

Aaron Wallace was a smaller version of Manny: shaved head, goatee, but not quite as stocky. Although he was equipped with a ballistic vest, his black T-shirt said CRISIS TEAM and he wasn't wearing a gun belt.

Aaron was talking with a red-headed runt, but Jack ignored the runt and introduced himself to the nurse. "We met up in 53 and you tore a strip off my ass for the way I handled a depressed, suicidal male."

"I remember that," Aaron said. He leaned to the side, peering at Jack's butt. "Your ass seems to have recovered."

Jack laughed. "It has."

"So you're down here now?"

"Back where I belong, more like it. Let's just say my time in 53 was a boring, temporary layover."

Aaron pointed at the scar running through Jack's right eyebrow. "Brought back a memento, I see."

"Yeah. Messed up at another EDP call. Learned my lesson, though. What have we got here?"

Aaron sighed. "A pain in the ass."

The ass pain was a few inches over five feet and weighed maybe a buck twenty with hair like a clown's red wig. All he needed was a red ball on his nose, but Jack doubted one would fit on a snout that twisted and busted.

"I'm gonna kill myself," Ass Pain declared.

"We could only be so lucky," Aaron griped. To Jack and Connor, he said, "This is Joey Horner. He threatens to kill himself about once a week, more if he's done something illegal. This is the third time we've dealt with him since Thursday and I'm getting ready to kill him myself."

"He nuts?" Connor asked.

"Not really," Aaron assessed. "More like a personality disorder:

he's an asshole."

Connor laughed. "Gotcha."

"I'm not an asshole," Horner cried. "I'm gonna steal a bottle of Tylenol and take all of it."

"Make sure you grab a big bottle," Aaron murmured under his breath. Louder, he said, "Joey, I know you're not going to kill yourself. You know you're not going to kill yourself. If you want a ride to the hospital —" Horner's face perked up "— jump on a bus."

Dejected, Horner stood his ground. "You can't leave me; you're a nurse."

"Joey, I get paid to help sick people," Aaron said through clenched teeth. "And you're not sick."

"You have to take me to the hospital." Horner sucked in a breath to carry on his tirade but Jack grabbed his arm, pulling him away from the frustrated nurse.

"Come and have a talk with me, Joey." As he dragged Horner out of earshot, the little man continued to demand a ride to the hospital.

"You're the police," he informed Jack and jabbed his finger at the scout car. "'To Serve and Protect.' That's what it says so you have to take me to the hos —"

"Do you have a dog?" Jack's quiet question cut Horner off in mid-rant.

"I used to," he replied slowly, suspiciously eying Jack. "But some asshole —" Horner stopped abruptly, truly seeing who was standing in front of him.

Jack smiled. He knew what it did to the eyebrow scar. "Glad to hear you don't." He pulled Horner in close. "Remember, I catch you with another dog and you'll be lucky if the hospital is where you need to go. We understand each other? Good. Now fuck off."

Horner scurried away, never taking his eyes off Jack. Only when he was a safe distance away did his courage reassert itself.

"Fuck you!" he screamed and gave Jack double fingers.

Jack jerked as if he meant to chase Horner and the little man bolted in terror. Jack watched, amused, till Horner disappeared around the community centre.

Too bad he didn't run into a tree. That would have been classic.

Aaron was nodding in approval. "That was pretty cool. It would've been better if he'd turned around and run into a tree or something. What did you say to him?"

"Just reminded him of something," Jack replied vaguely. "I'll tell you another time. Will he really chug a bottle of Tylenol?"

Aaron shrugged. "I doubt it. Every time I see him he says he's going to overdose. But even if he does, it won't kill him. If he takes enough Tylenol, long enough, it'll rot his liver but that's about all."

Jack cocked his head at Sue as she giggled with Connor. "What happened to the copper you usually ride with?"

"Holidays." Aaron scowled. "I'm stuck with her for the rest of the week. Hey! You obviously have a certain way with people. Maybe you should sub next time."

"Hm. Maybe I will. I like the uniform. Come on, Pest!" he hollered over his shoulder. "Time to get back to work."

Lying on the south side of Dundas Street just a stone's throw east of Filmore's was a forgotten parking lot, its surface a ragged, heaving mix of hard-packed earth and tired asphalt. The tiny lot held only three cars, two of them junkers that were slowly rusting into the ground and a Corvette, its black paint so new it gleamed in the feeble starlight.

Taylor ignored the wrecks, headed for the Vette and climbed in the passenger side.

"'Bout time, man. I was starting to think you weren't gonna show."

"The boss held us all back for a meeting," Taylor explained, not wanting to go into detail.

"I hated it when that prick did that." A lighter flared, casting

Rico's face in an orange glow as he puffed his cigarette to life. "Leaving that place was the best thing I ever done."

You say that like you quit and weren't fired.

"Am I right?" Rico cuffed Taylor on the shoulder.

"Absolutely," Taylor said, gazing out the windshield. He wasn't in the mood for chit-chat, especially with a moron like Rico. *Let's just get this done so I can go the fuck home.*

But Rico was in a happy, chatty mood, which was unusual for the big bodybuilder. "Damn fucking right it was a good move. Gave me time to concentrate on my business." He spread his arms expansively to encompass the car's interior. "What do you think of my new baby?"

"I thought you just got a new paint job." Taylor made a show of appreciating the ego extension he was sitting in. "Why'd you buy a new one?"

"Because I can, man! Shit, the other one was last year's model. Old. Time to upgrade." Rico dragged on his cigarette. He blew the smoke out through a crazy grin. "And I got the cash now, man, so why the fuck not?"

An uneasy quiver danced down Taylor's spine. Rico wasn't just in a good mood, he was downright cheerful and that made Taylor nervous. He knew Rico dealt in more than steroids and other illegal performance enhancers, but was the former bouncer sampling some of his own product?

"Yeah, I got some new customers now." Rico flicked his butt out the window. "They want quality, so they come to me and the cash is fucking rolling in."

Taylor nodded, not knowing what else to do.

"Lighten up, man." Rico cuffed him again then grabbed Taylor's shoulder. "You're putting on some size, man. Lemme see the guns. C'mon, man, show me."

Taylor obediently flexed his bicep, the paper-thin skin wrapping tightly around the hard muscle.

Rico nodded appreciatively. "Good definition, man. Good

size. I mean, you won't ever be as big as me but not bad."

Taylor shrugged. "Haven't got the genetics for that size."

Rico snorted. "Right. The *genetics*."

Taylor shot Rico a look. What the fuck was going on? Normally Taylor passed Rico the money in exchange for a new supply and Taylor was on his way.

"I like you, man," Rico said, lighting another cigarette. "That's why I got you the job at Filmore's. That's why I let you keep selling for me even after our little tussle." He sucked back a lungful and blew it out thoughtfully. "How long you been selling for me, man? Six months?"

"'Bout that." Taylor casually shifted in the seat, resting his hand on the door handle. He may have been working for Rico long before the steroid dealer got him the job at Filmore's but he still wasn't easy around him.

"I got a little worried when you disappeared on me for a few weeks, thought I'd have to find someone to take over your customers."

"I told you, I was in the hospital," Taylor told him carefully.

"Right, the hospital." Rico tapped his fingers against his lips, the lit end of the cigarette dancing in the darkness. "That was what? Three, four months ago?"

"Yeah. Just before you got me the job at the club." Taylor didn't like where this conversation was headed. His hand tightened on the handle.

"Well!" Rico exclaimed, slapping Taylor's knee. "Let's get down to business." He tossed his half finished cigarette after the first one. "You still selling to those assholes in the club?"

"A few."

"That's cool." Rico reached down between his feet and came up with a plastic bag. "Got all you wanted. Got the EQ, the Deca and Prope plus the growth hormone. Be careful with that shit, man. It'll thicken your waist, fuck up that nice vee shape you got going."

Finally. Taylor dug into his pocket and handed over a wad of cash. "Can you get me some coke?"

"No sweat." Rico waved the effort away. "For you?"

Taylor shook his head. He never touched that shit. "One of my guys wants some for a party. Couple hundred worth?"

"You bet. Oh, there's one more thing," Rico added, stopping Taylor before he could get the door open. "I've had to raise my prices. Demand, you understand."

Taylor eased down in the seat. "How much?"

"But for you, man, it won't cost a dime." Rico smiled a shark's grin. "All you have to do is blow me."

"The fuck I will," Taylor said with a half smile. He didn't know if the big man was joking or not.

"The fuck you will." And before Taylor could move, Rico had a gun pressed to his temple.

"What the fuck are you doing?" Taylor's head was pressed up against the passenger window, the gun's barrel gouging his scalp.

"Don't fuck me around, man!" Rico snarled. "I know all about you. Oh yeah, I do. I had some friends check you out. I know *allllll* about you." He bore down with the barrel, grinding it into Taylor's skin. "And unless you want me to blow your fucking brains out right now, you're gonna suck my dick."

"Go fuck yourself!"

"You don't think I'll do it, man? I'll put a bullet through your fucking head and I'll fuck the hole."

"Who'll sell your shit, then?" Taylor was grasping at shadows and knew he was seconds away from dying.

"I've got a whack of guys ready to take your place." He eased the pressure on the gun and carried on in a gentler tone. "But I like you, man, and all you gotta do is suck me off."

"Fuck you," Taylor told him, then groaned as the gun dug in.

"You don't think I'll do it?" Rico repeated. "You think I'm worried about the cops? Fuck the cops. I got friends who could make you disappear like you were never born." Rico cocked the gun and in the confines of the car it was as loud as a tomb door slamming shut. "What's it gonna be, man? Suck or die?"

In the end, Taylor didn't want to die.

Rico squealed the tires of his Corvette leaving the parking lot but Taylor never heard them. His fingers were desperately clutching the chain-link fence as his stomach heaved and heaved. He puked until there was nothing left and still his stomach clenched. He staggered away from his puddle of vomit and sagged against the fencing, tears streaking his cheeks. Tears of shame, tears of hate, tears of rage.

He crumpled to the ground. "Asshole," he hissed and slammed the heel of his hand against his forehead. "Asshole, asshole, asshole!" Each word was punctuated by the strike of his hand until he was hitting himself hard enough to blur his vision.

"Never again. Never fucking again," he swore.

He pushed himself to his feet and collected his bag of steroids. The neon lights of Filmore's throbbed garishly across the street and Taylor knew there was no way he could go back in there tonight, not with his humiliation so raw and exposed. He crept from the parking lot, his eyes searching the street and buildings to see if anyone had witnessed his degradation.

Once he was far enough along Dundas Street he flipped open his cell phone. "Hey, Gregory, it's me," he rasped, letting his emotions trickle into his voice to make him sound sick. "I just spent my break puking. Let the boss know I'm heading home, okay? Nah, I'm good, I'll walk. Yeah, see you tomorrow."

Walking slowly, hunched over his illicit stash clasped to his belly, he plodded up Pembroke Street. Lately the residential side street had suffered an influx of prostitutes, probably feeding off of the strip club's customers, but the sidewalk was mercifully clear as Taylor trod wearily up its length. He had no idea how he would react right now if one of those skanky crack whores approached him.

Shadows lay across the paved paths of Allan Gardens, banished intermittently by the few ornamental lights. Taylor ignored the drunks, the young man who asked him if he wanted to get high, the odd couple strolling hand in hand. He ignored everyone until he saw Sherry on the park bench, her head bobbling rhythmically in a man's lap. The sweep of her strawberry blond hair hid her face from him but Taylor knew it was Sherry. But it couldn't be Sherry. It couldn't.

He stopped by the park bench, not believing what he was seeing. It was Sherry.

But Sherry was dead.

The man had a hand resting casually on the back of Sherry's head, his own tilted back in ecstasy. Neither of them knew they were being watched. Not until Taylor clamped a hand on the man's exposed throat and used his other to pull Sherry up and fling her away.

The man was making gagging noises as he futilely fought against the vise that was squeezing off his breath. He stared at Taylor with panicked eyes. Taylor grimly noticed the man's penis was now lying flaccid in his open pants much like Rico's had after . . .

Taylor screamed wordlessly, an animal sound of pure pain and rage, and drew his fist back. He was going to beat Rico to death.

"No! Please stop!" Sherry lunged at Taylor, wrapped both her hands around his cocked arm. "He's my boyfriend. It's okay, I wanted to do it," she sobbed frantically. "Please don't hurt him."

Taylor looked at the woman clutching his arm. It wasn't Sherry, never had been. Sherry was dead. It wasn't Rico on the bench, pinned beneath Taylor's hand, just some scared kid, barely out of high school.

Taylor released his grip on the man's throat and gently backed away, his hands held out peacefully. The woman threw herself at her boyfriend and they wrapped their arms protectively around each other, but neither ever took their eyes from the maniac before them.

Taylor eased away. "I'm sorry. I thought . . ." he said, trying to explain, but it was useless. He retrieved his bag from where he had dropped it and hurried from the park. He never looked back until he was safely across Carlton Street but by then the couple — if they were still there — were hidden by darkness.

Confused, lost in a haze of painful memories, Taylor headed up Homewood Avenue. He was almost at Wellesley Street — a short walk along Wellesley to his apartment, then he'd be able to lock tonight away with Sherry and all the ghosts — when someone spoke to him.

"Looking for a date, honey?"

Startled out of black thoughts, Taylor looked up and found a young Asian woman wearing a tiny red dress staring provocatively at him. Her black hair was swept to one side, baring a slender length of vulnerable neck. Lips painted in scarlet smiled at him.

"Like what you see?"

Taylor nodded mutely, not trusting himself to speak.

"I've got a room if you've got the money, or we can go someplace closer if we're quick."

"Where?" he managed. He licked dry lips.

"Follow me, honey." She took him by the hand and led him across the street to a dark parking lot. The whore was slight in build and height and Taylor knew she would fall quickly beneath his hands. They all did.

They're weak, all of them. Whores and weaklings. Taylor's hands trembled with a fury he could barely contain.

The whore smiled at him over a bare shoulder. "Nervous or excited, honey?"

She guided him to a far corner of the half-empty lot, tugged him into the dark recess between a minivan and a fence. She leaned up against the van and ran her eyes appreciatively over Taylor's body.

"What do you want, baby?" she purred. "You wanna come in my mouth or my ass?"

Taylor's fist slammed into her cheek, driving her skull into the van's side window, starring the glass. She would have fallen to the ground had he not hit her again. Blood exploded from her mouth as Taylor's fist shattered her teeth. He grabbed her soft, enticing throat with a hand callused from countless hours of lifting heavy iron and pinned her to the van.

She looked at him, her eyes filled with terror and bewilderment. "I thought you knew," she uttered feebly. Blood flowed from her ruined mouth to spill over Taylor's hand.

"Fucking whore," Taylor snarled. "You're all fucking whores."

He hit her again. And again. She sagged limply in his grasp and bloodied sweat let her slip free of his hand. She collapsed bonelessly, striking the pavement with a meaty thud. Taylor knelt and studied her unconscious form. The strapless dress had slid down, baring the whore's small breasts.

He sat her up against the van, nudging her into place several times to keep her from toppling over. Her head drooped on her chest. Taking a handful of hair, he raised her head and began gently slapping her cheeks. He wanted her to be awake for her punishment. She groaned, eyelids fluttering.

"That's it, you fucking whore. Time to wake up. We ain't finished yet." He shoved her dress down, baring the whore to the waist. He studied her breasts with a loathing sneer on his face, drew his fist back.

A voice rang out in the night, freezing Taylor.

"Police! How ya doing?"

"Bud, I can't believe it's gotten qui — not busy." Connor corrected himself, not wanting to jinx them with the q-word.

The night had flown by in a blur of radio calls but now the division had slipped into a lull, a period of calmness that could last the rest of the night or explode in the next few seconds. Jack had his money on the explosion; it felt like 51 was just pausing to catch its breath.

And like all smart coppers, they had taken advantage of the respite to grab coffees. Jack's training officer up in 32 had taught him the rules of policing. The first rule, of course, was *Everyone goes home at the end of shift*, followed closely by *A smart copper is never cold, hungry or wet*. No Second Cup this time, however; Connor was driving.

"Want a quick arrest?" Jack asked, twisting in the passenger seat.

"Sure t'ing, man," Connor said in a bad Jamaican accent. "Whatcha got?"

"A hooker just took her john into the stairwell by the parking lot."

"Cool." Connor pulled the scout car to the curb. They were on Homewood south of Wellesley. A squat apartment building sat on the southeast corner and its visitor parking lot was behind it with the entrance on Homewood. Just off the sidewalk, thrusting up from the lawn like some Morlock well, was the stairwell leading down into the underground parking lot. The officers approached the concrete railing, their portable radios at low volume but with no other efforts at stealth; they knew the couple would be otherwise engaged.

The bottom of the short stairwell was thick with shadows but not enough to completely conceal the two figures below. Not the one bent over the stairs nor the one behind, thrusting vigorously.

Connor stifled a giggle and mouthed to Jack *one, two, three*. On three, their flashlights cut through the darkness, revealing all, and Connor announced in an unnecessarily loud voice, "Police! How ya doing?"

The john threw up a protective arm against the light while his other groped for his pants. The prostitute simply hung her head and muttered, "Aw, shit."

"Come on up, folks," Connor called out merrily. Once the busted couple climbed dejectedly up to the surface, Connor took the john off to one side while Jack dealt with the hooker. Tall, even without the stilettos, she smoothed her pink dress over thin hips while she waited for the questions to begin.

Jack tapped his pen against his head. "Your wig is a little off-centre."

"Oh, thanks." Her voice was a husky whisper.

"Name?" Jack asked, pen poised to write.

"Sheila."

Jack looked at her, waiting.

"Fine," she huffed. "Sherman. Sherman Moors."

"Thank you." Jack jotted down Sherman's date of birth, address and description.

"Hey, Jack," Connor called. He jerked a thumb at the john. "This guy doesn't believe he was fucking a guy."

"That ain't a guy," the john said indignantly. "If that's a guy, then that means I'm gay and I'm not a fucking faggot. I'm married with a kid and one on the way." He was young, mid-twenties at best, and had his chest shoved out like some tough-guy wannabe.

Connor was grinning immensely. "Hey, honey, tell this guy your name."

Sherman's shoulders sagged. Sighing, the prostitute tugged off the blond wig. "Sherman." His voice was flat, defeated, and Jack felt like giving Connor a smack.

The john handled the revelation rather poorly. "Fuck me!" he cried and fell to his butt, trying to sob convincingly.

Jack finished Sherman's Appearance Notice, his court date set for next month, and handed it to him with some advice. "Why don't you stay out of sight for a while? Grab a coffee or something. We'll send the idiot on his way but I can't guarantee he won't come back."

Sherman nodded, his wig back in place. "Thanks, but he won't be back. Not for that, at least. He knew what he was buying."

"Yeah, kinda figured that. Any problems lately, Sheila? Anyone causing trouble in the area?"

Sheila shook her head. "It's been busy but tame. I did hear something about a working girl getting beaten up a couple of nights ago over on Church."

It was Jack's turn to shake his head. "We haven't been told anything about that, but that's 52 Division and they tend to keep things to themselves. Have a good night, Sheila."

"You too, officer." Sheila headed back to her spot on Maitland Place, the division's track for transvestite prostitutes.

I never asked if she got paid. Jack glanced at the john, still huddling on the ground like he was some kind of victim. *Guess she did.*

Connor had the john on his feet by the time Jack joined them. "Time to go, buddy." Connor waved his hand along Homewood. "North or south, just get going."

"Sometimes this job really sucks," Jack commented as he watched the john trudge away.

"How so?"

Jack faced Connor. "Think about it. If that guy's telling the truth and he is married, what's he going to take home to his wife after butt-fucking a tranny without a condom?"

"So what's that got to do with us?" Connor asked as they headed back to the scout car.

"Don't you think his wife has the right to know her husband was having unprotected anal sex with someone from a high-risk group? But if we called her to let her know for her own safety and the kids', then that asshole could probably sue us and have us fired. It sucks."

"So make an anonymous phone call," Connor suggested.

Jack snorted. "I'm thinking about it. But it'd be pretty obvious —" Jack stopped and swept the parking lot with his flashlight.

"What is it?" Connor had his light out as well.

"Don't know," Jack muttered, heading into the lot. "Thought I heard something."

The parking lot was small, room for maybe twenty cars, but less than half of the spots were filled. Jack slowly panned his light over the cars, not knowing what he was looking for but sure he'd recognize it when he found it. He walked farther into the lot.

"Hey, Jack. Hold up." Connor had his head cocked to the radio mike clipped to his shoulder. "There's a stabbing at Sherbourne and Dundas. Let's go."

Jack clicked off his flashlight and ran over to the car. Seconds later the lot was splashed with flickering red light as the scout car sped off down Homewood. The flashing light was swallowed by the night and the lot was left in shadow.

Taylor watched the cops run back to their car and speed off. The breath escaped him in a relieved sigh. Close, too fucking close.

He looked down at the whore, slumped over on the pavement. A small puddle of blood, glistening a dark crimson in the weak fluorescent light, spread out from the whore's face. Taylor stared at the whore's face then her breasts, recalling the comments he had heard the cops making.

Could it be?

He yanked the whore's dress up over her hips and ripped aside her underwear. "Fuck me," he groaned. "You're a fucking man." Why, in God's name, would a guy want to be a woman? A weak, useless woman?

"You're still a fucking whore," he spat at the hooker. He wanted to stay and punish the little fuck some more but the close call with the cops had shaken his nerve. No need to press his luck.

The whore was whimpering, trying to lift his head. Taylor's boot lashed out, smashing his jaw. The whore fell back to the pavement to lie unmoving and broken in his own blood.

Taylor scaled the fence at the rear of the parking lot and vanished into the night.

"Those boots are toast, bud."

"Yeah, I know." Jack stomped his feet. "At least they're not squishing as much now. The blood must be drying."

Jack and Connor were standing in the laneway to the east of 310 Dundas Street. The laneway — Jack had learned just tonight that it had a name, Oskenonton Lane — ran north from Dundas up to Carlton Street and was a common shortcut for pedestrians and some cars if the drivers were willing to risk the potholes. There would be no cutting through the lane tonight.

Jack and Connor were the first to arrive on scene at the stabbing and had found the victim collapsed a short distance up from Dundas, the handle of a steak knife jutting proudly out of his chest. The victim was barely conscious and his breathing was laboured.

Mine would be laboured too if I had to breathe around a knife.

"5106 with a priority," Jack called over the mitre as Connor packed bandages around the knife.

"Units stay off the air for the priority. Go ahead, 5106."

"We're on the east side of 310 Dundas, in the laneway. We have an adult male who's been stabbed in the chest. We need a rush on the ambulance."

"10-4, 5106. DAS on the way."

The victim, a crackhead judging by his filthy, wasted body, was growing paler before Jack's eyes.

"Shit!" Connor cried out in frustration. "I don't know how many times this guy's been stabbed. He's fucking gushing blood."

Jack slapped on latex gloves and grabbed a handful of bandages from the scout car's first-aid kit. "Let's just put pressure over as many holes as we can find," he said, squatting beside Connor. And that's when the victim, in the last moments of his life, puked out a lungful of blood.

All over Jack's boots.

Sunday, 22 July
0210 hours

Jack stretched, feeling his spine crack beneath the ballistic vest. He checked his watch under the streetlight. 2:10. Overtime for sure. FIS had rolled up a while ago — not Manny's team, unfortunately — and started doing their thing. Powerful floodlights bathed the scene in brutal clarity. Jack could see the irregular puddle formed when the bloody vomit had spewed across his boots. It looked like one of those psychiatric ink blots.

Hm, looks like a butterfly.

"You got another pair of boots, bud?" Connor asked as he lounged against the scout car. They were blocking off the south end of the laneway and a good chunk of the sidewalk on Dundas. Police tape sagged limply in the muggy air. Yellow plastic party streamers.

"Yeah, I think so. I'll have to check when I get home." He grimaced at his boots and stomped again. Inside, the boots were still wet but the outside was drying quickly and semi-dried flakes of blood fell off. "If I don't, I'll be wearing running shoes tomorrow."

"Sandals might be better in this heat." Connor tore open the Velcro sides of his external vest carrier and flapped the front panel, fanning himself. "I don't know how you can wear the interior carrier when it's this hot."

Jack shrugged. "Few reasons."

"Such as?" Connor probed.

"Well, I think it looks more professional than the exterior and why do I want to remind the assholes I'm wearing a vest? Also, the exterior's a lot of handholds."

"Handholds?"

Jack nodded. "Long ago, well before our time, the dress uniform was the uniform of the day and the assholes were constantly using the cross strap as a handhold during fights. Coppers

70

had to fight management to get the strap removed and now we've just gone and given the assholes a bunch of handholds."

"It's not that bad," Connor commented as he secured his vest in place.

While Connor had his head down, Jack snuck up on him — not easy to do in squelching, blood-soaked boots — and grabbed the shoulder strap of his vest. Connor managed a startled "Hey!" as Jack yanked him off the car and shook him back and forth, like Justice playing with his favourite stuffed animal, before flinging him away. Connor staggered down the sidewalk several steps before regaining his balance.

"Yeah, I guess you're right," Jack mused. "It isn't that bad."

Connor, shamefaced, walked back to the car. "I get your point," he conceded, tugging his vest back into place. He settled against the car next to Jack. "Sheesh. You taking steroids or something?"

Shocked, Jack looked at Connor. "Why the fuck is everyone suddenly asking if I'm on 'roids?"

"Let's see." Connor ticked off the points. "You spend more time in the gym than Tank —" tick "— you tossed me around pretty easily —" tick "— and you do have a reputation for a short temper." Tick.

"I do?" Jack asked, genuinely amazed. "Wonderful."

"Well? Do you?"

"No, I don't. Do you?" Jack snapped and instantly regretted it. *Guess my temper is getting short.*

"Not anymore," Connor admitted.

This was Connor's night for shocking Jack. "You took 'roids? No offense, but you're not exactly huge."

Connor laughed. "You should have seen me before. I weighed a hundred and twenty-seven pounds. The guys in 53 called me Skeletor." He quickly held up a cautionary hand. "I prefer Pest, if it's all the same to you."

"What's it like? Taking steroids, I mean."

"I got some good stuff from this guy I know, did a few cycles and put on sixty pounds, if you can believe it."

"Sixty pounds?" Jack was impressed.

"Yup. Before I went on the juice, I ate like a pig, lifted as heavy as I could and avoided cardio like the plague and still couldn't put on any size. But with the 'roids, poof! Here I am. Well, not exactly poof. I still had to train my ass off."

"Would you ever do them again?"

"Fuck, no," Connor said without hesitation. "Being on them scared the shit out of me."

"How so?"

"Your emotions get . . . exaggerated. Whatever you're feeling, happy, sad, mad, whatever, you *really* fucking feel it. I was bouncing off the walls I was so happy or ready to kill someone. And you feel tight and bloated all the time. Yuck. But the worst was lying in bed at night listening to my heartbeat. I could feel it pounding in my chest." He shivered at the memory. "No thanks, not again. I'm happy the size I am."

"Hmm," Jack grunted. Scary shit, but it didn't matter because Jack wasn't considering juicing.

He wasn't.

"Well, don't you look . . ."

"Look like what?" Jenny demanded as she caught up to Jack by the station's back door.

"Well, if you were a guy," Jack claimed, "I'd say you looked like a bag of shit. But since you're too pretty to be a bag of shit, how about I say you look like you got ridden hard and put away wet."

"Oh, yeah. That's much better than a bag of shit." Her waist-length hair was hanging loose, looking as rumpled as she did, and she brushed raven-black strands from her face. "Gimme a break, I just got to bed a few hours ago." She lowered her sunglasses then hurriedly shoved them back in place, but not before Jack caught a glimpse of red-rimmed eyes.

"Ah, yes," he said, grinning knowingly. "The bachelorette party. Wasn't that Friday night?"

"It was, but for your information, it ran late. We just got back from Niagara Falls this morning. And also for your information, no one rode me. Although —" she fingered the wrinkled fabric of her shirt "— I do vaguely recall something about a fountain."

"I guess I'm driving tonight, then," Jack figured, chuckling.

"Unless you want to check me out on a breathalyzer. And by the way, smart guy, you're not looking so prim and proper yourself."

Jack smiled sheepishly. "Yeah, caught a homicide last night and did some overtime." He reached for the door but it suddenly slammed open, driving the handle into his sore ribs. He stifled a scream and doubled over. He would have fallen had Jenny not caught him around the waist.

The metal door was swinging shut and an enraged voice yelled from inside. "Fuck you, too! Next time fucking do it yourself!"

The door exploded open again and this time someone didn't stop to yell obscenities. A very pissed-off black man stormed out of the station, his rigid stance radiating his anger. He never spared a glance for Jack and Jenny.

"Hey, asshole," she began, taking a step after the male, but a firm hand on her arm kept her from chasing him down.

"Don't bother, Jenny. It ain't worth it."

She turned and found Rick Mason, the detective in charge of the Major Crime Unit, holding her back.

"Who was the prick?" she wanted to know. "I don't recognize him. He's not a cop, is he?"

"No. Just a rather unhappy CI, is all."

"So what's his problem? Someone do his cornrows too tight?"

Mason lifted his shoulders in a tired *I don't know* gesture. Some confidential informants were just assholes. "What's with Jack?"

After Jenny had caught him, Jack had settled down on the old picnic table next to the door. He was holding his side and trying not to puke from the pain.

"Jack's fine," Jack announced.

"You don't look fine," Jenny said, eying him critically. "If I didn't know better, I'd say you look like you just got kicked in the balls."

Mason nodded in agreement, his long grey goatee brushing his chest. The detective was a big man. Big shoulders, big chest, big belly. With his shaved head and goatee, all he needed was a mess of tattoos to pass as a biker.

"Hurt my ribs in the gym the other day," Jack explained. "The door handle caught me in the perfect spot, that's all."

"Should you be going on the road?" Jenny was still viewing him with a doubtful expression.

Jack waved her concern away. "I'm fine. See?" He stood up and drew a deep breath, successfully masking the pain that lanced through him. "Since when do you meet with an informant at the station, Rick?" he asked to divert attention.

Mason snorted. "He's a special case, you could say. Hey, it's a good thing I ran into you two. You're with me starting Tuesday. We're doing a john sweep and I don't have anyone to play hooker."

Jenny shook her head uncertainly. "I don't know how well Jack'll be able to shake his money maker with those sore ribs."

Mason grinned. "Guess we'll just have to make do with you and put Jack on backup. The area around Pembroke's been busy in the afternoons lately so we're starting at one. Dress slutty, Jenny, not you, Jack," he clarified and disappeared into the station.

"You're looking rather happy with yourself," Jenny observed.

"Why shouldn't I be?" Jack confessed. "I get to watch you strut your stuff looking all slutty."

"Hm." Jenny cupped her breasts. "I don't have enough in the boob department to show off cleavage. Guess you'll have to settle for staring at my ass."

"I always do," Jack said, opening the door for her. "I always do."

"Why are we doing a call in 52?" Jack wanted to know as he pulled the scout car to the curb in front of the emergency entrance to St. Michael's hospital. The heat smacked him in the face as he got out of the car.

Not a good day to be wearing black polyester and Kevlar.

"The text said something about the complainant living in 51. I guess the dispatcher figured the assault happened at home so the call got bumped to us. Just as well," Jenny said as she gently closed the car door. Loud noises weren't her friend today. "You know as well as I do that if 52 got the call they'd be turning it over to us as soon as they realized it happened on our side of Jarvis."

"Can't expect the Hollywood cops to give up their paid duties."

52 Division was the core of downtown Toronto, sandwiched between the armpits of 51 and 14. It held the financial and entertainment districts and was a preferred place to work due to its insanely high amount of paid duties. It seemed to Jack that a lot of 52 coppers avoided radio calls because they didn't want overtime or court to get in the way of the off-duty assignments for private companies. A detective from 52 CIB had once confided to Jack that the biggest dog fucker in 51 or 14 could come to 52 and be a star.

Guess that's what Boris did.

Armed with a radar gun and his ticket book, Boris had vaulted himself to the top of the heap of ticket writers in 51. Supervisors loved him because he put in such good numbers and coppers hated him because he was a dog fucker when it came to real police work.

52's loss is our gain.

The ER doors whooshed open and Jack and Jenny gratefully

stepped into the air conditioning. Even the short walk from the car had left them both sweating under their ballistic vests. The waiting room, like any city's downtown hospital, Jack imagined, was controlled chaos. The line at the triage was four deep, all the chairs in the waiting area were packed and not everyone was waiting patiently. Two stressed-looking security guards were explaining, probably for the hundredth time that hour, how patients were seen according to severity of injury, not in order of appearance. The stocky woman being enlightened by security had an equally stocky child in tow. The boy looked unconcerned, shoving Tostitos in his mouth as his mom argued with security.

"No, it's you who doesn't understand," she expounded, her voice rising shrilly. "My son needs his stomach looked at, he's in dreadful discomfort and needs medical attention this second."

Your kid needs to lay off the chips, lady.

Jack could hear the twin sighs as the guards launched into the explanation yet again. Jack wished them luck.

The triage nurse looked like she was deep enough into her shift to have lost sight of when it began but not far along enough to be able to glimpse the end. Jack could commiserate; he'd been there enough times himself. Hell, all shift workers had.

The nurse glanced up at them from her computer then scanned the area around them.

"Don't worry," Jenny said with a smile. "We're not bringing you anyone."

"That makes you the first two who haven't," she grumbled wearily. "But don't expect too much in the way of gratitude. I'm too damned tired."

"Got long to go before shift ends?" Jack asked.

"Ends?" She smiled bitterly. "I was supposed to go home three hours ago."

"Ouch," Jack and Jenny said in unison, eliciting a small grin from the nurse.

"We're looking for . . ." Jenny consulted her notebook. "Cindy Rutherford."

The nurse directed them to the Major section of the ER and they left her with their hopes for a quick end to her overtime. They found Cindy reclining in her bed and there was no doubting she needed to talk with the police.

Cindy's face, where it wasn't covered in bandages and gauze, was a mass of swollen, bruised flesh. The purple of the bruises was almost black, painfully vivid against the white of the gauze. Her right eye was hidden beneath protective bandages and her left was reduced to a mere slit through puffed flesh. The eye was so swollen that Jack couldn't tell if she was watching them or asleep.

"Yeah, some asshole did a number on her, all right," said the woman sitting next to the bed, reading the cops' expressions.

"Boyfriend?" Jack supposed but the woman sitting bedside shook her head. There was something familiar about the light-complexioned black woman, but Jack couldn't quite grasp it.

"You'd think so, but it wasn't. Just some asshole off the street." The woman stared at them, as if challenging them, and Jack remembered where he knew her from but Jenny got there first.

"You work the corner at Gerrard and Church, don't you?"

The woman's stare dissolved into a sneer. "So what if we work the streets?" she spat at Jenny. "That don't give some asshole the right to do this to her."

"I never said it does, and it doesn't," Jenny answered calmly, not rising to the woman's aggression. "But if this happened when Cindy was working, then it could mean a lot of potential witnesses. Other working girls, businesses in the area."

"I know you." The voice was weak, hesitant, but it captured everyone's attention. Cindy was sitting up straighter, her one usable eye creaked open and fixated on Jack.

"You do?" He didn't bother trying to put a name to her face; he wouldn't have been able to recognize his own face in that condition.

She slowly nodded, a mere shifting of her head, but her friend covered Cindy's hand with her own. "Try not to move, Star. The doctor said your ribs are all busted up."

Star? The name tugged at Jack's memory and suddenly he had her face in his mind. "I met you last year, didn't I? We helped you out at a john's apartment when he didn't want to pay."

Again, that agonizingly slow nod.

"I was working with Sy," Jack explained to Jenny. "It was the first call I ever did with Manny." He turned back to Cindy. "You'd just started working then. It wasn't the same guy, was it?"

A slight turn of the head. No.

That would have been too easy. "Can you tell us what happened?"

"Yes." Her voice was barely a whisper, buried beneath the weight of her injuries, but there was a core of strength in it and the officers nodded in approval.

"Then let's get started," Jack declared, taking out his memo book. "And if we're lucky, when we catch this guy he won't want to be arrested and we can arrange a trip to the hospital for him."

Jack wasn't sure, but he thought the corners of Cindy's mouth twitched in appreciation.

"... sixteen staples in her scalp and three broken ribs," the doctor intoned, concluding the lengthy list of Cindy's injuries.

"Holy shit," Jenny breathed. "Sounds like the bastard was trying to beat her to death."

"Well, she's lucky one of those ribs didn't puncture a lung." The doctor was young, recently out of medical school, but already the light in his eyes was aging. Although, Jack noted, that light certainly perked up whenever the doctor looked at Jenny. "If this happened early Thursday morning like she said, I'm amazed she was able to stay out of the hospital that long before deciding to come in."

"She didn't want to," Jenny told him. "Her friend was the

one who brought her. She was afraid she wouldn't be treated because she's a prostitute."

The doctor sadly shook his head as he cleaned his glasses. Slipping them back on, he asked Jenny, "Is there anything else I can do for you?"

"Actually, there is."

So Jenny noticed his interest, as well. Guess that's my cue to leave.

"I'll meet you out in the car," he excused himself, but Jenny stopped him.

"Don't go anywhere, moron. This is about you." She favoured the doctor with a dazzling smile. "My partner hurt his ribs and I was wondering if you could check to see that he didn't break anything?"

"C'mon, Jenny. I'm f —"

For the second time that day Jack choked back a scream as Jenny jabbed him in the ribs. Trying to stay as erect as possible — it would have been damned embarrassing to collapse in a room full of people — he glared at her.

"What was that for?" he managed while keeping a protective forearm over his side.

"Proving a point, dummy. Do you see what I mean, doctor?"

Oh, sure. He gets a smile.

"Point taken," the doctor assured her. Taking Jack by the arm, he led him to a vacant room. "Let's take a look at those ribs, shall we?"

"That was nice of you."

"What was nice of me?" Jack asked over the roof of the scout car.

"I saw you take Casey aside." Jenny opened her door and ducked in. "You let her know she was wanted, right?" she asked, adjusting the steering wheel.

"Yeah." Jack eased himself into the passenger seat, babying his rib as much as he could. "I told her to turn herself in tomorrow morning and get it taken care of. That way, she'll be out before Cindy's out of the hospital."

Jenny nodded in agreement and pulled away from the curb. They were on the way back to the barn to do Cindy's aggravated assault report. "How do you crack a rib doing squats?"

"It takes talent," Jack replied smugly, lounging in the passenger seat drinking a Diet Coke. Or as close to lounging as possible when wearing Kevlar and a gun belt. After being poked and prodded by the doctor — insult after injury after Jenny's little jab — Jack was more than happy to relax and sip on his version of a doctor's lollipop while Jenny drove.

"How can he be sure it's cracked without X-raying it?"

"He says the pain is too site-specific for bruising. He wanted to do X-rays but we would've been there for hours."

"That's fine, but how did you crack it?"

"When I got folded up under the bar the rib was either forced over or under the weight belt, that's all."

"Idiot," Jenny muttered. "That's why you're supposed to use a spotter."

"My spotter and I weren't talking that morning." He took a sip of Coke, musing. "Still aren't, now that I think about it."

Jenny let the comment about Karen slide and asked instead, "What are you supposed to do for the rib?"

"Not much. Take it easy." He looked meaningfully at her. "And not let anyone punch me in the ribs again."

Jenny ignored that comment as well. "Did Brian give you any painkillers?"

"Brian? Who's Brian?"

"The doctor, moron," she said gruffly, trying to cover a sudden blush.

She wasn't gruff enough. "Ah, so it's Brian now, is it?" Jack taunted, noticing the flush climbing up Jenny's neck. "So, when did you ask him out?"

"When you were getting dressed. When else? And, for your

information," she smugly enlightened him, "he asked me out."

"Good for you." Jack drank some, belched.

"What a gentleman."

"Always. Whatever happened to what's-his-name?"

"Don't you remember? He stood me up for a hockey game and that was a mistake he never recovered from." She sighed, thinking. "Fuck, that's pathetic."

"What?"

"I dumped him over three months ago but we both knew who you meant. I haven't had a date since. Fuck."

"Don't worry, you'll always have me." He reached over and playfully stroked her thigh. "I noticed you called me 'partner' while you were talking to Brian."

"Of course, that's what people expect us to call each other. It'd sound stupid to say you were my assigned escort for the evening. Makes it sound like I'm paying for you for the evening. And since I'm not . . ." She plucked his hand from her leg. "Did you rub Manny's leg all the time?"

"Of course not," Jack said defensively. "Just once in a while." His phone rang and he checked the call display. "There he is now."

"Probably needs a leg rub."

Jack shot Jenny a look then flipped open his phone. "Hey, Manny." He listened for a few moments, then said, "No problem. Give us a few," and hung up.

"Would you mind doing a food run for Manny?" Jack asked. "He's stuck at that machete homicide and didn't bring a lunch. Swing by a Pizza Pizza and I'll grab him a couple of slices."

Jenny nodded, goosed the car through the light at Parliament Street and headed north while Jack called the dispatcher.

"Go ahead, 5106."

"Before we head in to do that report, we're going to stop off at 40 Alexander Street to see the Ident unit. 10-4?"

"10-4, '06. Off at 40 Alexander. Let me know when you're heading to the station."

"Two slices and a Coke. That'll be ten even plus tip."

"Thanks, dude." Manny gratefully snagged the paper sleeves holding his lunch, unmindful of the grease seeping through to drip on his dark golf shirt. "I'll catch you next time."

"Cheap bastard," Jack griped with a smile. "You sure your partner didn't want anything?"

"Nah," he replied around a mouthful of cheese and pepperoni. "He brings a garden with him every day."

They were standing in the ninth-floor hallway outside the apartment crime scene. The uniformed copper from 52 who was stuck guarding the door while the Ident guys did their thing inside had appreciatively taken the opportunity to disappear for a while.

Probably went to check on paid duties.

"You know you can take time to chew, right, Manny?" Jenny was watching Manny with a queasy, disgusted look on her face. "My dogs don't eat their food that fast and they're both pigs."

Manny wadded up the first empty sleeve and chucked it in the McDonald's bag that was acting as a makeshift garbage can next to the old lawn chair beside the apartment door.

"Nothing like a copper's diet." Jenny poked Manny in the stomach. A stomach already easing out past the belt buckle. "If you aren't careful, Manny, that's going to get bigger."

Manny shrugged as he mowed down on his second slice. William Armsman, Manny to everyone except supervisors when they were pissed at him, was a big, imposing guy with a shaved head and goatee, but Jenny was right: he was going to end up huge, and not in a good way.

"I see you're taking advantage of being in plain clothes," Jack noted, indicating Manny's goatee. "But I thought goatees still weren't allowed in investigative positions, only old clothes."

Manny pumped his shoulders again, a silly grin on his face. "Until someone tells me otherwise . . ."

The apartment door opened and a tall, bespectacled man in a

golf shirt and khakis stepped out. "I *do* keep telling you, Manny. You just ignore me."

"That's because I know you're not serious, Al. Can I show them the front hall?"

The Ident detective waved them on. "We're finished there, so go ahead. I'm heading down to the van to get my lunch."

"Come on, guys. This is cool." Manny swung open the door and stepped back, beaming like a proud parent.

Jack let Jenny go first and bumped into her when she stopped just inside the doorway.

"Holy shit," they both exclaimed, softly and in perfect unison.

The front hall was small, no bigger than twenty square feet, with a solid wall to the right and a closet opposite. The floor, walls, closet doors and even the ceiling — Jack craned his head in disbelief to check — were shrouded in old blood, dried over the last few days to a rust brown. Protruding from the walls and clumped in the thick desiccated puddle like tiny, grotesque islands were pieces of bone, some with scraps of scalp and hair still clinging to them.

"Cool, right?"

Jack stepped back from the carnage. "Well, I'll never accuse a horror film of overdoing the blood again, that's for sure."

"What the hell happened in there?" Jenny shut the door behind her.

"Someone took a machete to the guy's head. Imagine hacking away at a block of cheese with a kitchen knife." Manny karate chopped the air. "Whack, whack, whack."

Jenny grimaced. "You're sick, Manny. You should fit right in at Ident. By the way, when you worked with Jack, did he ever rub your thigh?"

A puzzled little smile flittered across Manny's face as he looked from Jenny to Jack. "All the time," he confessed. "Only when he did it, he called me Jenny."

The Seaton House, the city's largest men's hostel, was a huge, bleak building. A sense of weariness and finality hung about the four-storey edifice and its faded, yellow-brick exterior appeared to sag beneath the burden of too many lost souls. The homeless, the mentally ill, drug users and alcoholics, all passed through the Seaton House's doors, adding their tales to the institution's near half century of history.

In the winter the hostel could be wedged to capacity, providing beds and meals to hundreds of men seeking shelter from the cold. But in the heat of summer, only the long-term clients who called the hostel home could be found haunting its halls.

As the sun sank below the skyline, mercifully dragging the worst of the heat with it, a handful of residents drifted aimlessly along the sidewalk abutting the fence that ran the length of the hostel. The head-high metal fence with its spearlike rods always reinforced the hostel's brooding, medieval feel to Jack.

Jenny pulled to the curb behind the crisis team's white unmarked Crown Vic. Jack slowly got out of the car, favouring his sore rib but trying not to show any impairment. He and Jenny headed for the front doors, their eyes constantly scanning the people and area about them. A cyclist in a dull red shirt, upon catching sight of the officers, did an abrupt U-turn back into the alley he had just come out of, nearly spilling himself off the bike. Jack smirked.

"If I was any more sensitive, I'd get a complex."

Jenny nodded. "Some people just aren't comfortable around uniforms, I guess."

On a warm evening such as this, the front steps — *All they need is a moat and portcullis* — would normally be populated with smokers, the odd card game and the occasional resident daring or stupid enough to sneak a forbidden alcoholic drink. Today the worn stairs hosted only three people: the cop and nurse from the CIT and one sorry-looking sack of shit.

Shit Sack, clad only in a pair of threadbare jeans, was having trouble staying upright even though he was sitting on the concrete steps. His forearms were braced on his wide-spread knees and his head, with its mop of unkempt black hair, hung listlessly over a puddle of vomit between his feet. As Jack and Jenny approached, Shit Sack's left arm slipped free of its mooring and he would have toppled down the stairs had he not caught himself. His hand, already dropping, splatted into the puke, splashing his bare feet. He held that position for a moment, then dragged the arm back up to the knee. He didn't wipe his hand clean. Jack watched as vomit slowly dripped from Shit Sack's fingertips.

"Hi, Sue, Aaron. I take it he's not EDP?" Jenny asked, gesturing to Shit Sack.

Sue twiddled hello with her fingers as she chatted on her cell phone.

"The call came over as EDP and he might be emotionally disturbed when he sobers up," Aaron said, "but right now, he's just piss-ass drunk. Can't hold his Gatorade and rubbing alcohol. I hate to dump this on you but there's no mental health issue here and my chicken dinner's getting cold."

"No problem. Do you have a name on him?"

"Lloyd Henry, Jack," Sue told him, snapping her phone shut. "Come on, big boy. Everybody's arrested Lloyd at least twice."

"Guess I'm just lucky." Jack snugged on a pair of latex gloves. "We've got him. You guys can take off," he offered, but Sue was already back on her phone and heading for her car. Aaron rolled his eyes and left, shaking his head.

"Let's get you home, Lloyd," Jenny suggested as she and Jack each took an arm.

"Home?" Jack inquired as they hoisted Lloyd to his feet. He hung limply between them.

"Cell thirteen, Jack," Jenny explained as they shuffle-dragged Lloyd to the car. "He probably sleeps there more often than any other place. Hell, he'll probably end up dying in there."

Jack nodded. "Home it is, then."

"When did Sue join the crisis thing?"

Jenny shrugged. "Couple months ago, I guess. Why?"

It was Jack's turn to dismiss the question. "No reason. First time I saw Aaron he was working with a cop whose head looked like a fire hydrant."

"Oh, him," Jenny giggled, knowing exactly who Jack was referring to. "He transferred somewhere or got his stripes or something."

Jack shuddered at the thought of Hydrant Head as a sergeant.

"You interested in joining the team?" she wanted to know.

"Nope. I'm happy where I am. Comfortable-looking uniform, though. Hold still, Lloyd." They were in the scout car parking lot waiting to parade their drunk and Jack had Lloyd leaning face first against the brick wall next to the sally port door. With his hands cuffed behind him — only idiots handcuffed prisoners to the front — and one of Jack's gloved hands pinning him between the shoulder blades, Lloyd couldn't move much, but that didn't stop him from wiggling.

"Hold still," Jack repeated. "You keep squirming around like that and I'll let go of you. See if I care if you take a face-plant in the pavement." Not that it would make much difference to Lloyd's face.

Lloyd Henry was one of a small group of Native Canadians living within the boundaries of the division. According to Jenny, who had heard it from members of the quarter-century club — coppers who had worked in 51 for twenty-five years or more — Lloyd had been getting hammered since before he was old enough to drink and he was as much a divisional mainstay as the old station house itself. He was in his late forties but looked a bad twenty years older. Lloyd had progressed, or fallen, from drinking hard liquor, to beer, to cheap beer, to the cheapest beer and now rubbing alcohol and cooking wine were his cocktails of choice.

This guy's liver must look like a used dishrag.

Besides being a lifelong alcoholic, Lloyd was also a well-known scrapper. Apparently, in his younger and not so inebriated years he had loved to fight almost as much as he loved to drink and had the missing teeth, crooked nose and misshapen knuckles to prove it. The broken web of veins across his distorted nose resembled a road map laid over a three-dimensional map of a mountain range.

But Lloyd's brawling days were mostly behind him, probably nothing more than dimly recalled memories slowly drowning in the alcoholic bog that was his brain.

"Gah fuh yo'sef," Lloyd gurgled.

"I think Lloyd just told you to go fuck yourself," Jenny laughed.

"That's what I got, too. Love you too, Lloyd. Now stay put." Jack leaned a little more weight on Lloyd's back, settling him down. "I hope Greene isn't parading."

"Fuck, no," Jenny agreed. "He takes forever. Yesterday, Paul and I brought in a guy for assaulting his own kid. The guy had a bloody lip and Greene asked him how he got hurt and if he wanted to lay a complaint against me for hitting him. I know they're supposed to ask about injuries and complaints, but he didn't have to encourage the fucker."

"And did he lay a complaint?"

Jenny shook her head.

"And did he have grounds?" Jack asked with a sly smile.

"I wonder what's keeping the booker," she said, avoiding the question.

"Greene's probably doing a sock check on the prisoners," Jack commented.

A lifer — forty-plus years on the job and counting — Staff Sergeant Greene held to the directives and practices from the time when he took his first steps in police boots. Stand-up parades with full uniform and equipment inspections, including sock checks — must be black — had only been the beginning of his rigid, backward-facing leadership. Morale had been quickly crushed beneath his polished issued shoes.

Open revolt had come when Jack had orchestrated Operation Underwear and the platoon had paraded in their underwear. The brazen display of unity and defiance had shaken Greene down to his regulated foundations, cracking the thin veneer of normalcy he exhibited to the world. Since then his acts of tyranny had abated and his appearance on parade was nothing but a ghostly memory. Greene was wounded but still dangerous, as Manny had discovered. Jack would not relax his guard until the man and his waxed handlebar moustache were gone from the station.

The sally port door rumbled up on its tracks and once it was high enough, the officers walked a shambling Lloyd into the garage. Navigating the four metal steps up to the door leading to the booking hall was an act of controlled stoogery. The steps were barely wide enough for two people abreast, let alone three, and Jenny and Jack had to take Lloyd up sideways. Jack found himself practically lifting their soused prisoner up to the landing and was thankful it was a short hoist; for someone on a liquid diet, Lloyd was damn heavy.

"Listen up, Lloyd." Jenny pointed to a sign posted by the door. "'Sections of this building including this area,'" she read loud enough to be picked up by the camera, "'are monitored by remote audiovisual recording devices. This equipment is now in operation and you are under observation.'"

"Fu' 'ou."

"That's right, Lloyd. Smile, you're on camera." Jenny pushed open the metal door with her foot and they ushered Lloyd into the booking hall.

Calling the booking hall a hall was rather grandiose, like calling a taxi a limo, but it was a well-trafficked room, as all prisoners coming in and going out of the station had to cross its worn concrete floor. There were two more doors: one for the prisoners headed to the CIB and one that lead directly to the cells. Lloyd would be taking the shorter of the two trips.

There was a small bench bolted to the cinderblock wall and Jack and Jenny carefully guided Lloyd's ass to its wooden slats. Seated, Lloyd tilted forward; with his hands behind him, he had nothing to brace against his knees. Jack and Jenny each put a hand on a shoulder, halting Lloyd in mid-topple. They cautiously removed their hands, ready to grab for Lloyd should he start to fall, but he stayed where he was, his dirty, sweaty torso canted forward, head hanging like a dead pendulum. A thin, silvery line of drool appeared from behind the curtain of Lloyd's greasy hair, reaching for the floor.

"Officers, can you tell me why this man is in your custody and present at my police station?" Greene was standing by the booker's desk, pen poised over memo book, a distasteful look on his face. Whether the frown was for Lloyd or his handlers, Jack couldn't tell.

"This male has been arrested for being intoxicated in a public place," Jenny justified, then quickly added, "at the time of arrest, the male was examined by the CIT nurse who determined he was not drunk enough to warrant being taken to the hospital." Jenny had obviously paraded drunks before the Staff before and knew to pre-empt an objection.

Greene stalked from behind the counter. He mostly stalked, rarely walked, and never strolled. Jack figured it was from being a small man in a big man's world. Greene wasn't exactly short, more average in size and build, but must have resembled a dwarf when sized up alongside his colleagues, since he was hired in an era when six foot was considered short for a cop.

"Son," he said, moving to stand in front of Lloyd. "Are you feeling ill?"

"Staff, I wouldn't —" Jack began, but Greene glared him to silence.

"Do you want to go to a hospital?"

Lloyd mumbled a low "Fu' 'ou."

"What was that?" The Staff leaned over to better hear Lloyd and that's when Lloyd, who had been power-chugging rubbing alcohol and grape Gatorade since noon, puked all over Greene's legs.

"We should give Lloyd a bloody medal." Lloyd had been lodged in cell thirteen, the drunk cell and his home away from wherever, more than an hour ago, but Jack was still grinning. He was half listening to the dispatcher as she gave out an unwanted-guest call to another car when Jenny shushed him.

"Jack, can you pull up the call she just gave to '09?"

"Sure thing." Jack tapped out the commands on the car's computer. "Heidi Dubaine," he read, "is calling in to have her boyfriend removed."

"What's the boyfriend's name? I thought I heard the dispatcher say Dean Myers."

"Hang on." Jack scrolled down the text of the call. "Yeah, Dean Myers. You know him?"

Jenny nodded as she swung the scout car in a U-turn on Shuter Street, bumping the wheels over the south curb. Crown Vics were notorious for their wide turning radius.

"Remember the twit I told you about? The one I brought in with the fat lip?"

"Yeah. And Greene tried to persuade him to lay a complaint. This the same guy?"

Jenny nodded again and Jack reached for the microphone. "5106, we'll take that unwanted guest on Whiteside."

"10-4, 5106. '09, you can disregard."

Whiteside Place was a little loop of a street in south Regent Park, home to a single high-rise. How the only building on a street that amounted to little more than a pimple on the south side of Dundas could be numbered 605, Jack never knew.

Regent Park was a sprawling housing complex packed with

squat apartment buildings, high-rises and townhouses, lane-ways and parking lots, good people and assholes. It was an infamous blotch on downtown Toronto. When Jack told people he worked in 51 Division, he typically drew blank looks. If he said the Regent Park area, people usually nodded and offered their condolences.

"Didn't you pinch this guy for assaulting his kid?" Jack asked as they passed into the lobby. No need to buzz for entry; locks in Regent Park didn't stay functional for long. "He should have conditions not to be here."

Jenny shook her head as she punched the elevator button. "I grabbed him over in Moss Park. This must be a different girlfriend."

The ride to the eleventh floor was done in jerky silence as the elevator hitched and groaned its way up. *Gotta start taking the stairs more often*, Jack told himself as the doors wheezed open with the floor of the lift a few inches shy of the hallway. They stepped up into the hall. The eleventh floor in 605 Whiteside Place was like the halls in any Regent Park building: dingy, dirty and malodorous. If the halls had been the veins and arteries in a human, the poor sap would have died ages ago from rotten circulation.

The apartment was at the end of the hall — *Of course it is, it's always at the end of the hall* — with a dozing male sitting outside the door, his legs stretched out on the scummy floor. He snorted awake and turned bleary eyes on the approaching officers.

"I ain't leaving till that bitch gives me my shit," he said from his seat on the floor. He crossed his arms and glared defiantly at them.

"We'll see," Jenny said. She stood by Myers's outstretched legs. "Well?" she asked, giving him her own glare.

Myers studied her for a moment then, with a sneering smirk, slowly withdrew his legs, stopping with his feet in front of Jenny's boots. His smirk deepened, a stain upon his already ugly mug.

His bottom lip still bore the cut Jenny had given him, partly healed. It looked like some rancid liquid was dribbling from Myers's mouth. Jack was coming to dislike Dean Myers rather quickly. He didn't know if Myers recognized Jenny but he was pretty sure the unfavourable impression Myers had made on her was still foremost in her mind.

Then she proved it was. She hooked her foot around Myers's ankle and swept his legs ahead of her, spinning Myers on his ass and dumping him fully on the floor.

"Excuse me," she said sweetly and stepped past him.

Myers made to get up, anger darkening his face, but Jack stopped him with a simple "Don't."

Myers paused, propped up on one foot and hand, obviously thinking; the strained effort was clear on his face. Finally, rational thought prevailed and he settled back onto his butt, instructing Jack, "Tell that bitch I want my shit."

"Who says common sense is dead?" Jack asked rhetorically as Jenny rapped on the door.

A young woman, old before her time, with frizzy strawberry blond hair and a baby cradled on a hip, opened the door. She jabbed a finger at Myers, spitting, "I want that piece of shit out of my house."

"I ain't in your house, bitch!" Myers declared from where he sat.

Jack threw Myers a cautionary finger, growling, "Enough!" at the same time Jenny snapped, "Quit it!" at the woman.

Miraculously, both parties quieted and Jenny turned to Myers. "You," she ordered, "stay put. You," she said to the woman, "inside."

The baby started to cry and the woman bounced him on a bony hip as she backed up to let Jenny and Jack into the apartment. The units in the Whiteside building were two-floored and this one had three tiny bedrooms crammed into the first floor. An incredibly steep, narrow staircase ran up from beside the door to the second floor.

"Can we talk upstairs?" the woman — girl really; Jack doubted she was old enough to be called a woman — asked over the baby's wailing. "I can put Rocky in his playpen."

"Rocky?" Jack whispered to Jenny as mom and son began the long climb up the stairs.

"Let's hope it's a nickname," she mouthed back.

Jack waved Jenny up the stairs before pointing at himself then twirling his finger to encompass the area around him. She nodded and left him to check the bedrooms. The rooms were tiny, cramped, with just a mattress in each one. A quick check of the closets and Jack headed up the stairs.

The stairs opened up into the living room and the girl was just straightening up from a playpen that had seen better days. Holes in the mesh walls had been mended with duct tape and the original white was a dingy ivory, matching the floor of the hall outside. Rocky was curled up with a stuffed Elmo, his cries snuffling off as he and his red-furred pal drifted off to sleep.

The girl put her hands on the small of her back and stretched, sighing in relief as her spine cracked audibly. Her oversized grey T-shirt proclaimed she was the WORLD'S GREATEST GRANDMOTHER.

I really hope that's her mother's shirt she's wearing.

"You're Heidi, right?" Jenny asked. "Can you tell us what's going on?"

"What's he doing?" Heidi asked, watching as Jack crossed the room to peek in the kitchen.

"Just checking to make sure we're alone, that's all," Jenny reassured her. "Why don't you sit down?"

Heidi sank onto a worn black leather couch that appeared older than Rocky's playpen. All the furniture was tatty and aged, except for the big-ass large-screen TV, of course.

Wish I could afford one of those, Jack thought as he positioned himself by the top of the stairs, keeping an eye on the door in case Myers thought about joining them uninvited.

Heidi ran her fingers through her frizzed hair then let them fall into her lap with a dramatic sigh.

"You look tired, Heidi," Jenny commented.

She nodded listlessly. "Yeah, I'm just tired of all of Dean's bullshit." She sighed again and turned a tear-rimmed eye Rocky's way. "I'm tired of him hitting us all the time."

Jenny looked knowingly at Jack and he dipped his head in agreement. Looks like things just got worse for their friend Myers.

Jenny was usually able to maintain a professional distance from the victims and the assholes she arrested. Hell, if she took every report or arrest personally, she would've burned out the first month on the road and spent the rest of her career riding a desk, safely tucked away from all the guns. But there was something about Myers that just got under her skin and refused to leave.

She and Paul Townsend had arrested the little dick yesterday for hitting his common-law wife and their two-year-old daughter. Now here he was, hitting another woman and her child.

"Is Dean Rocky's father?" *Please let it be no. Please let him have some other guy's genes.*

"He is," Heidi sniffed.

That's one strike against the little guy. Hope mom doesn't turn out to be strike two. Aloud, she asked, "When was the last time he hit you?"

Jenny stood near the other end of the couch so she wouldn't be looming over Heidi. Not sitting wasn't a matter of officer safety but personal hygiene. There was a simple rule in 51: never touch a crackhead or homeless person without wearing gloves and never sit on furniture unless you're positive there's nothing crawling around on it. No offence to Heidi's housekeeping abilities but Jenny had been in some Regent Park apartments where, instead of running when the lights came on, the cockroaches simply stayed put and stared at the trespassing humans.

"This afternoon. After he got out of jail." Heidi wrapped her arms around herself as if she was cold, even though it was hot in the apartment; Jenny was sweating under her uniform.

"Do you know why he was arrested?"

Heidi shook her head as dark tears started to drag her mascara down her cheeks. "He said some asshole cop grabbed him for something he didn't do."

Jenny was tempted to tell Heidi she was talking to the asshole cop but decided against it; no telling whose side Heidi would end up taking. Instead, she said, "He was arrested for hitting a woman and her daughter." Jenny squatted down before Heidi. "He hit his wife and his own daughter."

It took a moment for Jenny's words to sink in, then the puzzlement clouding Heidi's face shifted to anger. "That asshole! He said he left them." She jumped to her feet but Jenny eased her back down to the couch.

"Where did he hit you today?"

"Here!" Heidi yelled, yanking up the sleeve of her T-shirt. "This is what that asshole did to me." A red bruise, already darkening to purple, was wrapped around her upper arm as if someone had drawn the perfect imprint of a hand on her pale skin.

Jenny wondered what other injuries she'd find under Heidi's shirt and jeans. She had no doubt the girl's legs would give testimony to Myers's cruelty. Why else would Heidi be wearing jeans in this heat? And did Rocky's innocent skin bear any marks?

"Did Dean hit Rocky today?"

"Not today," Heidi sobbed as her sudden anger melted to dismay.

"But he has in the past?" Jenny prompted.

Sniffling back tears, Heidi bobbed her head. She balled up a fistful of T-shirt and wiped her face, smearing mascara across her cheeks.

Jenny took the moment to look at Jack and smiled when he nodded, slow and deliberate. She saw that his hands were already clenched in white-knuckled fists. It seemed he shared her feelings about this. If Myers was smart, he wouldn't give either of them a reason to express those feelings.

It didn't seem possible, but this was only their first day working together. Jenny felt comfortable working with Jack and their styles of policing, whether dealing with victims or assholes, meshed beautifully. And she liked it that he was a solid presence in uniform. Not that she was the type of PW to pick a fight then expect her male escort to step in when things got messy. Jenny had seen that happen more than once and it always pissed her off. Enough guys on the job were already against policewomen; no need to give them fuel for their arguments.

Jenny could handle herself in a fight and had surprised many a bigger man with her ability to scrap, but it never hurt to know your escort could hold his, or her, own when it was time to go hands on. Jack wasn't as big as Paul — then again, not many guys were — but the scar running through Jack's right eyebrow, coupled with the scowl that seemed to be his permanent expression these days, gave him a Terminator-like intimidation factor. No, she didn't mind working with Jack at all.

Now, if only I could find someone like him off the job.

The thought jumped into her head as she was looking at him and she shoved it aside. She had to admit, it wasn't the first time she'd had a romantic thought about Jack, but he was married and, on the rocks or not, married men weren't on her list. Period. And besides, they had a job to do right now and Heidi finally seemed to be getting herself under control.

"I'm just . . . I don't know." Heidi wiped at her cheeks again, widening the dark slick beneath her eyes. "We had a fight today," she confessed, breathing out her frustration. "I mean, we fight a lot. But everyone does, right?" she beseeched Jenny.

"People fight, sure, but not like that." Jenny pointed at the bruise on Heidi's arm. "He doesn't have the right to hit you or the baby."

"But this wasn't his fault," Heidi explained. "I kind of messed up, you know? He called me from jail to tell me he was getting out. I was supposed to get him some beer and I forgot. That's all.

I just got mad when he kicked me. 'Cause I was holding Rocky, you know?"

Jenny went cold and could almost feel Jack stiffening up across the room. "He kicked you when you were holding the baby?" she asked, not wanting to believe she had heard correctly.

"Yeah. That's when I got mad and called you guys. But it's okay now. I think you guys scared him enough. He won't do anything else now." Heidi smiled at the officers, a strained, hopeful smile. With her frizzy reddish hair and smeared mascara, she looked like the world's most pathetic clown.

"Heidi, we can't leave," Jenny began, but got no further.

Down the stairs, the apartment door banged open and Myers's nasal voice yowled up at them. "Bitch! I want my shit!"

Damn it! I forgot to lock the door.

Fuck! I forgot to lock the door.

Jack turned to head down the stairs, to keep Myers on the first floor, but the little wife-beating coward was already coming up the steps. Jack eased back; if Myers decided to fight — and part of Jack really wanted him to — a steep staircase wouldn't be the best location. Jenny moved from between the couch and coffee table to bar the way to Heidi.

Jack nodded inwardly, approving of how Jenny had positioned herself. He stayed by the stairs and had time to think, *Bloody hell, we work well together*, then Myers reached the second floor.

"What's taking so fucking long, bitch? I can't wait all fucking day." Myers stepped into the living room and stopped, glancing from his girlfriend huddling on the couch to the two officers and back to Heidi. "Now fucking what?"

Jack clamped a hand above Myers's right elbow. "You're under arrest for domestic assault, that's what."

"The fuck I am!" Myers pulled away from Jack while shoving him in the chest with his free hand.

Myers wasn't a big guy — Jack was sure the leather jacket he was wearing wasn't concealing anything — and Jack barely felt the shove. Still holding Myers's right arm, Jack grabbed his jacket and yanked him close, intending to finish the fight with a quick head-butt. Myers may not have been big, but he was fast and twisted his head away. Jack slammed his forehead into Myers's neck.

At the same time, Myers drove a knee up into Jack's groin. But they were both off balance and Jack only took a glancing blow. It was enough, though, to shoot a flare of pain from his balls up to his throat.

Fuck this.

Jack stepped closer to Myers and flipped the smaller man over his hip, hauling him down. Jack's rib screamed in protest. Myers hit the floor hard and Jack landed on top of him, making sure to drive a shoulder into Myers's chest. The impact blasted the air from Myers's lungs as it ripped agony through Jack's side.

Heidi was shrieking in the background. "Dean, stop fighting! Dean! Dean!"

Jack snapped a look at Heidi to make sure she wasn't about to latch onto his back and saw that Jenny was holding her by the couch. The girl seemed more intent on screaming than interfering.

"You good?" Jenny called when she spotted Jack looking her way. She had her mitre in hand, ready to put over the assist.

"I've got him," Jack assured her through gritted teeth just as Myers bucked underneath him. Myers was squirming like a worm skewered on a hook, but even without the extra twenty pounds of equipment, Jack must have outweighed him by a good fifty pounds. Myers's efforts weren't amounting to much.

Then the guy went for Jack's eyes. Jack pulled his head back and felt Myers's nails scoring the skin by his right eye.

I don't need another scar, fuckhead.

"Stop fighting and calm down!" Jack yelled at him, hoping Jenny was keying her radio. Nothing like having a recording to play back when the asshole complains. "Stop fighting me! You're under arrest!"

But Myers wasn't listening and his free hand was groping for Jack's eyes again.

The words of a defensive tactics instructor came back to Jack. Words to live by. *Don't fight to put on the handcuffs. Put them on after the fight is over.* And Jack intended to finish the fight.

See how you like being hit by someone bigger than you, fuckhead.

Jack drove an elbow into Myers's mouth and the busted lip, just beginning to heal, split open, spewing blood in a crimson fountain. Jack cocked his elbow back as Myers's hand shot up. In surrender this time.

"I give up! Don't hit me again!" he pleaded and Jack wondered how many times Myers had heard those exact words.

Jack grabbed Myers's arm and levered him onto his stomach. Trapping Myers's arm between his thighs as he knelt on the smaller man's lower back and neck, Jack ordered Myers to put his other hand behind his back. Jack took out his cuffs and snapped the cold steel into place. Only then did he ease his weight off Myers.

If this was a movie, I'd say something witty, Jack thought glibly as the sounds of crying filled the apartment.

Heidi was on the couch sobbing into her hands, her frail shoulders hitching with each ragged breath. Rocky was on his feet in the playpen, chubby fingers clutching the dirty mesh as he wailed out his fear and frustration. His Transformers T-shirt had ridden up in back, revealing an old bruise colouring his side.

"Ow! C'mon, boss, please. That hurts."

At Myers's squealing, Jack realized he had unconsciously shifted his weight onto Myers's neck. He got to his feet, making sure the little coward's neck bore the brunt of his weight as he pushed himself upright. He hauled Myers off the floor.

Once he was standing, Myers's nerve reasserted itself. He turned to Heidi.

"Don't you say a fucking word, bitch! Not a fucking —"

"Enough!" Jack grabbed Myers by the elbows and spun him into the stairwell, holding him over the steep drop at arms' length. "Tell me why I shouldn't drop you, you little piece of shit. I'd be doing Rocky a favour."

"Oh, fuck, boss. Please don't," Myers blubbered, the tough wife-and-child-beater gone. "I'm begging you."

"Jack," Jenny said softly. She shook her head when Jack looked at her.

"You're lucky this time, fuckhead." Jack pulled Myers into the living room. "And if you have any brains in that head, you'll keep your mouth shut. It's a long way down to the scout car and we may take the stairs."

Monday, 23 July
0820 hours

"You're useless, boy. Useless. I have no son."

Taylor knew he was dreaming, but every word of his father's cut him, every punch, every slap delivered pain.

"Please, Papa," the young Taylor begged from his knees. "Don't hit me anymore."

"Quit your mewling, boy. Take your punishment like a man." His father's hand, callused and strong from years in the mines, landed again and again. Taylor tried to protect himself, covered his head with his arms, but this only infuriated his father more. The miner swatted his thirteen-year-old son's arms aside and rained more discipline down on his head.

Minutes later, his father, a big man with a big belly, staggered away, gasping for breath. He collapsed onto the old, broken couch, a man old and broken before his time.

"What are you doing lying on the floor?" he roared. "Get me another beer!"

The young Taylor shuffled into the kitchen, his vision to the left already darkening as the eye swelled shut. He pulled open the fridge door, the squeal from the hinges a touch of normalcy in the boy's chaotic world. But there was no beer in the fridge, nothing at all except for his father's severed head.

His father's eyes, open but dead, cold but alive, glared at the boy. "You killed me, boy! You killed me just like you killed your mama and sis. You killed your family!"

Taylor screamed as blood gushed from his father's mouth; despite the gory torrent his father was still yelling. "You killed your family! You killed your family!"

Taylor slammed the fridge door and threw his hands to his ears but still he could hear his father. "You're useless, boy! You killed your family!"

"Shut up!" Taylor shrieked. He ran into the living room, tripped, fell. When he looked up, Rico was smiling down at him, a needle in one hand, his dick in the other.

"Want some?" he asked, waggling the syringe. "All you gotta do is suck me off."

"The boy can't even do that right," his father proclaimed from the couch. "He's useless."

"Go away! You're not real!" Taylor huddled on the floor, curled into a tight, protective ball. "You're not real," he sobbed. "You're not real."

Then hands, gentle and caring, tugged at his arms. Taylor lowered his arms, his strong, muscular arms, to see Sherry kneeling before him. She had on the Maple Leafs jersey he had bought for her and the sun streaming through the balcony doors lit up her blond hair, blond with the faintest hint of red — his Dusty Rose, he had called her — so that it framed her beautiful face like a halo.

"Sherry," he wept, knowing this was a dream.

"It's okay, baby," she shushed. "Everything's going to be okay."

"No, it's not," he cried, feeling the old hate and revulsion stirring in his belly. An ugliness that needed, wanted, to be vomited out.

"Let me make you feel better." Sherry reached for the zipper of his jeans but he grabbed her wrists.

"Don't," he pleaded, fearing what was to come.

"It's okay, baby. I don't care." Her hands, somehow free, were pulling down his zipper.

"Don't!" Yelling this time. He seized her wrists and the anger and hate inside him flowed free. "Don't you fucking touch me."

Sherry was on the balcony, the wind whipping her hair into a fury. "I'll tell!" she screamed at him. "If you leave me I'll tell!"

Taylor went to her, his hands held out to her. In supplication or violence?

Then Sherry was falling, falling, and the ground rushed up at Taylor.

Taylor jerked awake.

"Fuck me," he muttered. He lay in his bed, watching the dust motes drift lazily in the hazy sunlight as he waited for his heart to slow its thundering pace. He wiped sweat from his forehead, not knowing or caring if it was from the dream or the heat building in the confining bedroom.

He groped for his watch on the milk-carton night table. 8:20. So much for getting a decent sleep. He knew that, in the aftermath of the nightmare and the heat that was slowly converting the room into a sauna, sleep would be impossible. He went to the air conditioner and knelt in front of it as if praying, beseeching God or the gods or whoever the fuck was up there to put a hold on this heat. The pitiful breeze limping out of the labouring AC unit was just cool enough to dry his sweat-soaked skin.

He headed for the washroom but avoided the mirror; the

person inside it was someone he didn't want to face today. Not after last night.

"Fucking Rico."

With his name, memories of last night rushed back and Taylor quickly dropped to his knees over the toilet, spewing out what little there was in his stomach. His stomach heaved repeatedly, painfully, but there was nothing left in him. He dropped the lid, flushed and weakly pulled himself up till he was able to sit on the edge of the tub, his forearms braced on the toilet.

No, there would be no more sleeping today, perhaps not for quite some time.

He pushed himself to his feet. "Might as well get my ass to the gym."

Blevins Place was a little blip of a road — more a pretentious driveway, really — looping off Shuter Street in south Regent Park. It boasted two of the five high-rises in the southern half of the housing complex and there was nothing about 14 Blevins to differentiate it from any of the other filthy, worn-out, run-down government housing buildings. It looked the same, it smelled the same. And it didn't smell good.

They met their complainants, two housing guards, as they headed for the elevator.

"Hey, guys," Jenny greeted. "You called about abandoned children?"

"Yes, we did," the older of the guards confirmed, speaking with a soft Jamaican accent. His lean frame was tall and proud in his immaculate uniform and the lines in his dark complexion, plus the fringe of grey hair, proclaimed a lifetime of experience, not old age. His partner looked young enough for this to be his first summer out of high school; he hadn't blinked since laying eyes on Jenny. Jack hoped the kid didn't start drooling.

Jenny introduced herself and Jack to the pair.

"A pleasure, miss," the senior gent stated with a dazzling smile.

He took Jenny's hand. "I'm Autry and this young pup is William."

"Bill," the pup corrected and Autry rolled his eyes.

"What do we have, Autry?"

Autry waited as the elevator doors slid open; he stepped aside to let the police in first. Inside the metal box — it stank worse than the lobby: fermented urine — Bill punched the button for the eighth floor while Autry pulled out his memo book. He flipped to the proper page, seriousness sliding over his face.

"The neighbour in 812 called," he began as the elevator laboured upward. "She heard the baby crying, but no one answered when she knocked. She called us because the mother likes to go out and leaves the children behind. Last month, we found the boy down in the lobby."

"How old is he?"

"Three," Autry said sadly. "Somehow he got on the elevator."

"Where was mom?" Jack asked.

"I believe she and one of her boyfriends were busy getting drunk somewhere." Autry did not sound impressed.

"But we don't really know if the kids are alone right now?"

Autry cocked a skeptical eyebrow at Jenny. When the elevator reached the eighth floor, he led the way down the hall.

Hm, not the end of the hall, Jack noted with surprise when Autry stopped halfway along the hallway.

Jenny knocked, a civil *Come to the door, please*. When no one answered, she banged, a standard *Police, open the door*, and a baby started crying somewhere in the apartment. Out came the baton and Jenny clanged its metal butt against the metal door. More of an *Open the fucking door, now* knock.

Still no answer and the crying sounded as if the baby was the only one coming to the door.

Autry handed Jenny the pass-key and judging from the set of her jaw and the way she thrust the key into the lock, Jack figured the mother's only chance of getting out of this alive was if she was in the apartment and already dead.

Jenny opened the door and nearly tripped over the baby sitting on the floor. The little guy — or girl — was sniffling pitifully and wearing nothing but a diaper — and had been for some time, if the smell had anything to say about it. Jenny scooped the baby up and handed him, dirty diaper and all, to Autry. The guard had no choice but to accept the infant, but by the way he folded his arms protectively around the little guy, Autry didn't seem to mind. With a thumb lodged firmly in his mouth, the baby gazed at Autry in awe. His other hand sneaked out to pat inquisitively at the old man's face, as if he was saying, *Hey, we're the same colour. How about that?*

Like the Whiteside apartments where they had arrested Mr. Girlfriend-Beater Myers, the units in 14 Blevins were two storeys. The stairs leading down to the lower level — so steep Jack wouldn't want to navigate them in the dark, stone sober — were steps from the front door. And there was nothing blocking them off, nothing preventing the baby from suffering a lethal tumble if he ventured too close to the precipice.

Jack caught Jenny's eye and gestured at the stairs. She nodded, a grim, pissed-off expression clouding her face. She drew a deep breath and bellowed, "Police! Anybody fucking here?".

The rooms on the entry floor — the bedrooms — were empty and Jenny asked, concerned, "Where's the boy? The three-year-old."

She took the lead down the stairs to the lower level and they found the baby's brother asleep on the parquet floor in front of the television. The room was as hot as an open furnace and Jack felt light-headed as the heat wrapped around him. The closing credits to an animated film scrolled across the TV screen, flickering light across the sleeping boy's body.

Curled on his side with only his arm for a pillow, the boy never stirred as they approached him. He was shirtless and even from across the room, he appeared frail and sickly thin, his ribs far too prominent beneath his dark skin. Jack's anger, already seething from finding the baby next to the stairs, began to boil.

"Someone's going to answer for this," he swore quietly.

Jenny nodded in agreement as she knelt to wake the boy. While she bundled him up unresistingly in her arms — *is it good or bad that he goes to a stranger that easily?* — Jack picked up the DVD case. Disney's *Aladdin*. He flipped it over and his anger reached new heights.

He held the case up to Jenny, speaking through clenched teeth. "The running time is ninety minutes. Does that mean their mother has been gone that long?"

"Could be. The call was already forty-five minutes old when we got it." She ran a hand over the back of the boy slumped in her arms. "Call for an ambulance, Jack. He's hot and his skin is bone dry."

Jenny carefully climbed the stairs, one hand supporting the boy, the other gripping the railing. Jack followed her up, keeping close in case she slipped under the child's weight, although Jack doubted Jenny considered the boy a burden. Going up the stairs, Jack had the dispatcher order up an ambulance, amazed the mitre worked within the apartment. The Service's portable radios were notoriously crappy when . . . well, just notoriously crappy.

Jack watched the muscles in Autry's jaw bunch with tension when he saw the boy in Jenny's arms.

Jenny headed for the door. "Let's get them downstairs. We can meet the ambulance out front."

They gathered in the hall outside the apartment and while Jack was locking the door, he heard Autry say, very quietly, very furiously, "That's the mother."

A rather rotund black woman was walking toward them, her beaded braids swinging with each ponderous step. They watched in silence as she approached, Jack — perhaps all of them — waiting and hoping for some sign of concern or apprehension on the mother's face. After all, how often does a mother find her young children in the arms of police officers outside her apartment?

Apparently, for this mother, often enough.

She calmly stepped up to Autry and reached for the baby, no more troubled than if she was taking a bag of groceries.

Jack stopped her with a hand on her arm. "Are you these children's mother?"

She spared Jack's hand a disdainful glance. "Ya," she spat, the word heavy with Jamaican patois, before sucking her teeth derisively at him. "Give me my baby," she demanded of Autry.

"I don't think so," Jack declared. "You're under arrest." The hand on her arm went from stopping to gripping.

"What?" she shrieked. "What for?"

"For abandonment," Jack explained, an angry, satisfied tone to his words. "For leaving your children alone and in danger. Now, put your hands behind your back."

"You can't arrest me," she yelled as she tried to pull free of Jack's hold. "Ah ain't done no'ting wrong."

Jack clamped her arm, his fingers sinking into flabby flesh. He jerked her toward him and snarled in her face, "You're under arrest. If you keep this shit up, you'll be going to the hospital first. Understand?"

"Oh, Jesus, help me!" she cried and flung herself to the floor. The sudden drop caught Jack unawares and her sweaty arm slipped free. "Jesus, Jesus! Help me," she wailed as she rolled on the dirt-encrusted floor.

Any other time, Jack might have found her performance ludicrous, but at the moment it was anything but amusing. Annoyed, disgusted, he squatted and grabbed a flailing arm. She was still crying out for Jesus to save her and banging on the floor with her free hand, as if Jesus was a downstairs tenant. Jack reached for the other arm but there was too much of her to lean over and the arm was too sweat-slick to grab.

"God-fucking-damn it, woman. Hold still!"

"Jesus! Save me!" she howled, thrashing her blubber around.

Jack's anger at this self-righteous, uncaring ass was about to break free but then Autry was there, kneeling across from him and snagging the woman's free arm with two hands. He twisted the arm up none too gently behind her back, eliciting a cry of wordless pain from her.

Jack nodded his thanks and took the arm. As he snapped the handcuffs on he spared a quick look at the children, afraid of how this embarrassing scene with their mother would be affecting them. The boy was still asleep in Jenny's embrace and the baby, now held awkwardly by Bill, was staring at the loud woman on the floor in a puzzled yet unconcerned way.

Jack hauled the blubbering woman to her feet and pressed her to the wall. "Why don't you go down with the kids first?" he suggested to Jenny. "That way, they don't have to listen to this piece of garbage."

"Good idea," she said, staring at the mother with what looked to Jack to be complete and utter revulsion. The mother undoubtedly had no idea how lucky she had been that Jenny's hands hadn't been free.

Jenny and Bill, with the kids safely in hand, disappeared into the elevator. Once the doors rattled shut, Jack took the whimpering woman by one flabby arm and walked her down the hall. Her pleas for divine intervention had subsided in volume, but as soon as Jack started her walking she must have realized where she was headed; she threw back her head and hollered.

"Jesus! Help me!"

"Enough!" Jack roared. "That's . . . fucking . . . enough!"

Stunned into silence, the woman stared at Jack, blinking owlishly at him. "Ah ain't done no'ting," she protested.

"Nothing?" Jack repeated, astounded. "Nothing? Your baby could have died falling down those stairs and your son is so dehydrated he's unconscious. And you think you haven't done anything wrong? Fuck me." He turned away from her in disgust and jabbed the elevator button. "And just in case you cared," he added over his shoulder, "the baby's fine. I don't know about your son."

"Jesus, Jesus, Jesus," she chanted and Jack knew she wasn't thanking Him for looking after her children. "Jesus, help me. Jesus, help me," she whined, gaining volume. *"Jesus, h —"*

There was a sharp, piercing *crack!* as Autry slapped the woman across the face. "Now you be quiet like the officer said," he warned her. "Or you'll be getting another one."

"Ah ain't done —"

Slap!

The woman's head rocked sideways, both cheeks tattooed with Autry's handprint. The security guard glared at his country-woman with an intensity and hatred that Jack would not have thought the old gentleman capable of.

Autry leaned in toward the mother so they were almost nose to nose. "I don't want to hear another word out of you, woman." He stepped back and studied her head to toe, as if mentally weighing her value. It was clear she came up wanting in his evaluation. "You disgust and embarrass me, woman. I came to this country to give my children a better life. I worked hard so they could go to school, get educated, be better than their father is. I left Jamaica to get away from the likes of you." His lip curled in a very un-gentlemanly sneer. "Living off welfare, the charity of others, because you're too lazy to work. Always wanting, demanding, thinking only of yourself."

He held up a warning finger as she drew breath to speak. "Don't you be calling to Jesus, woman. You don't deserve His help and you sure don't deserve those babies He gave you. Now you just shut your mouth and keep quiet or you'll be getting another one."

She looked to Jack for help but only found Autry's feelings mirrored in his face. Defeated, she hung her head and cried quietly to herself.

"That's better." Autry straightened his shirt and faced Jack.

"I'm sorry for what I did, officer, but it needed doing. If you need to charge me for what I did, I understand."

"You didn't do anything that my partner and I weren't thinking, Autry. As far as I'm concerned, you did nothing wrong." The elevator door creaked open and they stepped inside. Jack deposited the woman in a corner before turning to Autry. "And, in my opinion, your kids don't have to be better than you. If they grow up to be just like you, they'll be damn good people."

51's Youth Bureau was a tiny office — what office in the station wasn't small? — tucked into a corner on the second floor. The YB detectives were handling the case against Cantrice Morgan, the less-than-stellar mother, because of the age of the victims. The little guys — the baby was a boy, after all — were safely with Children's Aid but no doubt would be returned to their inattentive mother once she was released on bail.

"Some people just shouldn't be allowed to breed," Jack declared.

"No argument here," Jenny agreed. They had the office to themselves, the Ds having headed home for the evening, and were just finishing their notes.

Jack chuckled. "I wish you had been there when Autry tore a strip off her ass. It was a thing of beauty. Bet it won't do any good, though." He sighed and drained the last of his Diet Coke. Belching gently, he chucked the can at the recycle container.

Jenny watched the can arc into the blue bin. "Don't you ever drink anything else?"

"Hey, I've got water out in the car," he protested. "I just wanted something a little stronger after that call, and they frown on us for drinking on the job."

Jenny nodded her understanding. "Makes you wonder why some people have kids."

"Because the government gives them money?" Jack suggested.

"My, aren't we cynical tonight." She closed her notebook and stretched in her seat. She felt her spine cracking and popping. Damn, but the vest and gun belt did a number on her back. Not to mention carrying the boy around; he got heavy after a while.

From across the back-to-back desks, Jack watched her stretching. "I notice you've started wearing your vest under your shirt," he commented once she was done emulating a cat.

"I heard Pest telling Paul what you said about the externals and it makes sense." She paused. "Were you just checking me out?"

"Nope," he said sincerely.

She cocked an eyebrow at him.

"Honestly," he swore. Quietly, he added, "Couldn't. The damn vest was in the way."

Jenny laughed, then threw out a question. "Do you still want kids?" The question surprised her as much as it seemed to catch Jack off guard. *Where did that come from?*

He was silent for a moment, then shook his head. "Honestly, I don't know. But with all the trouble between Karen and me right now, I'm just glad we don't have any. I've actually been thinking about it — having kids, I mean — a lot lately. Ever since Karen tried to get pregnant without telling me," he admitted, his voice tightening over the last words.

Jenny heard the pain in his voice and wanted to help but there was only so much she could do; she was concerned her feelings toward him could get in the way or be misinterpreted.

"What about you?" Jack asked. "Do you want kids?"

"Me?" she squawked. "My sister has two and that's enough for me. Don't get me wrong, I love them to death but it's really nice to be able to give them back when they start to cry."

"I didn't know you had a sister."

"Two, actually. I'm the middle child."

"The problem child," he amended.

"Damn straight," she confirmed, smiling. "Both of my sisters are married and there's two grandchildren already so the pressure's off me."

"Lucky you," he grumbled. "Nothing like parents, or in-laws, pushing for grandchildren."

"Your parents are on the grandchildren bandwagon?"

Jack shrugged. "Don't know. We're not exactly on speaking terms."

"Oh, Jack, I'm sorry. Do you mind if I ask why?"

He didn't answer right away and Jenny feared she had pried into forbidden territory. Partners or not, some areas were off limits.

"Dad was against me being a cop," Jack said at length. "He had dreams of me following in his footsteps and taking over the practice but there was no way I was going to do that."

"What's he do?"

Jack fell silent again, then, sighing, "He's a lawyer."

"Oh," Jenny said softly. Lawyers and cops, water and oil.

But it got worse. "A defence lawyer."

"Oh," she repeated. Forget water and oil. Try fire and gasoline. "I can't see you being a defence lawyer."

"Neither could I and when I told him I was going to be a cop, he acted like I had . . ."

"Stabbed him in the back?"

Jack snorted. "More like slit his throat. I'm an only child so when I refused to take up the family occupation, Dad saw his legacy die, but the thought of being a defence lawyer made me want to puke."

Jenny nodded. "I can understand you feeling that way now, but why did it bother you so much then? You were what? In high school?"

Jack slumped in his chair and scrubbed his face with his hands. "Yeah. I hadn't even thought of joining the job but what Dad did just seemed wrong." He sat up, an earnest, troubled look on his face. "You see, Dad wasn't one of those lawyers who defended people he thought were genuinely innocent. Oh no, not Dad. He always said, the guiltier they are, the more they'll pay. And Dad got paid a shitload."

"What about your mother? What did she want you to do?"

"Mom tried to patch things up a few times but . . ." He shrugged again. "They divorced while I was in university. Dad remarried a year later." He grinned humourlessly. "Upgraded to a newer, younger wife."

Jenny suddenly understood Jack's dedication to the job and why Karen's and her parents' efforts to get him to quit hurt so much: he had lost his parents, his family, because of the job.

"Is that why you became a cop?" she asked gently. "Because of your dad?"

Jack laughed scornfully. "That's the best fucking part. I don't think it had anything to do with him being a lawyer. I wasn't trying to piss him off but I couldn't have picked a better occupation if that was my intention." He paused and Jenny could see he was reliving some unpleasant memories. "Honestly? I couldn't think of anything else to do. All I knew was that I didn't want to be a lawyer. Good thing I like the job, huh?" he joked sourly. "How about you? How come you're a cop?"

Jenny smiled but her thoughts were troubled. Jack could say his revulsion of his father's profession hadn't been a factor in his choosing to be a police officer, but how could it not? His father also sounded very similar, painfully similar, to Jack's father-in-law.

My God, Jack, how much stress are you under?

"So, how come you joined?" he prompted.

"Because," she explained with a sultry smile, wanting to soothe the wounds she had uncovered. "I look good in black, silly."

Night was descending on the city, an inky darkness that did little to cool the air. Jack had his arm out the passenger window as Jenny slowly cruised the pathways of Allan Gardens.

"The air feels oily, it's so humid. Makes you almost wish for winter."

Jenny immediately pointed her finger to Jack's temple and cocked her thumb. "One more comment like that and I'll have to kill you."

He eyed her sideways. "Not a big fan of winter, I'm guessing."

"If it isn't warm enough for me to go into the backyard with my bikini on," she told him, lowering her 'gun,' "then it isn't fit for humans."

"You're going to be a joy to work with come winter."

She flashed him a sinister smile. "We'll get along fine. As long as I don't have to get out of the car."

"Oh, joy," Jack groaned and Jenny patted his leg in sympathy.

The park was busy as twilight crept into full night. No empty seats could be found on the benches dotting the pathways, the excess spilling over onto the cement lips of the flower beds. Dogs and their owners roamed the grassy areas, most of the furry companions enjoying a romp off leash. At the sight of the scout car, owners hurried to leash their dogs, but the cops just waved them off. Dogs running loose kept the drunks and crackheads out of the park, or at least down to a tolerable level, and besides, there were worse things going on in the city than a dog chasing a ball or squirrel. Unless you were the squirrel, of course.

"Hey, Jenny," Jack said, brightening up. "Stop here. There's someone I want to talk to."

Jenny eased the car to a stop in front of the park's greenhouse and Jack got out, taking his water bottle with him.

Damn, it's hot. Hot and sticky.

Two men were sitting on a bench and as Jack approached, the grubby one — the liquid in his bottle looking a touch too murky to be water — suddenly remembered somewhere he was supposed to be and wandered away, as quickly as he could nonchalantly.

"Guess he didn't wan' t' talk t' you, Officer Jack," the remaining man said by way of greeting, an amused smile on his tired face.

"I have that effect on some people." Jack extended his hand and asked, concerned, "How are you doing, Phil?" Phil was well into his eighties and Jack realized with that age came some wear and tear, but the wrinkles in Phil's black skin — dark skin that had a definite unhealthy grey tinge to it — appeared deeper than before and the bones in his face more prominent.

"I'm doin' okay, I guess." Phil smiled, but the frailty of his handshake — swollen, arthritic knuckles aside — belied his words. "Don't know whether t' curse or bless this weather. Too hot t' sleep but it feels good on my bones."

"And how's my buddy Bear doing?" Jack knelt and held out a friendly hand to the little dog hiding under the bench.

Phil laughed. "Go on, Bear. Go say hello." He gave the dog an encouraging nudge with his slippered foot and Bear, all fifteen or twenty pounds of him, tentatively crept out from under the bench to sniff warily at Jack's fingers. Bear was a chubby hodge-podge of different breeds on skinny legs and his coat had as many hues of brown in it as his lineage had fathers. He was a skittish little guy but with Jack's familiar scent, Bear's stubby tail set to wagging and he hobbled forward to butt his head against Jack's hand. Grinning, Jack obediently scratched behind Bear's ears.

Bear slowly, arthritically worked his way down to his belly then rolled — tipped over, really — on to his side. His foreleg rose beseechingly and Jack started on a tummy rub. Bear's tail thumped the ground in doggy bliss.

"Bear ain't never bin much for strangers but he sure likes you, Officer Jack." Phil chuckled at his friend's silliness but the chuckle hoarsened into a rasp, then a cough. Convulsions racked the old man's body as he fought for control of his breathing. Jack watched anxiously from where he knelt with Bear, prepared to summon an ambulance if Phil's coughing fit worsened.

At length, the hacking subsided and Phil wiped his lips with the back of an unsteady hand. "Damned cigarettes," he muttered. "Payin' me back, they are."

Phil's eyes brightened and he straightened up as best he could when Jenny joined them. Jack introduced her and Phil took her hand courteously.

"My apologies, my dear, for not gettin' up to properly greet you but these old bones jus' don' wanna move today." Phil winked at Jack. "She's a helluva lot better lookin' than the las' one you was workin' with."

"Manny," Jack explained.

"Then I would certainly hope so," Jenny said.

"I've been hearin' a rumour, Officer Jack."

"Oh, what's that?"

"You remember that little shit I told you 'bout? The one abusin' his dog?"

"He doesn't have another dog, does he?"

"No, he don'," Phil said, smiling at the sudden vehemence in Jack's voice. "But he's bin goin' 'round sayin' some big cop stole his dog." He dropped his voice to a raspy confidentiality. "Cop with a big scar through his eye."

"Is that so?" Jack asked, raising his scarred eyebrow in mock surprise.

Phil nodded solemnly. "It is."

"Well, if he believes he's the victim of a crime, then he should report it to the police. I, personally, wouldn't know anything about it." Jack paused, then smiled. "Did I mention that I have a new dog?"

Phil cackled delightedly. "I knew you was a good man," he managed around his mirth but once more, his laughter degenerated into hoarse coughing. The two officers waited, patient but concerned, for the fit to pass. Even Bear, after labouriously rolling back to his belly, had a wary eye fixed on the old man.

The coughing passed with a final shudder running through Phil and he pulled a handkerchief from his back pocket. "'Scuse me," he mumbled before spitting into the cloth and wiping his lips.

A sad smile touched Jenny's lips. "Those damned cigarettes?"

Phil nodded wearily. "Oh, yeah." He reached down to give Bear an affectionate pat as the old dog waddled his way back underneath Phil's legs.

"Excuse me, officers," a tentative voice said from behind Jenny. A young Asian man waited patiently for Jenny to face him before pointing off past the greenhouse. "There's a man and a woman over there and it looks like he's going to hit her. I think they might be boyfriend and girlfriend maybe."

They said their goodbyes to Phil and Bear and headed around the greenhouse, forgoing the car for the short walk.

"You have quite the soft spot for the old guy, don't you?"

Jack nodded. "And Bear. I told you how I met him, right? The asshole in the rooming house beating up both of them?"

"You did. It's one of the things that endeared me to you," Jenny said with a teasing smile.

"What? That I kick down doors without warrants to arrest people?"

"Well, that too." She gave him a playful nudge. "I figured anyone who cared for animals that much couldn't be a complete loss."

"I'm not a loss?"

She nudged him again, harder this time. "I said, not a *complete* loss."

"Gee, thanks."

The domed greenhouse was the centrepiece of the park and expansive enough to effectively cut the grounds in half. Before they even rounded the building they could hear two voices, predominantly a male's, raised in heated anger. Even if they hadn't been able to hear the yelling, Jack and Jenny could have found the domestic just by following the stares of everyone in this section of the park.

At the rear of the greenhouse sat a round concrete pond, no more than fifteen feet in diameter, a ring of benches encircling it.

Its waters were a favourite cooling spot for canines on hot days but Jack would've balked at letting Justice wade in there, having seen some local hounds — the two-legged kinds — using it as a communal bathtub.

A young couple, university age, were currently the only ones near the pond; everyone else was giving them plenty of space but no privacy. Although, at the volume of their voices, privacy would have required several city blocks.

"You're a fucking whore!" the man — more of a boy in Jack's opinion; an adult knows better than to have a screaming hissy fit in public — shrieked, inches from the woman's face. He was a big, blond kid in a sleeveless top and jeans. *Football or rugby*, Jack thought.

"Oh, good, idiot." Jenny smirked. "That'll win her back for sure."

The woman, another blonde, was a fraction of the kid's size and cowering on a bench, trapped between his muscular arms as he leaned over her.

"Quite the gentleman," Jack agreed. Then, as they drew nearer, he announced firmly, "Hey! That's enough!"

The kid and his reluctant captive turned at Jack's shout, the woman's face registering immense relief, the kid's immense pissed-off-ness.

The kid straightened up as the officers approached, his jaw set in an angry clench. Unless the idiot had hit or threatened the woman, all they had right now was a domestic argument and so far, there was no law about yelling at someone.

At most, if we have to push it, Jack thought as he kept his eyes on the big kid's hands and Jenny moved off to the left — just because it looked like no crime had occurred didn't mean one hadn't or wasn't about to — *we've got him for causing a disturbance.*

Jack really didn't want to bother with an arrest or a fight; it was just too damned hot.

After glancing at Jenny and dismissing her — Jack was

reminded of how the steroid monsters from The Keg had shrugged her off as if she was not a threat — the kid took a couple of steps to meet Jack away from the bench and snarled, "You're not needed here."

"Glad to hear it," Jack said. "But you'll understand if we check for ourselves."

Cause Disturbance, at best, Jack was thinking. Most likely just a uniformed intervention in a lovers' quarrel, couple of 208s filled out and everyone's on their separate ways. Then the big idiot went and fucked that all up.

"I said, you aren't needed here." The idiot stepped forward, planted a hand on Jack's chest and shoved him.

You fucking . . . ". . . moron," Jack finished aloud. "Now you're under arrest." If there was one rule Sy had hammered home in his short time with Jack, it was that no one laid hands on a police officer. No one.

While the big idiot had his eyes fixed on Jack, Jenny slid in from the side, probably intending to clamp her hands on the guy's right arm. If the police gods were smiling, then the idiot would realize fighting two cops wasn't such a bright idea. Worst case scenario, she'd take one of his arms out of a fight, giving her partner a significant advantage. But the gods must have been pissed off or looking somewhere else because the guy's hand shot out, snake fast, and grabbed Jenny by the throat. Effortlessly, he hauled her onto her toes and held her there.

Jack lowered his shoulder and exploded into the guy's ribs, meaning to knock the idiot from his feet and then deliver some punishment, but the sudden, sharp pain in Jack's rib robbed his tackle of strength and the guy only staggered back a few steps but kept his balance. His free arm whipped under Jack's chin and clamped around his throat.

Fuck. He's choking both of us at the same time.

Jack reached for a leg, still hoping to get the guy off his feet, and that's when he heard Jenny's baton, her steel baton, whacking off the guy's skull. Heard it and felt it, the impacts sending miniature shock waves through the guy's body. And she might as well have been hitting him with a pillow. The guy didn't fall, buckle or even stagger. All he did was grunt every time the metal slammed into his head.

Jack forgot about trying to grab a leg and pulled out his own baton. A quick flick and the metal weapon snapped open to its full length. Jack had never hit anyone with the baton and it felt like it was quivering eagerly in his hand, anxious for its first taste of flesh and bone. Or that could have been Jack's brain starting to go fuzzy from the lack of oxygen.

Jack had been taught in the college not to strike any joints — knees and elbows especially — with the baton if it could be avoided. Less serious or permanent damage meant fewer lawsuits, Jack had figured at the time. But Jenny was already whaling away on a prohibited body area to no effect so Jack reasoned all bets and rules were off.

He kept his eyes fixed on the guy's left knee and swung the baton as hard as he could. Granted, bent over as he was, and with a cracked rib, he wasn't able to get his whole body behind the blow but it still landed hard on the outside of the knee. Jack didn't wait to assess the result and swung twice more, targeting the same joint.

It felt like he was hitting a fucking tree.

The guy tightened his arm around Jack's throat and Jack realized the man — had he really thought of him as a boy? — wasn't going to let go until Jack was unconscious. And an unconscious cop was a dead cop.

Jack planted his feet, sank his hips and surged forward as powerfully as he could. The guy started backpedalling, slowly at first, then faster as Jack pumped his legs like he was doing a heavy set of squats. Once the guy's legs were moving quickly enough, Jack stuck his baton behind a leg and the three of them went crashing down.

Right into the pond.

The water wasn't deep, about a foot, so it did little to cushion the impact as the guy landed on his back. Jack dug his shoulder in under the guy's ribs so that when they landed, all of Jack's weight drove into the boy's diaphragm. Above the splash, Jack heard the guy's breath blast free of his body. The grip on Jack's neck suddenly slacked off and Jack pulled his head free. He reared up, his baton spraying a fan of water as he drew it back.

But Jenny beat him to it.

As the idiot's head cleared the water, she shoved her pepper spray into his face and doused him at point-blank range. The guy screamed as the spray bit into his eyes and skin and began to burn. And Jenny continued to blast him. In seconds, the idiot's face and hands — he'd been trying to block the spray — were bright orange from its dye.

The idiot finally exhibited some intelligence and threw himself face down into the water, but pepper spray was an oily, clinging bitch and it would take more than a quick dunk to wash it away.

Jack grabbed an arm and with a sudden, savage twist had it pinned behind the guy's back. He was tempted to keep the idiot submerged until he was cuffed, but figured that wouldn't be the best course of action with all the bystanders. He yanked the idiot to his knees and repaid the chokehold with one of his own.

"Calm down!" Jack yelled, more for the bystanders' benefit that the idiot's. "Put your other hand behind your back. Do it and we'll clean that shit off of you. Do it now!"

Jenny grabbed the idiot's left arm and, none too gently, 'helped' him place it beside the arm Jack had trapped. A couple of metallic clicks later and the idiot was safely cuffed.

"I don't know about you," Jack said to Jenny. The idiot was slumped against the side of the pond, his face a dripping bog of snotty orange. Five minutes of thrashing his face in the water had cleared most of the pepper spray. Most, but not all, and Jack figured the idiot had earned a slow burn for the trip to the station. "First the freaks at The Keg and now him. I'm starting to feel kind of small and weak."

"I think you did this on purpose," Jenny told him, waving her hands at her soggy uniform.

Jack coughed then spat. Fuck, he hated pepper spray. "How's that?"

"I think you just wanted to see me in a wet shirt," Jenny said, striking a provocative pose.

"Yeah, but the damn vest is still in the way."

Manny snorted so hard Coke blew out his nose. "Ow," he complained around a mouth jammed full of pizza. "The bubbles burn."

"Serves you right for eating like a pig," Jenny admonished him.

Jack had just reached the part of the story where they'd taken the impromptu swim and, obviously, Manny had found that rather amusing. Jack waited for his friend to compose himself before continuing.

Manny whistled appreciatively when Jack was done. "Three times in the knee and nothing?"

"Not then, but when he left the station later, he could barely put any weight on it. His head was a mess of lumps, too."

"Serves the guy right," Manny mumbled around more pizza. "You don't touch a cop, man."

"Actually, he turned out to be an okay kid once he calmed down," Jenny said.

Jack nodded. "He even complimented me on how I swung my stick."

"Really?" Jenny asked.

"Yup. Never mentioned you, though," he added with a smug smile.

Jenny stuck her tongue out at him.

"Promises, promises," Jack said.

"You need guns like these to inflict some damage," Manny declared. He hit a double biceps pose, pizza slice in one hand, Coke in the other.

"You keep eating like that," Jenny warned him, "and what muscle you have will disappear under all that cheese and pepperoni."

"Never happen," Manny said, tearing off another chunk of grease wheel. "I've got a fast metabolism."

Jack just shook his head while Jenny asked, "How many more nights are you going to forget to bring your lunch here?"

Manny waved his hand in answer until he swallowed. "We'll be done tonight. Did I tell you about this?"

"You showed us the front hall," Jack reminded him.

"Cool, right? But did I tell you who he was?" Manny was grinning like a kid with a new toy. "The guy who got his head chopped up is the brother of a pedophile on trial right now."

"The one at district court? I thought I heard on the news there were problems with the search warrant."

Manny nodded. "Yeah, that's the one. Mason's in charge of it, did you know? He stopped by here after court today, says it looks like the guy is going to walk."

"So somebody decides to play judge and executioner but gets the brother instead." Jack snorted. "Sucks to be the brother."

Grinning, Manny nodded and chomped down on more pizza.

Tuesday, 24 July
0253 hours

Jack leaned against the scout car's trunk and gazed at the cloudless sky. Drawing a deep breath, he slowly sighed it out, imagining it was taking all the accumulated crap from the day and releasing it up to the stars.

"Whatcha thinking?" Jenny plunked herself down on the trunk, resting her feet on the bumper.

"We did some good today, didn't we?" he asked, keeping his eyes on the night sky. There weren't all that many stars out. From inside the city, even on a cloudless night, the heavens were never clear. Jack thought there might be some deep, hidden meaning in that but was too tired to figure it out.

"Yeah, we did," Jenny said, a smile touching her words. "And yesterday. Let's hope that Myers prick gets DO'ed this time."

"Well, the Ds were asking for a detention order," Jack contemplated while he unhurriedly rolled his neck from side to side. "Assaulting a different girlfriend and child within two days should get him some dead time but you never know. It's up to the courts, not us."

"Don't I know it," Jenny sighed. She leaned back on her hands and joined Jack in his study of the stars.

It was a few minutes to the end of shift and they were the last of the evening cars back at the barn, but Jack wasn't all that eager to leave and Jenny seemed content where she was.

"We should get the kids together some time, now that Justice is doing well," Jack offered, wanting to say something and feeling like he was back in high school, trying to work up the nerve to ask out the prettiest girl in class.

"That'd be cool. Hammer and Mugsy would love to meet him." Jenny's Rottweiler and pug were frequent visitors to the station and unofficial 51 mascots. "We work well together, don't we?"

Caught off guard by the sudden topic shift, Jack blurted, "Yeah, it's hard to believe we've only worked together for two days; it feels longer."

Jenny laughed. "Feels longer in a good way or bad?"

"In a good way," Jack stumbled. He turned to face her. "You know what I mean."

She laughed again, but her smile smoothed the sting from it.

Jack smiled, embarrassed and amused by his awkwardness. High school? More like grade school.

"Listen, Jenny, what would you think about . . ."

"You want to pair up?" she asked, putting him out of his misery.

It was Jack's turn to chuckle. "You'd think things like this would get easier over time."

"Geez, Warren," she mocked, nudging his shoulder. "It's not like we're going steady. So, what do you say?"

"Absolutely. But shouldn't I be the one asking?"

"'Cause you're the guy? Nuts to that," she scoffed. She hopped off the car and grabbed her duty bag. "I'm a woman for the new millennium. Better get used to being told what to do."

"Yes, ma'am," he replied, falling in beside her as she headed for the door. "Or should I say partner?"

"Partner," she agreed and Jack smiled; the night was ending on a good note.

But the night, as Jack was soon to learn, was not over.

Jack eased open the front door and a wet and cool black nose poked through the crack between door and frame.

"Hey, Justice," Jack whispered, reaching blindly to rub behind the dog's ears. Without the front hall light — whenever Jack came home at odd hours he kept to the dark as much as possible so as not to wake Karen — the predominantly black shepherd was all but invisible.

Scratching Justice's ears, Jack could feel the dog's body quivering as his tail wagged enthusiastically. Even after four months of greetings like this, Jack still wasn't tired of it. It didn't matter what kind of day he'd had or what his mood was or what time it was, Justice was always at the door waiting for him, ecstatic his master was home.

"You need to go outside?" Jack asked in a low voice and Justice huffed in reply.

Damn, he's smart, he marvelled as the two of them made their way to the kitchen. Jack slid open the door and Justice scampered across the deck to disappear into the shadows draped across the yard.

The night was warm, a breath away from being hot — Jack was amazed Karen didn't have the AC on — and Jack settled down on the deck, forgoing a chair to prop himself up against a post and stretched his legs out at the top of the steps leading up from the lawn. A moment later, Justice reappeared and bounded up the stairs in one effortless leap. He plopped down onto the deck, resting his chin on Jack's thigh.

"All done?" Jack sank his fingers into the thick soft fur on his dog's neck, luxuriating in its feel, and felt the last of the day's tension dissolve. Anxiety and stress had become close ... not friends, but associates of Jack's since that asshole Kayne had become a big wet spot on Rosedale Valley Road. The SIU investigation, the open wound that Karen's attempted pregnancy had left between them. Justice. His job. Her parents. And now the fight over being back on the road.

Too much shit. Just way too much shit.

Jack dropped his head back against the post, searching the stars once more for answers. The sky was clearer out here in the burbs, away from the city and its constant haze. The stars were brighter, sharper, and the darkness between them deeper and so much blacker.

The door slid open, closed. Jack followed Karen by ear as she stepped down to the deck's lower level.

"I thought I heard you come in." She dragged a lounge chair close to him and sat — *perched, really, she's too tense to sit* — on its end.

Justice's eyes twitched in her direction then closed again. He gave no other indication of her presence.

"I tried not to wake you. Sorry."

She shook her head. "I couldn't sleep." She was wearing an

old housecoat and her dark blond hair gleamed softly in the starlight. "How come you're out here?"

Jack hoped it was his imagination, but he thought there was a tone of . . . something in her voice as her eyes flicked to Justice. *There's no love lost between them*, he judged sadly but construed it was no time to tell Karen she shouldn't be jealous of a dog.

He's my dog, that's all. "Wasn't ready for bed. Just needed some time to unwind."

"Thinking anything in particular?" The question was harmless in its context but the way she brushed her hair back over her ear as she asked it told Jack it wasn't empty to Karen.

I don't want to get into anything tonight. He returned his eyes to the stars as he told her, "Remember when we were in Arizona? How many stars there were out in the desert? How bright they were?"

"I remember," she sighed and this time there was no mistaking the hue of her words. Sadness. Was she recalling better times when there was no tension between them?

"What happened to your face?" She had been asleep when he got home last night and had been gone in the morning; this was the first time she'd seen the scratches. It was a simple question. A razor blade in the dark.

He touched the twin marks next to his eye, left by Dean Myers. "Just some scratches. Nothing major." A thought crossed his mind — a gift from the stars? — and before Karen could respond, he asked, "How about we go to Ted's for breakfast tomorrow? We haven't been in a while. I could go for some of their peameal bacon and pancakes."

"We can't. We're going out to brunch with Mom and Dad, remember?" Her hair had slipped free. She brushed it back. "What happened to your face?"

Bloody hell. "It's nothing, really. I got into a fight when I arrested a guy for assaulting his girlfriend and their baby." He rubbed the scratches to show how insignificant they were. "Just a couple of scratches." *No need to say the asshole was trying to gouge my eye out.*

Karen hung her head over her clasped hands. Her hair draped forward, hiding her face from him.

"Just some scratches. Just a fight. Oh, Jack." Karen sounded not sad but disappointed, like a teacher mourning the failure of a once promising student. "How many more 'justs' are there going to be, Jack? How many before I have officers showing up at the house or the school to tell me you're dead? That it was *just* bad luck."

"Oh, come on, Kare. It's not like I get into a fight every day. Hell, I hurt myself worse in the gym."

"You've been on the road four days, Jack," Karen pointed out sadly. "What if this —" she imitated him rubbing his temple, rather sarcastically, Jack thought "— had been an inch the other way? *Oh, it's just an eye, Kare,*" she mimicked him. *"I've got another one."*

Jack felt Justice stiffening under his hand and realized the dog was reacting to him. Jack relaxed the hand on Justice's neck and slowly unclenched his jaw. He drew a cleansing breath in through his nose, held it momentarily as he visualized the tension draining from his blood, then gradually freed it to the night air.

"Do you know what I arrested him for?" he posed quietly. No tension at all.

"It doesn't mat —"

"Yes, it does matter," he interjected sharply. Well, maybe some tension. "He assaulted his girlfriend and their baby, Kare. And not just today. Weekly. They're both covered in bruises. And yesterday, *just yesterday,*" he spat, "Jennifer arrested him for beating up his other girlfriend and her baby. So I'm not going to complain about a couple of scratches."

"It doesn't matter what you arrest them for, Jack. Whether it's murder or shoplifting, one of them is going to kill you someday. And then it won't matter one shit what you were arresting them for."

Jack's anger was beginning to rumble, quietly and down deep, but still, it was stirring. Did she have no faith in his abilities? Why did she have to see the scars as reminders of near misses? Why couldn't she see them as victories, as proof of his strengths and his dedication to her?

"I won't let some piece of shit kill me, Karen," he vowed, almost growling. "It won't happen."

But it was obvious she didn't believe him. "How can you be sure of that?"

"Because I have you to come home to," he snapped.

Silence.

A soft breeze wafting across the deck was all that passed between them for minutes. Jack was pissed and he'd be damned if he was going to be the one to break the stalemate. He let his gaze drift over the starry sky, concentrated on the feel of Justice's fur beneath his fingers and tried to let go of his anger.

But Karen was her mother's daughter and Evelyn Hawthorn's stubbornness was legendary — although she would call it determination or willpower. Even though Jack knew his last comment had caught Karen unprepared and shocked her into silence, it didn't mean she'd be the first to breach the quiet. They had already sat long enough with nothing said; if Jack didn't rein in his pride, they'd still be sitting here when the sun came up in a couple of hours.

But he certainly wasn't going to apologize; he had nothing to be sorry for.

"I forgot to tell you," he ventured, "I'm starting early tomorrow. At noon, so I won't be able to join you and your parents for brunch."

"Typical," she decided, staring off into the shadows beyond the deck.

"Typical?" *What the fuck does that mean?*

She turned to face him, an ugly twist to her lips. Lips, Jack suddenly realized, he hadn't kissed, or been kissed by, in a long time.

"I know you don't like my parents, Jack, but if you don't want to see them just say so. You don't have to make up excuses."

Excuses? God, it's like she wants to fight. "We were told today at the beginning of shift," he justified. "It was a busy night and I forgot to call. That's all."

"We?" she asked suspiciously.

Oh, fuck. Despite Jack having never worked with Jenny, Karen nurtured a mistrustful jealousy of his new partner. The two women in his life had never met and all Karen knew of Jenny was her distorted reputation as a party girl. All thanks to a friend of Karen's who worked in 32 Division and who had been more than happy to regurgitate rumours and gossip.

"Jennifer —" not Jenny, not around Karen "— and I are doing a hooker sweep with the Major Crime guys and they want to start early."

"A hooker sweep?" she asked dubiously, as if he was making up something.

"Yeah. The PWS pose as hookers to grab the johns and the rest of us will be backup."

"She gets to act like a whore," Karen mused. "How fitting."

More stirrings down in his belly, hot and harsh. "Damn it, Karen, that's not fair. You haven't even met her. You have no idea at all what she's like."

"If you think so highly of her, Jack, why don't you two become partners?" She threw the question at him. When he didn't answer, she moaned, "You did, didn't you?"

"I was going to tell you —"

"When? How long were you going to keep it a secret from me?" There was venom in her voice.

"Bloody hell," he muttered. Jack was holding tight to his temper but the more Karen refused to listen, the stronger it grew.

"We just paired up tonight and I'm telling you now. I wasn't hiding it."

"So how long have you wanted this? Did you have to wait for Manny to get kicked out of the station?"

"Bloody fucking hell," he muttered, running his free hand through his hair. His right hand was still buried in Justice's fur, pulling as much calmness as he could from the shepherd. "I haven't been planning this," he explained, frustrated that he had to. "Hell, yesterday was the first day we worked together." He snapped his teeth shut, far too late to stop the words from coming out; he knew as soon as he uttered them how wrong they were to say to Karen.

She laughed. A scornful, mocking sound. "Didn't wait long, did you, Jack? Did you decide to marry me on our second date?"

"It isn't the same, Karen, and you know it."

She was crying now, her tears shining streaks in the moonlight. "You're an asshole, Jack."

The accusation was a knife in Jack's guts. Karen, no matter how heated the argument, how ferocious her ire, had never hurt him as she just had with those simple, little words. His anger, a strengthening inferno, was extinguished beneath those words, a bonfire snuffed out by a tidal wave.

He went to her and knelt before her. "Karen, if it means that much to you, I won't work with her. You're the one I love, not her."

He reached for her hands but she snatched them away. "Do what you want, Jack. I don't care. You can be her first customer tomorrow and fuck her in your car. I just don't care." She stormed into the kitchen, slamming shut the sliding door, rattling the glass in its frame.

Silence once again slid over the yard.

Jack stared after his wife, his face frozen in disbelief. He knelt on the deck, shocked into immobility until Justice, whimpering softly, nudged his head under Jack's arm. Jack gratefully wrapped his arm around his friend.

What the hell was happening to his marriage?

"She called you an asshole?"

"That she did." Jack laughed, an empty, hurt sound. "But at least she didn't call me a fucking asshole, right?"

Jenny didn't join in on his laughter. "That doesn't sound good, Jack. What are you going to do?"

He shrugged and sipped his Diet Coke. In the office's thick, stale air, the pop's icy sweetness was ambrosia. Jack and Jenny were in the second-floor Major Crime office waiting for Mason and his crew. The shades were drawn, casting a dim pall over the cluttered desks and filing cabinets but doing little to dispel the room's mugginess.

Jack stretched, then rolled his shoulders. "I'll tell you, that futon in the basement sucks, that's for sure."

"You slept in the basement?"

Jack nodded, bobbing the pop can as he drank. "Kind of got the hint when I found the bedroom door closed. And nope," he said, anticipating her next question, "I didn't see her this morning. She'd left by the time I got up." He grimaced. "I imagine she and her parents had an interesting conversation over brunch."

"Did someone say brunch?" Jason "Tank" Van Dusen strolled — as well as anyone of his size and bulk could stroll — into the office with an expectant grin on his face that quickly faded. "Aw, no food."

According to his self-written legend, Tank was the world's only sumo wrestler–Viking love child. His gigantic bald head sat neckless on his enormous shoulders over his equally massive body. Tank refused to weigh himself, claiming the last scale he had stepped on had broken, but anyone who doubted the legitimacy of his nickname had never seen him bench-pressing a bar bending under the weight of its plates or handling the unit's two-man battering ram by himself.

"Sorry, Tank," Jenny apologized. "You can have a sip of Jack's Coke if you want."

"Ew, diet." Tank shuddered before squeezing in behind his desk. "You're looking good, Jenny."

"Thanks, Tank. Just my usual crack-whore outfit." Jenny's wardrobe consisted of a stained T-shirt, worn jeans and scuffed high heels. Her waist-length hair hung in a loose ponytail. Her normal French braid would have been safer, but it was a hairstyle not many crack whores took to.

"You good to go, Jack? Heard you got some busted ribs." Tank was rummaging in his desk and came out with a protein bar.

"I'm good. Just one cracked rib, that's all. So, unless some john puts up a fight, I'll be fine."

"Johns usually ain't the aggressive type." Tank ripped open the wrapper and bit the bar in half. Around a mouthful he said, "And if someone does want to scrap, we'll just sic Kris on him."

"Who am I beating up for you now, babycakes?" Kris Kretchine asked, gliding through the door. Kris was a competitive female bodybuilder with enough muscle mass to make most men jealous. Or nervous. Jack knew his ego wouldn't be able to handle a comparison of biceps with Kris. Despite her size, she moved with a liquid grace that hinted at the speed that had earned her a college scholarship for track and field. Her spiky blond hair was frosted with blue today to match her T-shirt and Jack couldn't help but notice how the material strained over her substantial breasts.

Jenny smacked Jack in the shoulder.

If Kris was aware of Jack's stare she let it slide. On her way to her desk she stopped behind Tank and gave his bald pate a loud smooch.

Tank giggled then blushed crimson when he spotted Jack and Jenny staring at him. "She does it for luck," he explained sheepishly.

"Does Mason kiss you, too?" Jack wanted to know just as the Major Crime detective walked in.

"Who do I kiss?" he wanted to know.

"Do you guys time your entrances, or what?" Jack looked to Jenny for support and she just shrugged, a bemused smile on her face.

Mason studied them for a moment then turned to Tank and Kris, but neither of his crew could help him out. "Whatever," he mumbled, sitting down. His chair creaked in protest. "Damn it, Tank," the burly D snarled. "Quit stealing my chair."

"Sorry, boss." Chagrined, Tank exchanged chairs and when he sat down, the chair didn't just creak, it screamed. While everyone was waiting to see if the chair would dump Tank on his ass John Taftmore, the final member of Mason's team, waltzed into the room.

"Tank take Rick's chair again?" When Taftmore spotted Jenny his face lit up, a stupid grin and his acne scars dropping his visible age back into high school. He ran his fingers through his mop of unremarkable brown hair then sidled over to Jenny. His tall, gangly build added to the teen illusion.

"Hey, Jenny," he crooned, the stupid grin becoming a repulsive leer.

"If you even think about touching me," Jenny warned him, "I'll kick your balls up into your throat."

Taftmore paused in mid-sidle, his leer faltering, clearly assessing the legitimacy of Jenny's threat. At length, common sense won out, or maybe his balls reminded him of an incident involving Jenny and a chair. Whichever, he nodded to Jack then sauntered over to his desk. Kris gave Jenny a thumbs-up while Tank snickered around the last of his protein bar.

"Is Sue coming?" Kris asked once Taftmore and his wounded pride had sat down.

Mason shook his head. "She's tied up on the nut squad so it's just Jenny today. Which works out 'cause Taft and I have something else to work on." He ran his hands over his short-cropped hair. The big detective was looking tired.

"Court not going well, boss?"

"Court fucking sucks, Tank." Mason slapped his hands on the desk. "Fucking defence lawyer. He convinced the judge the search warrant was no good so all the evidence we got in the apartment and on the computer is inadmissible. We're fucked, totally fucked."

"That the pedophile case?" Jack asked.

Mason nodded glumly. "Yeah. Did you know the prick actually filmed himself having anal sex with a twelve-year-old boy? We've got it but thanks to that fucking lawyer none of the files in the computer are worth a shit." Mason's voice was tightening as his face reddened. "We have proof, beyond any fucking doubt, that this asshole raped this boy and he's going to walk. Fuck!"

The office was silent, the only sound the detective's slowly easing breathing. "All I can hope for is to drag this out a few more days and run up his lawyer's bill. What a clusterfuck."

"That reminds me, boss," Tank ventured. "Homicide called. They want you to give them a call when you get in."

"Well, I'm not fucking in yet."

"Didn't think so."

"That about the machete thing over in 52? Manny said you stopped by the scene yesterday."

Mason eyed Jack before answering. "Yeah, somebody offed the pedophile's brother by mistake."

"Too bad."

"Yeah," Mason agreed. "Too bad." The big man shook himself. "Enough of that shit. The whores have been working Pembroke lately and the residents are complaining to the boss and he complains to me," he spelled out for the officers. "Now, I was hoping not to spend more than a couple of days on this; we've got more important things to do than pinch some businessmen looking for a cheap fuck. No offense, Jenny."

Jenny waved it off then shot a warning finger at Taftmore. The boy detective constable wisely shut his mouth.

"Grab as many as you can so the superintendent can show the numbers to the residents, but don't bother hiding while you're processing the pricks," Mason instructed. "If the other johns see their buddies getting pinched, maybe they'll get the idea and move on."

"It's a waste of time," Kris opined. "All we're doing is moving the whores to another street."

Mason agreed jadedly. "And then another batch of residents will complain and we'll move the girls on to yet another street. Fuck," he grumbled. "When is someone going to clue in and just legalize the damned thing?"

"Legalize and tax it," Kris added. "Could probably pay off the national debt."

"It certainly would make enforcing it a lot easier." Mason held up a hand, ticking off points on his thick fingers. "If a girl's caught hooking without a licence, she gets pinched. No recent medical checkup, pinched. Hooking under age, pinched."

"Set up legal brothels," Tank suggested. "Safer for the workers."

Kris nodded. "It'd do away with pimps."

"They could have price wars," Taft declared joyously. "Can you imagine the commercials?"

"Another legitimate argument ruined by Taft logic," Kris proclaimed despondently.

To Jack, the discussion had the feel of a well-worn subject and he could sympathize with the Major Crime officers; rousting crack whores and scooping johns didn't seem all that major.

"All right, get out of here," Mason ordered then gestured everyone back to their seats. "Fuck, I'm getting old. My mind's fucking going." He scrubbed his face again. "You two," he said, looking at Jack and Jenny, "took a report Sunday for an assault on a hooker."

Jack nodded while Jenny clarified, "Aggravated."

Mason cocked an eyebrow so she carried on. "Guy picked her up at Church and Gerrard. She took him to her normal laneway and the guy just beat the living hell out of her."

"Any description of the suspect?"

Jack was already flipping back through his notebook. "Male white," he read when he found the right page. "Young, early twenties most likely. Short brown hair, clean shaven. Muscular but not like a bodybuilder."

"So it isn't Kris," Taftmore announced.

"Shut the fuck up, Taft," the other three MCU coppers said together.

Practice makes perfect, Jack guessed then went back to his notes. "That's it, except for a strong jaw. No description on the car except for small and dark-coloured."

"When did that one happen?" Mason asked.

Jack checked his notes. "Wednesday night, close to midnight."

The detective nodded. "As of Saturday night, we have a second one."

"We didn't hear anything about it on parade yesterday," Jenny pointed out.

"Didn't get reported till yesterday evening when the victim regained consciousness."

"Another hooker?"

Mason nodded grimly. "A tranny got beaten half to death in the parking lot off Homewood."

"Whoa," Jack interrupted. "Lee and I did a tranny and her john by that parking lot Saturday night. What time did it happen?"

"Right around the time you gave those two their papers; we checked your notes."

"Did that fucker come back?"

Mason heaved a sigh. "That's what we thought. It certainly would have made things easier, but we tracked down your hooker and spoke to him. He said our victim headed into the parking lot with a trick just a few minutes before she hooked up with the one you pinched her with." Mason shook his head. "Damn it, I hate talking about trannies. I don't know whether to call them he or she and keep getting fucking confused."

"It happens to guys your age, boss," Tank offered.

Mason glared at Tank and the big sumo Viking found something interesting on his desk to study. "Your tranny," Mason said, turning back to Jack, "couldn't give us any description beyond white male."

"Fuck me," Jack suddenly exclaimed. "I thought I heard something in that lot. Fuck, it was probably him."

"You didn't check it out?" Mason wondered aloud.

"We were going to, but then the stabbing came over and we headed down to that. Fuck," he swore in frustration.

"Bad luck. Happens all the time."

Jenny spoke up. "Are you sure it's the same guy? Our victim was female and you said this one was a tranny. Could some john have just freaked out when he realized the hooker was a guy?"

"It's possible," Mason conceded. "The tranny's Asian and a john wouldn't know he wasn't dealing with the real thing until it was too late. But the description, as shit as it is, matches: male white, young, dark hair, muscular build. So for now we're treating it like it's the same guy." Mason pointed a finger at Jenny. "You see anyone that might be this guy and you signal for a high-risk takedown. Got it?"

"Got it."

"Good." Mason swept the officers with his eyes. "Well? Get the fuck out of my office."

Pembroke Street was a little one-way running south off Gerrard Street, opposite Allan Gardens. The homes lining the asphalt were two- and three-storey and old, their bricks having endured decades of seasons. The front yards were small, the trees shading them mature and just as weathered as the houses. It would have been a quiet, picturesque street, except it was in 51 Division.

The Seaton House, that granddaddy of hostels, was just one street over and George and Pembroke were connected by well-travelled laneways at the north and south ends of the streets. Crack central, the intersection of Sherbourne and Dundas streets, was just one tiny block away and Pembroke was a major artery feeding the heart of the drug trade.

And the ladies of the night — or afternoon or early morning; crack whores didn't keep regular schedules — frequently worked the sidewalks, laneways and doorsteps of Pembroke Street. It wasn't uncommon for residents to step out onto the front porch to collect the morning paper and interrupt a "business transaction." When the oldest profession began to occupy too much of the neighbourhood, the ladies and their clients had to be encouraged to change locale.

Which was why Tank and Kris were heading over to Pembroke with Jack and Jenny in the back seat of the banged-up and abused Ford Taurus.

Jack listened to the engine's irregular sounds. "What year is the car, Tank?"

The big cop shrugged, his meaty shoulders overflowing the sides of the driver's seatback. "Dunno. Two, three years, I guess. Why?"

"I'm suddenly not feeling so bad about my Taurus."

"Tank has that effect on cars," Kris commented. She reached over to stroke the back of Tank's bald head when the sumo-Viking began to pout. "It's okay, Tanky. I'm just teasing."

Jack watched avidly the way Kris's fingers toyed with Tank's ear, then turned to Jenny, mouthing *Tanky* to her. She bobbed her shoulders, an amused smile touching her lips. Her shoulders weren't nearly as wide as Tank's and came nowhere near to spilling out of her seat, but they did interesting things to the front of her grey T-shirt.

Jack pulled his eyes away — reluctantly — just as Tank turned onto Pembroke. There was an Aboriginal community centre on the southeast corner with a miniature parking lot behind it. The laneway starting at George Street cut across Pembroke to open up farther over at Sherbourne Street, leaving the parking lot open on two sides. Tank backed in to give him and his partner — Jack wondered if the term "partner" could be applied outside of work then decided it wasn't any of his business — a clear view of the street.

Kris twisted around in her seat to face Jack and Jenny. Tank watched them in the rearview mirror; Jack doubted the big cop could turn that easily in the confines of the small car. As it was, Tank had the seat back enough so Jack was almost sucking on his own kneecaps.

"Okay, Tank and I are going to stay in the car —"

"With the air conditioning," Jenny interjected.

Kris smiled. "Someone has to, and besides, you don't want to be near Tank when he starts to sweat." Tank shook his head as if to say, *No, you don't.*

Kris gestured over her shoulder at a yellow-bricked semi-detached house on the west side of the street. "There's a bag of bottled water back there; you guys may need it. Jenny, hang out by the semi there, closer to the south end. Jack, see the porch at the north end? Grab a seat there. That way, when a car pulls up to talk to our little money-maker here, we'll all be in his blind spots in case we need to sneak up on him.

"Now because the car will be between us," she went on, "Tank and I won't be able to see your signal, but Jack will. There should be an empty beer can somewhere back there, Jack. Just hang on to it and when Jenny signals for the pinch you make like you're taking a drink. Tank'll pin the john in with the car and we'll lay some paper on him. Jenny, as we're processing him, disappear into the lane so any other passing johns won't associate you with us. We all good? Let's do it."

"'Let's do it,' she says," Jenny grumbled as she and Jack crossed the street. "They've got the AC. We've been outside thirty seconds and I'm already too hot."

"You could never be too hot for me," Jack assured her with a sombre face then broke into a grin. "Actually, I'm tempted to inquire about your prices."

With her own solemn expression, she told him, "You couldn't afford me."

"Don't you give a partner discount?"

"That's with the discount."

"Ouch." They were in front of the semi, street numbers 114 and 116; the front yard of weeds and dead grass would give Jack an unobstructed view of his partner as she fished for johns. "I think I'll just settle for watching your ass. It's my job, after all."

"Don't you mean cover my ass?"

Jack flipped his hands up. "Watch, cover. Same thing."

"Well, remember to check out my feet every once in a while; I won't be signally with my ass." Jenny gathered up her T-shirt and knotted it below her breasts to bare her midriff. "Ah, much better."

"I didn't know your belly button was pierced."

"Gives the guy something to play with on his way down." Leaving her partner open-mouthed and speechless, she headed out to peddle her ass.

An old, beat-up Toyota that made Jack's Ford look like a floor model rolled to the curb, the engine wheezing heavily. The passenger window lowered in jerks and Jenny sauntered over to her first customer of the day. She gave the back seat a quick scan — empty — as she approached the car, then leaned into the open window, crossing her arms beneath her. She hissed as her bare skin touched the door's metal, heated beyond belief by the gruelling sun. She rolled her forearms forward so they rested on the cooler side of the window partition. Her sunglasses shielded her eyes from the john as she swiftly but thoroughly examined him and the car's interior.

The inside of the Toyota was as dilapidated as its exterior but clear of weapons or anything suspicious. Unless it was tucked away somewhere, of course. The driver was in far better condition than his car. Asian, middle-aged, with a predatory glint in his eye, he stared at Jenny like a hungry cat spying a tasty mouse.

Jenny smiled; this one was going to be easy. She bet herself she could have him hooked and reeled in within twenty seconds. "You looking for some action, hon?" she purred.

"You know it, baby. But the question is —" he leered as he twisted in his seat to face Jenny and brought his knee up "— can you handle my action?" Grinning proudly, he let his right leg fall open.

His pants were undone and there was no doubting he was ready for action. Jenny felt like she was being stared at by a third eye.

"What type of action you looking for?" she asked with a husky breathlessness before slowly licking her lips.

"I want you to wrap those luscious lips around my dick and suck it." If nothing else, the john certainly couldn't be criticized for shyness.

Hooked.

"Sounds good to me, hon. How much you gonna give me?"

"Forty. Fifty if you let me come in your mouth."

And reeled.

Now to land him. Out of sight to the john, Jenny casually crossed her ankles. Behind her, on his porch, Jack raised his beer can and seconds later Tank was lifting the john out of his car.

"Speak no English! Speak no English!" the john was squawking as he tried to keep his pants from slithering down his legs. His third eye was suddenly looking not so potent.

That's one.

The stench didn't slap Jenny in the face so much as shove itself up her nose. She nearly gagged but covered it with a lopsided smile.

"Looking for some action, hon?" she invited as she casually shifted back from the open window. The car was a big fuel-guzzler, sleek and glossy. The driver may have been a big guzzler himself, but he was far from sleek and glossy. Oily, but not glossy.

He was a chubby, small man perched behind the wheel of his road boat. What little hair he had was slicked across his sun-burned scalp. His suit jacket was folded neatly on the passenger seat and Jenny could see that, despite the cold blasted out by the air conditioning, the john had sweated huge stains into his shirt. The car reeked of body odour and she had to keep reminding herself smells couldn't physically touch.

The john stared straight ahead, nervously kneading the steer-ing wheel. He had yet to look in Jenny's direction. She felt a pang of sympathy for the man.

"I'll give you fifteen dollars to have sex with me," he said to the windshield.

Fifteen! Not that much sympathy.

Jenny crossed her ankles.

"It sure is hot, isn't it?"

Jenny wiped sweat from her brow then peered at the john seductively over the rim of her sunglasses. "It's very hot," she said suggestively.

"Are you all sweaty?"

"All over." She smiled, almost leered, then slowly winked at the john. She couldn't believe she had resorted to winking, but this john was refusing to be hooked. First he had cruised by sev-eral times; his flame-red pickup wasn't hard to miss. Then, when he'd finally stopped with his window-shopping, he talked about the weather — *It's hot, you idiot* — and now he wanted to know if she was sweating. She felt like giving him the finger and telling him to fuck off but there was no way she was going to let him slip free after spending so much time with him.

"*All* over?" He rubbed his stubbled chin as if he was contemplating a grave decision. "I watched you, you know, when I drove by."

Duh. I'm surprised you didn't drive into a parked car.

"You're wearing high heels. I like that." Mr. Pickup rubbed his chin again. "Yeah, a lot better than sandals."

"You like my shoes?" *How about I brain you with one of them?*

Mr. Pickup was starting to breathe heavy, almost pant. "Yeah, I do. I bet your feet are real sweaty in them."

Bingo! Now I know how to hook you. Jenny let a smile slowly, sensually spread across her lips. "And what do you want to do with my hot, sweaty feet?"

Mr. Pickup leaned toward Jenny so much he was practically crawling into the passenger seat. "I wanna suck on your toes," he said fervently.

Does that count as a sex act? Jenny was sure it would be for the john, but it might not be enough for the courts.

She pouted. "Is that all?"

"Then I want you to jerk me off with your feet." The john was all but trembling with excitement.

Now that's more like it. Time to reel this fish in. "How much? I got real pretty feet."

"Is eighty enough?" Mr. Pickup asked trepidatiously.

Mr. Fifteen Dollars oughta talk to you. "That's just fine, hon."

The afternoon was a steady stream of johns: married johns wanting what the wife wouldn't give; businessmen johns looking to blow off some corporate steam; cabby johns — cheap bastards — offering to trade a free ride for sex and even one john couple anxious for a threesome. The latest was a knob hoping for a birthday freebie.

Jenny blew the knob a little kiss and left him in the hands of the MCU cops, then cut across the brief front lawn to join Jack on the porch. She held back a smile when she noticed his eyes dip as he quickly checked her out. She didn't mind; he wasn't blatant or stupid about it. Not like the knob back there. He'd stared at her breasts so intently she could have been holding her badge next to them and he would have never noticed. She knew Jack was attracted to her and she wasn't stupid enough to deny her similar feelings.

Why are the good ones always taken?

That Jack was one of the good ones she had no doubt, wouldn't have paired up with him otherwise. But he was a man in pain. The constant fighting with his wife and her parents — if Jenny ever met either of those nosy, interfering asses, she would gladly teach them not to fuck with her partner — was inevitably eroding his spirit. When he had come to 51 last summer, she had seen a gleam, an excitement in his eyes. Now that light was gone and in the shadow left behind lurked something that Jack kept buried deep inside himself, hidden away from those around him. It hurt her to see him slowly buckling under the pressure.

Oh, damn. I think I'm falling for him.

But there was no rule against caring for your partner and if she could rekindle that light, that gleam, even for a moment by flirting or showing off her flat stomach, then that's what she was going to do. Jack needed a safe place, a place where he could forget about, and escape, the stress and hassle of his personal life. And if that place turned out to be the inside of their scout car, then so be it.

"You're looking awfully serious," Jack commented as he handed her a bottle of water.

Jenny cracked the bottle and took a long pull. She was tempted to dump the rest over herself — damn, it was hot! — but a wet T-shirt might take the whole flirting thing a bit too far.

"Just an idiot," she explained. "That guy was so damn stupid I probably could have gotten him if I was in uniform. Trust me," she went on when Jack raised a disbelieving eyebrow her way. "There are guys that stupid. Last time I did a sweep, Mason didn't tell me till the day of — all I had was a Toronto Police T-shirt and I still got guys. I just told them some cops gave it to me and it meant other cops should leave me alone."

Jack laughed. "Some guys just can't think with both heads at once."

Kris was waving at them. "Hey, Jack. C'mere for a sec."

"Duty calls," he said, excusing himself.

Jenny downed the rest of the water and snagged another bottle before ducking into the laneway to keep out of sight of potential pinches.

She leaned against the brick wall. The sun may have been settling on the skyline but the bricks still held the heat that had been baked into them all day. The heat was uncomfortable on her shoulders but, damn it, she was too tired to stand up by herself.

Who would've thought strutting up and down the sidewalk could be tiring? Damn, I should have grabbed Jack's chair.

The heat from the bricks was starting to feel good on her back, loosening muscles she hadn't known were tight. She closed her eyes and sipped from her bottle.

Damn, I'm one pooped crack whore.

Jesse Polan was horny.

Horny and sore. A stay in the hospital will do that to a guy. Two days without a piece of rock or a piece of tail. And those fucking bitch nurses acting like their shit was gold or something. Fuck.

I should get a fucking bigger gun. A big fucking AK fucking gun and waste those high-snotted bitches.

Teach those bitches for getting security on his ass. So what if he'd been whacking off? It wasn't like he'd touched the nurse while he was stroking it. And was it his fault they'd left his stretcher bed in a hallway? Fuck them.

Jesse shot a finger in the general direction of St. Michael's Hospital then doubled over, clutching his broken ribs. The sudden movement started his head spinning and black dots slewed across his vision as the laneway spun around him. He staggered over to a car and collapsed on its hood, only to jerk back as the hot metal seared his forearms. The laneway was whirling madly and Jesse dropped to his butt, the impact pounding another wave of nauseating pain through his ribs.

The doctor may have been right. Maybe he should have stayed in the hospital.

Groaning, Jesse reclaimed his feet. He may have a dent in his head, one of those fucking percussion things, but he wasn't dumb enough to lie in the laneway; someone would fucking run over him thinking he was a bag of fucking garbage. And if someone fucking did, would the fucking cops do anything? Not fucking likely. Did they do anything when he told them people were trying to kill him? Fuck, no.

Bet some of those fuckers that jumped me were fucking cops.

He carefully walked back to the car and even more carefully knelt down to view his face in the side mirror. Something that looked like it belonged in one of those zombie movies stared back at him. His left eye was hidden beneath a mass of swollen, purple flesh. His other eye was just as colourful but not puffed up, thankfully.

"Yeah, fucking lucky me," he whined.

His nose, broken at least twice before, was splinted as straight as possible with a wad of fucking tape holding it in place. It looked like he was wearing a fucking white tent in the middle of his face. His lips were a mess of cuts, some stitched shut. He knew his body was just as mangled and his arms bore wounds from trying to protect himself.

I should fucking sue the cops. I fucking told them I was a marked man.

But they'd wanted to know why people wanted to kill him

and Jesse wasn't about to tell them that. No fucking way. The stupid fucking cops hadn't known but everyone else had. Just because he'd been running with that fucknut Kayne while he was slicing up people's faces. Jesse told anyone who'd listen that he'd had no choice, that Kayne would have killed him. Tried to tell them that he, Jesse, had actually held Kayne back, had stopped him cutting when that crazy motherfucker wanted to slit some throats. But no one listened and after months of hiding, he'd been found. Found and beaten almost to death.

But no one would fuck with him now. He'd made a stop right after getting out of the hospital. The next asshole fucker who got in his face would be as dead as that fucking Kayne.

That fucking cop. Twice now, that motherfucker had fucked up Jesse's life. But no more. No one was going to fuck him up anymore.

Patting the hard bulge under his shirt, Jesse Polan slowly but deliberately walked up the laneway behind the Seaton House in search of some crack or pussy. Whichever came first. He wasn't picky.

The man had come out from the laneway behind the Seaton House and Jenny watched as he limped in her direction. Someone had laid the boots to the poor bastard something fierce. His face was a colourful mosaic of swollen flesh and bruises, made all the more vivid by the startling white splint over his nose, and by the way he was hobbling along, she was sure someone hadn't spared his body.

Jenny expected him to simply shuffle on past; no one in that condition could possibly be interested in sex, but he surprised her. And not for the last time.

He stopped in front of her, close enough for Jenny to smell the sick sweat coming off him. "Hey, baby, how about you and me go somewhere and fuck?"

"Aren't you a charmer," she told him as his eyes unabashedly trolled over her body. Jenny fought back the urge to shudder. Where Jack's earlier appraisal had been subtle and, in a way, complimentary, this creep's blatant inspection was palpable, an oily touch sliming her skin.

Despite her revulsion, she didn't sucker him into a communicate charge. She knew she could, he didn't look all that bright, but anyone busted up to that extent deserved a touch of sympathy.

"What's that supposed to mean?" With his lips stitched up, the creep was having a hard time talking. His words were coming out all mushed together but there was no mistaking the tone. The creep was getting angry, but Jenny really didn't give a damn.

She lowered her sunglasses, and there was nothing seductive about the gesture this time. She fixed him with her cop stare and said, "It means I'm not interested. Keep walking."

The creep pulled back but didn't retreat. "Fucking bitch. Just like those fucking high-snotted bitch nurses."

"Whatever. Take a hike." She tossed her head in the direction of Pembroke.

"Bitch," he spat and turned away. But kept turning and when he was facing Jenny again he had a gun in his hand.

"Shit," she breathed and then he was on her, the revolver jammed painfully into her ribs.

The creep clamped his left hand over her mouth and dug the gun in harder. "You listen to me, bitch," he sneered. His breath reeked. It smelled like some small, diseased rodent had crawled into his mouth and died. "I'm gonna fuck you, bitch. Dead or alive, I'm gonna fuck you. You understand?"

Jenny nodded beneath the creep's hand. He smiled, showing rotting teeth behind his ruined lips, and cautiously removed his hand.

"You fucking scream, bitch, and I'll fucking shoot you. You fucking got that?"

"Yeah," Jenny whispered huskily. "Let's get started." She

dropped her hands to his belt buckle, her left forearm resting against the inside of his gun wrist.

"Can't wait now, can you, bitch?" His left hand slid down from her face to her breast, squeezing greedily.

"Like that?" Jenny asked. She had his belt undone and could feel his eager hardness behind the zipper.

"Yeah, bitch. Keep going," he sighed, and his eyelids slipped shut.

Jenny swept her arm out to the side, pushing the gun away, and at the same time drove her knee into his balls. The creep gagged deep down in his throat and his legs sagged under him. She grabbed his gun hand and twisted the palm skyward, locking the elbow joint in a tight arm bar. Bent over, his free hand clutching his groin, the creep was unable to defend himself as Jenny snapped two vicious kicks into his body, driving her shin hard into his ribs.

He hit the pavement like a sack of shit and Jenny plucked the gun from his unresisting fingers. The creep was curled tight, clutching himself, but managed to glare up at her.

"You fucking bitch," he choked out.

Jenny smiled sweetly at him. "That's *Officer* Bitch to you, asshole."

Taylor flipped open his cell phone. "Hello?"

"Hi, Taylor. It's Sandra. I hope you don't mind but I got your number from Gregory."

Why would she be calling him? He suppressed a tremor of — what? Alarm or anticipation?

"Are you still there?"

Taylor shook his head. "Sorry. What can I do for you?"

"Gregory said you have his car. I was wondering if I could get a lift to work. Amy's not feeling well so she's staying home."

Relief. And disappointment? "Yeah, no problem. Where should I pick you up?" He jotted down the address on Drewry then realized where he was. "I'm actually close by. If you don't mind being a little early, I could come and get you now."

"That'd be nice. Maybe we could grab a coffee or something before work," she suggested and that unknown quake ran through Taylor's body again.

He closed the phone and sat still, tapping the cell against his chin. Part of him wanted to see Sandra outside of work, perhaps try for something normal, that elusive goal he believed he had found with Sherry. He had had less than a month with Sherry but in that brief period he had lived as the man he wanted to be. The anger, the shame, the guilt, all laid to rest. But that had been before that night, before that hooker had —

No. Best not to relive that horror. Unconsciously, he rubbed his hands across his chest. His hands were trembling but, again, from fear or excitement?

He had one last stop to make before meeting Sandra; he could not imagine her wanting to accompany him as he made the last of his steroid deliveries. As he started the car he wondered, not for the first time, why he did it, sold for Rico, but the answer was obvious: he couldn't afford the apartment and the steroids from Rico on the money he made at the club. Selling let him keep both.

A quiet voice timidly spoke up. *But why use it at all?*

He recognized the voice as that of his sister, Sara. She hid deep in his mind, too weak to reveal herself except in times of confusion and doubt. Hers was a voice he never liked to hear.

"Go away. Leave me alone," he whispered. "Leave me alone. You're dead."

But she would not rest easy. *You don't need it*, she insisted. *Be who you are.*

"I am who I am," he rumbled. "Who I want to be. Now fuck off, you snivelling little bitch."

Sara's voice, her ghost, fell silent but the seeds of doubt she had so swiftly and precisely sown took root, growing and spreading like poison, reaching deep into Taylor's soul. The ire, entwined as always with self-loathing and doubt, intensified, burning ever stronger until it was a rage he could barely contain.

At York University he rid himself of an order of Deca and GH to a university linebacker, a student whose scholarship depended on his gridiron success. Taylor wound his way through the parking lot back to his borrowed vehicle, grumbling under his breath the whole way. He passed a van and spied himself in the passenger window.

He stopped and stared at his reflection. The man staring back at him was not yet old but his youth was masked by eyes that had seen much sorrow and anguish. Skin drawn taut over a solid brow and chiselled jaw gave his face strength beyond its years. But for all the power and confidence his body and visage exuded, he saw only a small boy cowering from his father's wrath and haunted by the ghost of his sister.

Taylor screamed, an inarticulate bellow of rage, and slammed his fist into his mirrored self. His first punch spiderwebbed cracks through the glass; the second shattered it completely.

His rage vented, drained for the moment, he trod wearily to Gregory's car, heedless of the blood dripping a trail of red from his scored knuckles. It was not until he was pulling out of the parking lot that he became aware of the blood. Swearing incoherently, he jammed his fist against his thigh, pressing the cuts to his jeans to inhibit the bleeding. By the time he reached Sandra's house on Drewry Avenue, the blood was no longer flowing, only oozing where it had not congealed into soft, ugly scabs.

Sandra trotted down the driveway, a vision of blond hair, pink tank top and black shorts. Taylor looked at her, at the smile she gave him, and felt dead inside.

Better that than the other.

She jumped into the car and before Taylor could react gave him a quick kiss on the cheek. "Thanks so much for picking me up."

"Um, no problem," he stammered, then feeling more was needed, asked, "you live here?"

"Only in the basement," Sandra told him as she belted up. "Amy and her boyfriend live upstairs. Taylor! What happened to your hand?"

She reached for his hand but he curled it away. "I . . . fell. It's nothing."

The drive down Yonge Street was slow, congested by traffic and road work. "You know the old saying," Sandra joked. "There's two seasons in Toronto: winter and construction."

Taylor grunted and Sandra said no more, but Taylor could see her watching him, studying him. Some time later she asked him if he wanted a coffee or something cold to drink. He didn't but told her yes to be polite; he was feeling guilty and embarrassed for rudely ignoring her during the drive.

Second Cup coffees in hand, they resumed the drive, the AC in Gregory's car performing well enough that the hot beverages didn't seem too out of place.

"Is that the right time?" She tapped the digital readout on the dash. "I didn't realize it was so early. I don't have to be at work for another hour at least."

"Sorry," Taylor said glumly. "I shouldn't have picked you up so early."

But Sandra was quick to reassure him. "No, it's not that. I just meant that if you're not in a hurry we could stop somewhere to finish our coffees and chat, maybe."

He turned to her and gave her what felt like a genuine smile. Tired and little, but genuine. "Sure, I'd like that."

"I know the perfect place." She directed him off Yonge Street onto Rosehill Avenue. Leaving the car, they ventured out into the heat.

"Is this okay for you?" Sandra posed. "I can't believe you're wearing jeans. Why don't you take your shirt off at least?"

Taylor shook his head firmly. "I'm okay."

She looked at him questioningly, clearly puzzled by his defensive attitude, but shrugged her slender shoulders and let it go.

They strolled through an open park that was, in defiance of the broiling sun, teeming with people. A game of ultimate Frisbee ebbed and flowed alongside a soccer match while children and dogs splashed in the artificial ponds and streams birthed from the central fountain.

Taylor gazed about, a sad, faint smile in his eyes as he watched the children playing. "I've never been here before. It's nice."

Sandra nodded, sipping on her coffee. "I grew up around here until . . ."

"Until what?"

"Until my mother died," she admitted then sighed, a breath full of lost hope.

"I'm sorry. I didn't mean to upset you."

"It's okay." She smiled, tossing her hair, and Taylor recognized it for the protective act it was. "I moved away when my dad got remarried," she elaborated, her voice hard and bitter. "His new wife didn't like me and since I wasn't the one fucking him, he took her side."

Hearing the pain in her words, he blurted out, "My family's dead," and instantly regretted it.

"All of them?" Sandra whispered, shocked.

Taylor nodded, clamping his jaws shut. *You've said enough, asshole. Shut up.*

But Sara's ghost disagreed. *Tell her. Let her in.*

Sandra didn't pry and they walked in companionable silence until they reached the east end of the park where it dropped away into a heavily wooded ravine. Running a finger along Taylor's sweaty brow, Sandra joked, "I think we better get you out of the sun before you melt." She guided their steps to a service road that curved down into the narrow valley and its cooling shade.

The air was indeed cooler within the deep green shadows but still held enough heat to mould Taylor's shirt to his body with sweat. The sounds of the city, a harsh constant background, also faded as they descended into the vale and the knot that was binding Taylor's guts loosened ever so slightly. At the ravine floor, the service road became a smaller paved path, but Sandra tugged Taylor away from the asphalt.

"This way is nicer, less people." She led him onto a dirt trail that hugged a small stream as it crooked and flowed through the ravine. The path was well-worn, packed hard into the earth and wide enough in places for two to walk abreast. Sandra slipped her hand into his and he did not pull away.

"What happened to your family?" The question was gentle and caring, not accusing, but even so Taylor flinched. Sandra immediately apologized. "I'm sorry. I shouldn't have asked."

Tell her, Sara whispered.

"It's all right," he said at length. "It's just that I haven't talked to anyone about my family since my girlfriend."

"Your girlfriend? Oh, I didn't know." Sandra tried to pull her hand free but Taylor held onto her.

"We broke up months ago," he told her and was happy when her hand relaxed in his grip. He almost added, *She killed herself a few days ago*, but held that in, as painful as it was.

If you leave me I'll tell!

His hands, reaching for Sherry, then Sherry falling. Falling.

Taylor clamped his eyes shut and willed Sherry away, forcing her memory down into the depths with his sister's ghost. When he opened his eyes, he found Sandra looking at him, concern on her face.

"You don't have to talk about it if you don't want to," she told him.

Taylor gave her a shaky smile. "She . . . didn't take the breakup well." He lifted Sandra over a fallen tree and thrilled to feel her skin beneath his hands. When he set her down she kept one of his hands on her waist and curled her arm around him.

Her touch and the loss of Sherry —

If you leave me I'll tell!

— unlocked memories Taylor had believed laid to rest a lifetime ago.

"I was a twin," he revealed. "I had a sister. Her name was Sara. My mother killed her."

Sandra's hand flew to her mouth. "Oh my God."

Taylor smiled weakly at her in reassurance. "Not on purpose. We — my parents, Sara and I — lived in Sudbury. Dad worked in the nickel mines. God, he was an asshole."

Pulling Taylor after her, Sandra climbed the ravine's slope for a ways before settling on a fallen tree a distance from the path. Wordlessly, she drew him down beside her and with his hands clasped in her own, silently encouraged him to share his pain.

Taylor's eyes drifted past her, focusing on distant times.

"He drank and he beat us. All three of us, but Mom and Sara more than me. I was never good enough for him. He didn't care about school but in sports I was never good enough, never strong enough, never fast enough. I used to listen to him beat Sara, telling her how useless she was, how she should have been a boy. If Mom tried to stop him, she got it worse. Eventually, she stopped trying to protect us.

"Dad drank and Mom started taking Valium. By the time I was thirteen, she was stoned most of the time. What a useless cunt. She let her husband beat her kids and just sat there smiling like some fucking drug addict. And that's what killed Sara."

Taylor paused, freed one hand to wipe tears from his eyes. He drew a deep shuddering breath and plunged on.

"One day at school Sara got her period. It was her first one and she was wearing this white dress and it got covered in blood. She kept begging me to have Mom pick her up. I guess she was really embarrassed." Taylor sniggered, a heartless sound barely above a growl. "Dad was drunk, of course, so Mom came to get Sara but she wasn't much better. On the way home, she crashed the car, killing herself and Sara. She was thirteen years old."

"Oh, Taylor, I'm so sorry." Sandra squeezed his hands as tears trickled down her cheeks.

But Taylor didn't hear Sandra. He was too deep into the past; he could not retreat. All he could do was push ahead, see the hellish journey to its end.

"Dad blamed me, of course. Said I should have made Sara walk home, said I should have known women were weak and had to be told what to do. Said it was my fault, for relying on Mom." Taylor laughed again, a hollow sound. "You know, I don't know if he even cared that they were gone; I never saw him cry. He just drank more."

Taylor sighed heavily, the journey almost done. "He ended up losing his job and we moved to some shithole town outside of Sault Ste. Marie too little to even have a name. I tried to please him, tried to be the son he wanted, but I was never good enough. He died when I was eighteen."

"And you've been alone ever since?"

"Pretty much," Taylor said with a sad smile. "I moved to Toronto. Thought I could start a new life here on my own. I've been here four years now and haven't got shit to show for it."

"That's not true," Sandra argued. "You have a good job, friends at work and you have me . . . if you'll have me." She caressed his cheek, kissed away his tears, met his lips with hers.

A passion, a need, flared alive in Taylor's soul, and he pulled Sandra to him, wrapped her in his powerful arms. The taste of her lips, her tongue, swept away the bitterness in his mouth that was Rico. One hand was entwined in her hair; the other slid to her breast. Sighing into his mouth, Sandra pulled aside her halter top, bared her flesh for his hand. Her hands travelled the length of his arms, kneading the muscles that quivered under her touch, slid over his shoulders and onto his muscular chest.

Taylor suddenly snatched her hands from his chest and held them away from him in a crushing grip.

Sandra cried out. "Ow! Taylor, you're hurting me."

"Oh! I'm sorry, I'm sorry." He freed her hands and slid away from her, hunching protectively against her touch.

"Taylor, what's wrong?" She extended a hand but pulled back when he cringed.

"My . . . chest. I have . . . scars," he confessed, his voice ashamed and hurt. "My dad . . . burned me." He glanced at his watch and surged to his feet. He held a hand out for her. "Come on. We should get to work."

"Are you okay?"

"Yup. See?" Jenny hiked up her T-shirt to show her ribs were bruise-free. At the station she'd unknotted her shirt and let it hang loose. No way was she going to give Taft a show.

"That's good, but it's not what I meant," Jack replied.

They were standing by Jenny's Accord in the station's personal parking lot. The sun was down and the sky was that deep indigo shade just before true dark. The evening had stolen some of the clamminess from the air but there was enough left skulking on the faint breezes to remind the city that it would return with the sun.

"I meant, how are you feeling? You don't get a gun pressed into your side every day."

"I'm . . ." She paused, considering. "Okay. Really."

"Good," he breathed out, as if he had been fearing her answer, then his face twisted up in a grimace. "I should have been there to help. Not that you didn't handle him perfectly by yourself but I shouldn't have left you alone. Not unarmed." His head was bowed, his shoulders slumped, and to Jenny it seemed that invisible weight he'd been carrying for so long had just doubled in mass.

"Jack." She placed a soft hand along his jaw and tilted his head up to meet her eyes. She was always amazed that they were the same height; for some reason she thought of him as taller. His brown eyes — with flecks of green in them, she'd learned working with him yesterday — were heavy with pain and an anger she could see him turning on himself.

Having a gun pulled on her had definitely rocked Jenny and she doubted she'd be sleeping all that well over the next few nights, but she wasn't about to share that with Jack. She knew he still carried, to this day, guilt over Sy's death. It was a piece of the burden he silently bore and she'd be damned if she was going to add to it.

"It wasn't your fault," she told him, locking her gaze on his. "It was Polan's choice, his actions. Not mine. Not yours. And if you'd been with me, he would've walked right on past and attacked the next woman he saw. So, really, it was a good thing I was there by myself. And if you'd come around while he still had his gun, you probably would have shot him. And how bad would that have looked?"

Jack laughed, shaky and uncertain. "Yeah. Shooting the one witness from the bridge that the SIU weren't able to track down. Yeah, I thought about that."

"You were . . . lucky, that's for sure," she said, but had been about to say *pushing your luck*. Back in the laneway Tank had called for a scout car to transport Polan to the station — the MCU unmarked cars didn't have caged back seats — after a side trip to the hospital to make sure Jenny's kicks hadn't shoved a broken rib into a lung or some other organ. Connor Lee and Paul Townsend had been the officers dispatched and they wasted no time bundling a handcuffed Polan into the back seat.

Tank and Kris were on Pembroke finishing off the last john while Jenny gave Connor and Paul the details of Polan's arrest — she'd gotten his ID from the hospital bracelet he was still wearing. The uniforms had their backs to the scout car and their eyes on Jenny's stomach so she, watching over Connor's shoulder, was the only one to see Jack head for the cruiser. He opened the rear door to duck inside briefly and was lost to her sight. She could still see Polan's head through the rear window and wasn't too surprised to see it violently jerk to the right. A moment later Jack was out and closing the door.

She was confident Jack didn't know she had seen him hit Polan. An elbow most likely, with the close quarters of the back seat. But why? Jack wasn't the type to go after a handcuffed prisoner. She didn't think it was because of who Polan was and what he had done to Jack with Kayne; Jack had had murder in his eyes long before they'd learned the creep's real name.

No. Jack had stepped over a line he had once told her he would never cross because of her, but who did he really want to punish? Polan or himself?

What was that old saying? Still waters run deep. She just didn't want Jack to drown in those waters.

"Hey, it was a good day," Jenny declared. "We scooped a bunch of johns, got a homicide in the making off the streets and you got to check me out in my slut clothes."

Jack brightened a bit. "Yeah, it was a good day."

"What was your favourite part?" she asked with a teasing smile.

"You have to ask?" he laughed, sounding more genuine this time.

"If you liked me today . . ." She opened her car door. "You're going to love me tomorrow."

She drove off, for the second time that day leaving Jack speechless.

Jack watched Jenny drive off then climbed into his old Ford. He slumped back in the seat, a haggard sigh escaping his lips as his hands quivered on the steering wheel. He stared at his fingers, watching them shiver in the heat before gripping the wheel to still them. How close had he come to losing Jenny today? When he had sprinted into the laneway and seen her holding that gun, an icy fear had seized his stomach. She had been doing the sweep unarmed, so that meant the asshole had pulled a gun on her. Never mind that he was crumpled at her feet like a mashed-up rag doll, the fucker had pulled a gun on her.

How close had she come to being shot?

It couldn't happen again. Not because of him. He grabbed his left shoulder, wrapping his hand over the tattoo that lay beneath his shirt.

God, I miss you, Sy.

He should have never let Jenny go into that laneway alone, not unarmed. A partner, a friend, had already died because Jack had failed and it was a scar he would carry on his soul to the grave.

He knew what Jenny, what Karen, what the psychiatrist would say to his guilt, but none of them had been there. None of them had let Sy's life bleed away between their fingers. God, it was almost a year ago and the pain was still as sharp, a knife tearing apart his sleep, a horror that would give him no peace.

What? Like I deserve peace? I let Sy die and today Jenny came God knows how close.

He wearily shook his head. He was exhausted; the fear and anger had consumed him and it had taken all of his control not to choke the life from Polan when he had leaned into the back seat of the scout car. He was sure no one had seen him elbow that little fuck in the head, sure no one had heard him warn Polan to never touch his partner again.

And then at the station when Jenny had told Jack who Polan was . . . Suddenly it had been too much for Jack and he had rushed to the bathroom where he had vomited until his stomach had clenched painfully on nothing. Then he had huddled on the floor, gripping the toilet as spasms trembled through his body.

Now he waited as the tremors quieted in his hands and he was once again in control of himself. He started the car and classic rock thumped from the speakers. He flinched at the sound and hurriedly scanned the radio stations until he found one playing calm classical music. Better.

The music and the routine drive home, up the winding

parkway and along the bland, familiar 401, lulled his fears, soothed his anxiety. As he reached the edge of Toronto proper, he exited the highway at Port Union Road. A short drive north brought him to Twyn Rivers Drive.

The rough asphalt road dropped abruptly into a huge forested wilderness and as Jack left the streetlights behind he felt the last of his angst flow out the window to be lost in the darkness. The road snaked along the valley floor and after passing over an old-fashioned single-lane bridge, Jack came to a parking lot that opened up on his right. Gravel pinged off the Ford's belly as the old car jounced over potholes. He passed several parked cars and gave them their privacy before easing to a stop and killing the engine.

Jack closed his eyes and simply listened to the sounds around him. The ticking of the motor as it cooled, the burble of the river flowing peacefully in the darkness, the buzz of night insects. He listened to everything and to nothing. It was quiet here, peaceful.

I should bring Justice here for a walk. He smiled at the picture of Justice splashing in the river in search of fish. *I wonder if Karen would join us?*

The thought of his wife reminded Jack that she had been with him the last time he had come to this spot. Again, almost a year ago. The night of the crack-house search warrant. The night he had been shot at.

He smiled in the dark. Karen had been the one driving, the one to choose to stop in this parking lot. She had attacked him with a frantic passion, fucking him madly. That had been a good day, possibly the last time he had been truly happy. Then Sy. The constant fights with Karen. Charles Anthony taking Karen hostage. Jack killing him. Kayne.

Was he going to add losing Karen to the list?

He sat up and wiped away the tears that had crept unnoticed down his cheeks.

Time to go before some cop comes along and finds me alone in the car while everyone else down here is with someone.

It was time to go home and see if it was not too late to save his marriage. The engine reluctantly chugged awake and Jack drove out of the darkness and back into his life.

The living room lights were on as Jack pulled into the driveway and his stomach fluttered at the sight. Whether in anticipation of seeing Karen or trepidation, he didn't know.

Maybe a bit of both.

Justice was by his customary spot at the door. The shepherd slept in the front hall until Jack came home, no matter what shift Jack was on, then went with Jack to the master bedroom. And then it was to sleep on the floor by Jack's side of the bed.

"Hi, hon." Karen stepped into the front hall from the living room, a tentative smile on her face.

It was the first smile Jack had seen from her in weeks and it melted the apprehension in his belly. "Hi, Kare." He took her in his arms and buried his face in her blond hair, breathing deep of her scent as he held her tight.

"We've been waiting for you," she said, taking his hand and leading him to the living room.

We? Oh, fuck.

Karen's parents, George and Evelyn Hawthorn, were sitting in those damned wing chairs, a gift from the Hawthorns. Jack had come to loathe the chairs; they were too pretentious for him. The leather-covered chairs were a constant reminder of the influence Karen's parents had on their life. Jack had hoped Karen would throw them out after Charles Anthony had bound her to one, but the leather upholstery had been replaced and the chairs had resumed their sentinel duties in the living room.

Maybe I could teach Justice to chew on them.

"Mom and Dad stopped by earlier," Karen explained as she hugged — clutched? — Jack's arm. "Since you were getting home early tonight, they decided to wait and see you."

I'm sure they did. "Hello, Evelyn. George," Jack greeted civilly but on his guard; Karen's parents never just *stopped by.* "Listen, Karen. I need to run upstairs and change. I'll be quick."

"Don't bother changing on our account, Jack," Hawthorn told him. "We're all casual this evening."

Casual for Hawthorn was a golf shirt and slacks that probably cost more than two of Jack's suits. Karen's father looked like he'd dropped a bit of weight; his middle-aged bulge definitely seemed smaller, but at the same time the grey at his temples appeared to be making inroads on his dark hair.

"I'll just be a minute. I was working in old clothes today and spent most of it in the sun." Jack disengaged his arm from Karen. "Back in a sec."

Jack headed up the stairs, Justice a furry shadow behind him. In the washroom, he stripped off his shirt while Justice sat in the doorway watching him. Jack rinsed his face and ran a cold washcloth over his chest and arms. Even without the vest, he'd sweated like a bastard. How Jenny had handled standing out in the direct sunlight, he didn't know.

"Well, what do you think?" Jack asked Justice. "Does this have the feel of a relaxed visit or an ambush?" Justice huffed softly. "Yeah, me, too."

Relatively clean, Jack reached for his own golf shirt then paused. Grinning wickedly, he grabbed a black tee with CABBAGE-TOWN BAD BOYS stencilled across the back and a skull and cross-bones over "51" on the breast. A copper had sold the shirts as a fundraiser for the station's gym.

"If I'm going to war, I might as well carry my flag," Jack rationalized. "And you've got my back, right?" he asked Justice and the shepherd came over to nuzzle against Jack's thigh.

Karen frowned when she saw the shirt but she hid it so well Jack doubted her parents saw it at all. Jack settled onto the couch next to Karen, facing her parents across the glass coffee table. Justice curled up at Jack's feet.

"Feeling better, Jack?" Evelyn asked as she brushed at the sleeve of her blouse in case Justice had dared to taint the silk with any dog hairs as he passed her chair.

"Much better, thank you. Thanks, hon." Jack accepted a mug of tea from Karen and eased back on the couch, a content smile on his face. If they were here to gang up on him, he might as well let them have the opening barrage.

Hawthorn fired the first salvo. "I understand you've been cleared by the Special Investigations Unit."

"I have," Jack confirmed. *And do I detect a note of disappointment in your voice, George?*

"And you're no longer working in the station?"

"Thankfully, no. I'm back on the road."

"And you're now partnered with a female officer who has a rather dubious reputation." This from Evelyn. She was eying Jack antagonistically and Jack figured it had nothing to do with his new partner.

Jack's smile disappeared. He rocked forward and set his mug on the table then fixed Evelyn with his own confrontational glare.

"I see Karen has kept you up to date. My new partner is Jennifer Alton. She's a good friend, a good cop and a good person. I feel lucky to be working with her."

"You can understand our concern, I'm sure," Evelyn countered. "Working with a woman of such . . . loose morals."

Jack laughed harshly and felt Karen flinch beside him. "Loose morals? Let me guess," he said, turning to his wife. "You got that from your friend in 32, right?"

"I did and —" she started but Jack cut her off.

"And nothing. Your friend is too lazy and scared to go out on the road so she kissed ass until someone put her at the front desk and all she's given you is gossip." He surveyed the faces before him. "Do you really think I'd pair up with someone whose greatest talent is fucking other cops?"

"Jack, there's no call for such language," Hawthorn reprimanded.

Jack conceded his father-in-law a point. "Perhaps not, but you have to understand how I feel."

"Oh? And how is that?" Hawthorn asked, slipping into his mentor persona, which probably worked so well with his admiring university students.

"I know the two of you didn't just 'stop by' and this is far from a social visit. It feels more like an intervention."

Hawthorn tapped a finger against his lips thoughtfully. "An intervention? And what would we be trying to save you from?"

Jack rolled his eyes. "Enough. Let's just lay it all out, shall we? Evelyn, you're probably pissed at me right now for finding out about your baby plan and depriving you of a lever to use against me."

Evelyn opened her mouth to protest but Jack ran her over. "But you, George, are most likely ecstatic Karen's not pregnant. But I wonder, did you even know about their little plot? I'd guess not. But it doesn't matter. Now you can get back to convincing Karen to leave me."

"Jack! Dad isn't —"

Again, Jack cut her off. "He is, Karen. He's been after you to dump me since our first date. Your dad hates me and your mom hates what I do for a living."

"Hate is a strong word," Hawthorn cautioned.

"Yeah, but it fits."

Evelyn quickly jumped in. "Don't you see why we're concerned, Jack? This time last year you would have never been so confrontational."

Jack smiled and it was grim. "Maybe I just got tired of being your husband's punching bag and your puppet."

Justice must have heard the tension in Jack's voice. He sat up and nosed his head under Jack's hand.

"And that dog is another example," Evelyn added. "You brought it home without even consulting Karen. Bringing in a dog of that size and unknown temperament . . ."

"Oh, yeah, he's vicious," Jack joked, rubbing Justice's ears.

"And his name, Justice," Hawthorn added, picking up where his wife left off. "As in street justice, I assume. Karen told us how you . . . relieved the original owner of the dog."

"Relieved?" Jack laughed. "Why not use something a little more blunt? How about I stole him? Or, actually, I committed robbery because the theft was accompanied by violence. And, yes, we both dished out a bit of street justice. What was I supposed to do? The asshole had him tied up and was beating him with a metal pipe."

"Don't you see?" Hawthorn persisted. "The dog's mere presence is a constant reminder to Karen of what type of person you have become."

"He's a constant reminder of the good that can be done down in 51. But enough of this," Jack declared, waving a hand to encompass the four of them. He shifted to face Karen and took her hands in his. "Karen, I love you and I want to be with you, but I was a cop before we met. I was a cop when we were married and I never said anything about it being a temporary job. Why do you want to take something I love away from me?"

Karen pulled her hands free and her words were ice. "Because I don't know who you are anymore."

"Oh." Despite everything that had been said, Karen withdrawing from him hurt Jack the most. She wouldn't look at him and there was no way he was going to beg her, not with her parents here.

In a flat voice, with the pain and tears hidden away, he said, "I guess there's nothing left to say, then."

Jack got up and walked out of the room, Justice at his side.

Jack was sitting on the steps leading down to the backyard. Justice was curled up beside him, the dog's weight against his leg a comforting presence. Jack was working on a bottle of cider as he stared out into the darkness. In the distance he could hear the passing of cars and wondered if the drivers were happy with their lives. Or were they running away from their problems?

Jack knew showing his back to his troubles was not the solution but the thought of jumping in the car with Justice and buggering off was undeniably appealing. He chuckled grimly and Justice whined.

Jack scratched behind a furry ear. "Yeah, I know. It's not an answer."

But, God, it was tempting. Especially with the Hawthorns sitting inside. He had come home with the hope of patching things up with Karen. Instead, she and her parents had jumped him. That same old fucking argument two nights in a row.

Ease off, Jack. It won't help, going down that road and getting all pissed off.

He blew out his frustration and took another swig of cider.

The kitchen door slid open. Jack hadn't bothered with the lights when he had come out; they flashed on, leaving him squinting in the sudden brilliance.

"Hiding in the dark?" Karen accused.

Guess she didn't come out to apologize. "Nope. Just enjoying the night," he replied, struggling to keep his voice neutral.

"You were quite rude to my parents." She was standing behind him and he knew he should turn and face her but right now it just felt like way too much effort. Instead, he sipped his drink.

"Well?" she demanded.

"Did you know," he said to the darkness, "I came home tonight hoping we could talk, maybe work things out? But instead I get ambushed by you and your parents."

"We didn't ambush you," she scoffed.

"Well, that's what it felt like to me." He sighed then stood to face her. "Why are you always different around them? Why do you always give in to their wishes?"

Karen folded her arms across her chest defensively. "I don't.

We all care about you, that's why they're here."

"But you do act differently," he insisted. "I used to think you stood up to your parents, your dad especially, but now I see what you were doing. You always did what he wanted but just differently enough to tell yourself you were defying him."

"This isn't about me, Jack."

"No, it isn't," he conceded sadly. "It's about *us*. Tell me, Karen, did you ever approve of me being a cop? I know it's not prestigious or well paying enough for your parents' liking, but was there ever a time you were content to be a copper's wife? Or was the plan all along to get me to quit and get a different job?"

"You just don't get it, do you? This isn't about you being a cop," she insisted, sidestepping his questions. "It's about how you've changed. Do you realize that in less than a year, you've killed two people?"

"Well, forgive me for shooting the asshole who broke into our house and was going to kill you," he said rather sarcastically. "And the other one was going around mutilating people. Not exactly the type to submit peacefully to being arrested. And his death was an accident. Hell, even the siu said that."

"Of course, an *accident*."

"Are you saying you think I deliberately killed him?" Jack was angry she would ever say such a thing, hurt that she would think it.

"I never would have had to doubt that with the man I married. And I deserve better than this."

"Karen . . ." He stepped toward her but she backed away, thrusting a hand out at him to stop.

"Don't touch me, Jack. Dad's right, you're becoming some sort of savage and I don't want you touching me. If you want to fuck someone, go see your girlfriend."

Jack was ready to explode, to let loose the stifled anger churning his guts. "Damn it, Karen! I told you —"

"I don't believe you!" she screamed. Abruptly, she composed

herself, as if her outburst had shocked her as much as it shocked him. A cold mask slid over her face. "Why don't you go sleep with her tonight? Because you damned well aren't sleeping with me."

The kitchen door slammed shut behind her and the deck lights cut off, plunging Jack into darkness. He stood there for a very long time.

Wednesday, 25 July
1112 hours

Heavy-metal music blasted from the speakers, deafening as it howled off the cinderblock walls in the small workout room. Jack was alone in the station's gym and had the music cranked to an almost painful volume, but he was oblivious to it. The music's anger was nothing compared to the rage that gripped him, the rage that lashed out as he hit the punching bag.

Every time his right fist slammed into the heavy bag his rib screamed in pain but he only swung harder. His shins were red from striking the bag and he thought the knuckles of his left hand were bleeding, rubbed raw by the worn gloves. He ate the physical pain but it couldn't mask the pain he felt deep inside.

The music suddenly dropped.

"Cripes, Jack. You trying to go deaf?" Tank brought the music back up to a reasonable level.

"Was in the mood for something loud."

"I guess." The big man eyed Jack speculatively. "You okay? Last time I saw someone hit something like that, it was Kris beating the shit out of some poor bastard who called her a dyke then goosed her."

Jack laughed. "Man, I'd love to see the guy stupid enough to goose her."

"Before or after she was done with him?"

"Both, just for the full effect. Thanks, Tank. That was the first laugh I've had all day."

"I aim to please, my man. If you want to be alone, I can get out of your face. I just came in to do some stretching."

"No, I'm good. Stretch away."

As he settled down on a mat, Tank asked, "Does the bag have a face on it?"

Jack snorted. "My in-laws'." *And I guess my wife's, too, but I'll keep that to myself.*

"Say no more. We've all had our share of those." Tank spread his legs and leaned forward until he was close enough to kiss the mat. Besides being ridiculously and deceptively — so many people just saw a fat guy — powerful, Tank was also as flexible as a ballerina.

Jack plopped down on a bench and stripped the gloves off. Sure enough, the knuckles of his left hand were four islands of raw, brutalized flesh.

Tank was watching him from between splayed legs. "You sure you're okay, Jack? Your fingers look sore as hell and I can't imagine it felt very good hitting the bag with them."

Jack brushed the big man's concerns aside. "Pain can be therapeutic."

"Yup, it can be." Tank twisted where he sat and lowered his upper body along one leg.

Jack went over to the fountain to rinse his knuckles, wincing as the cold water hit the tender skin. "Guess I'll have to hide these from my wife or she'll think I've been in another fight."

"Not a big fan of the job?" Tank was now bent double over the other leg.

"Not the job, not my partner, not my workouts." Jack snickered as he flicked water from his hand. "Hell, she's all but accused me of taking steroids. Sometimes I think I should juice myself to the hilt and see what she thinks of that. Hell, after running into those two steroid monsters the other day, I'm tempted to shoot up myself. I've never felt so fucking small before."

Tank sat up, a thoughtful expression on his round face. "Well, if you ever were interested in trying something," he ventured, "I could probably help you out."

Jack sat silent for a moment, considering. "Probably not a good idea," he decided, shaking his head. "The way things are in my life right now I don't need to worry about 'roid rage and shit like that."

Tank giggled, a rather surprising sound to come out of such a large body. "That's been exaggerated and hyped up by everyone against performance enhancers. The ones that have problems with *'roid rage* —" he crooked his fingers around the phrase "— are either the dummies taking way too much for too long or they were an asshole in the first place and just use the 'roids as a scapegoat."

"Really?"

"Absolutely. Do I look like I have a problem with my temper?" Tank was back to resting his elbows on the floor between his splayed legs.

"Not like that, you don't."

"You take the right dosage of the right stuff and there's no trouble. A lot of the morons juicing are buying shit from drug dealers and injecting themselves with stuff labelled 'Veterinary Use Only.'"

"What's it feel like to be on steroids?" Jack was interested. Not tempted, just curious.

Tank grinned. "Remember when you were eighteen, twenty? Work out all day, fuck all night, sleep for a couple of hours then get up and do it all over again? Like that. More energy, faster recuperation time. And having more energy, size and strength sure ain't a bad thing on our job. Especially down here."

"Hm. Sounds interesting but . . ."

"Hey, man. No pressure. Just offering."

"Thanks, I appreciate it." Jack also recognized the trust Tank was placing in him by having this discussion. He wasn't sure how much shit it could cause Tank, but it would undoubtedly be enough to drown in.

"Good that you're here too, Jack." Detective Mason stood in the doorway leading to the men's change room. "Tank, I need you up in the office with the rest of us. Jack, we're going to be tied up for a couple of hours. Why don't you and Jenny grab one of our cars and keep yourselves busy? Come back in around two and we'll start the sweep."

"Wanna buy some crack?" Jenny asked.

"Sure," Jack agreed quickly. "Regent Park or somewhere else?"

"Let's try the park."

"The park it is." Jack swung off Regent onto Dundas. They were driving the MCU's old Ford Taurus and Jack squirmed in the seat. "No offense to Tank but it feels like I'm trying to sit in a bathtub."

Jack parked on Oak Street and they cut across River Street to enter Regent Park. Despite the sweltering weather and the deserted walkways and lawns — anyone with half a brain was somewhere air-conditioned — Jack was confident they could find a dealer. Unlike cops, a dealer was always around when you wanted one.

It was just a matter of finding one and convincing him they weren't cops.

When Jack had told Jenny the sweep was on hold, she had downgraded her look from crack whore to crackhead. Unfortunately, in Jack's opinion. She'd had her shirt tied up again and the strings of a thong visible above low-riding jeans. A good look for a sweep but kind of hard — okay, impossible — to hide a gun. She'd lowered her shirt and swapped her heels for some runners.

Jenny shifted to Jack's left side, touching his tattoo and sending a pleasant shiver running through him. Jack was wearing an old denim shirt with the sleeves cut off and the tattoo — an angry angel bearing a sword — was exposed to the light.

"'Simon, Never Forgotten,'" Jenny read, quoting the banner under the angel. "That's nice."

As they strolled along, trying not to look like cops — Jenny may have been succeeding but Jack, with his regulation haircut, didn't blend in so well — Jenny slipped her hand in his. He knew it was just for appearances but his stomach still did a quivering tumble.

"Are you okay, Jack? You're trembling."

"You have that effect on me, I guess," he joked, silently begging his hand to stop its embarrassing shudder.

They wandered the stairwells, exchanging sun-seared heat for stale heat, gloomy and oppressive. They crossed from building to building, zigzagging through the park, never bothering to climb above the first floor; dealers tended to position themselves near as many escape routes as possible.

They came out of 259 Sumach Street and Jack gratefully sucked in a lungful of humid, polluted air. "Fuck! It stank like an outhouse in there."

"A very old outhouse," Jenny added. She plucked the front of her T-shirt from her belly and flapped it in the stagnant air. "I could use a drink."

"Good idea. I think all the dealers are taking their afternoon siestas."

Sweaty from the heat and irritated by the lack of success, they trudged up the sidewalk, heading for Gerrard Street and a convenience store.

"I say we grab a drink then head back to the car. Either there's no dealers about or one of us is scaring them off," Jack decided, casting an accusing eye at his partner.

"One of these things doesn't belong," Jenny chimed as she tossed her waist-length hair. "Me? Or Mister Clean-Cut and Muscle-Bound?"

Jack perked up. "You think I'm muscle-bound? Wait, is that good or bad?"

Before Jenny could answer, a shirtless man rode up beside them on a bicycle, his black skin glistening with sweat. He looked them over, his eyes lingering on Jenny.

He must have approved of them, because he asked, "You lookin' to buy, mahn?"

"We've been looking all over," Jack complained. "Ain't no one selling."

Their new friend flashed them a toothy grin, a gold incisor winking dully in the sun. "Ah seen you lookin'. Ah can help you, mahn. Deval —" he crooned the name, Deeee-vahl "— will take good care of you."

Deval's Jamaican accent was about as genuine as his gold tooth, but he could try to pass himself off as a Russian czar for all Jack cared. As long as he had some crack to sell.

Straddling the bike's frame, Deval walked it onto the sidewalk. "Let's take our biz'ness someplace private so Five-Oh don't see us."

The east side of Sumach below Gerrard was a short stretch of townhouses and Deval led them to a small corner at the north end. Bordered on two sides by brick walls, the patch of grass was shaded by an old maple tree. As they stepped off the sidewalk to the grass, Deval asked how much Jack was looking to buy.

"A forty piece," Jack told him, rubbing a hand across his mouth. "I ain't got much money."

Deval shoved his hand down the front of his pants, then displayed a cluster of crack cocaine in the palm of his hand. The yellowed rocks were of different sizes but Jack estimated it to be about a hundred dollars' worth.

"How 'bout more'n forty, mahn? A little more crack never hurt."

Jack smiled. *I can't believe he just said that. I can't wait to say that on the stand.*

Deval interpreted Jack's smile poorly and grinned in return.

They stepped into the shade of the tree where its thick trunk and low-hanging branches screened them from the traffic on Gerrard. Deval was still astride his bike and had unknowingly placed himself between a tree and a plainclothes cop. Jenny, like any good crackhead girlfriend, was hanging back while her man conducted business. She also happened to be between Deval and Sumach.

"So, mahn, how much will it be?" Deval was still smiling like a used-car salesman.

"Just forty. Can't afford no more." Jack licked his lips then wiped them again.

Deval studied him momentarily then shrugged. He selected two pieces of crack — the two smallest twenty pieces Jack had ever seen — and tucked the rest back down his pants.

Excellent. Don't want you throwing away all the evidence.

Deval offered up the rock, but when Jack reached for it, he snatched his hand away. "Money first," he chided, as if Jack had just committed a heinous social blunder.

Jack patted his pockets, keeping an eye on Deval as he stepped closer. Deval's eyes narrowed in suspicion then flared wide in sudden understanding and panic.

Jack reached for the hand holding the crack. "You're under ar —"

Deval jumped off the bike as Jack's hand clamped around the dealer's wrist. Deval pulled against Jack's grip and Jack stepped forward, but his legs became entangled in the bike. Jack fell onto the bike and one of the pedals jammed painfully into his hip. He managed to hang onto Deval and dragged the dealer to his knees.

Deval heaved once more and his sweat-slick skin slipped free from Jack's grasp. He scrambled to his feet just as Jenny hit him from the side. He stumbled, dragging Jenny with him and she wrapped her arms around his thighs in an attempt to bring him down. Deval caught his balance and drove a fist down into Jenny's face. She hung on and Deval cocked his arm back, a sinister smile on his lips.

Jack charged Deval and hit him with an outstretched arm across the throat, slamming him into the hard ground. Jenny pounced. What air was left in Deval's lungs after Jack's clothesline blasted loose when Jenny dropped both her knees into his chest and stomach.

Gasping for air like a landed fish, Deval offered no resistance as Jenny flipped him onto his belly. She pulled her cuffs out of her back pocket and snapped them on.

Kneeling on Deval's back, she smiled up at Jack. "I got to admit, Jack. Working with you sure isn't boring."

"Hey, Jack, I forgot to tell you. You won't believe this but I went in there yesterday."

Jack looked up from the keyboard; he could type well enough but still needed to look down for the number keys. "Went in where?" he asked Connor.

Jack and Jenny had been in the detective office for the last hour doing up the paperwork — *why do we call it paperwork when it's on a computer?* — on the dealer Deval, better known as Peter Richardson. Connor and Paul had come in a few minutes ago with a whining suspect — soon to be a whining accused — and Jack had had a brief shock when he thought it was Dean Myers in for his third count of domestic assault. It wasn't him, just another cowardly piece-of-shit wife beater.

"The Second Cup, man. I went inside! Tell him, Paul." Having just finished his prisoner's strip search, Connor was pulling off the blue latex gloves. He dumped them in the garbage then dropped himself in the chair across from Jack, looking quite pleased with himself.

"It's true," Paul confirmed. "The Pest actually dared to step foot into the dreaded Second Cup. And emerged alive."

"Congratulations, Pest. And it doesn't bother you that you were probably in a bunch of fantasies that night?"

Connor paused, giving Jack a petulant look, then, "You would have to say that, wouldn't you? Anyway, I was going to say it wasn't bad inside. It was like a . . ."

"A coffee shop?" Paul proposed.

"Yeah! It was just like a coffee shop," Connor declared, sounding rather amazed.

"Imagine that," Jack commented, turning back to his paperwork.

Detective Mason stuck his head in the CIB. "Jack! How much longer you two going to be?"

."The body's already been lodged, Jenny's submitting the drugs right now and I'm just finishing up the show cause." Jack did some quick guesstimations. "Say twenty minutes, half an hour, for us to finish the paperwork and do up our notes?"

"Sounds good. Tank and Kris will be waiting for you in the MCU."

Jack reached for Deval's criminal record and managed to keep from gasping at the pain as his cracked rib screamed at him. He huddled in the chair with his arms wrapped protectively around his side. Falling on that fucking bike then hitting Deval with a clothesline had hurt like bloody hell and only his pride had stopped Jack from puking after the brief fight.

At least I didn't let that fuckhead see how much it hurt. Wouldn't want Deval thinking he caused it. And I don't think Jenny saw how bad it was, so that's good.

He tried a tentative deep breath and when the rib only groaned, he went back to typing.

Jenny gets punched in the face — she'll have a helluva shiner — I fall on a bike and the pedal digs a hole in my hip. What more could go wrong today?

I wonder what else can happen today?

Jenny studied her reflection in the mirror. The skin around

her right eye was a swollen, angry red.

On the plus side — she smiled — *I bet it helps me scoop more johns today. Who'd expect a copper to be sporting a black eye?*

Drugs submitted — Deval had had a rather substantial cache tucked away in his shorts — she headed to the lunchroom to grab Jack and herself something cold to drink.

I hope we don't get into another scrap today. I don't think Jack's rib can take much more. She smiled again, partly amused, partly pissed at her partner's attempts to hide the pain he was feeling. *Damn macho stupidity. He won't say anything's wrong until he's in the hospital.*

Mason was in the lunchroom ahead of her, at the vending machine, selecting one of the cold, measly hamburgers the prisoners were fed. "You two just about ready to go?" he asked, taking half the burger in a single bite.

"Ugh," she grimaced. "How can you eat that?"

"Desperately." He wagged the half burger at her. "You going like that?"

"Hang on." Jenny hiked up her white T-shirt and tied it off just under her breasts. "Better?"

Mason nodded, swallowing. "But lose the gun. It clashes with your pink thong."

"Duh." She ducked as the detective took a playful swing at her on his way out. She pumped the pop machine full of coins, grabbed two Diet Cokes and headed back to the CIB. Instead of going up the stairs by the lunchroom, she headed for the front desk, intending to pick up a new memo book — the one she had was just about finished. At the last second she veered away from the staff sergeant's office, remembering Staff Greene forbade anyone lower than himself in rank to use the office as a passage from the hall to the front desk.

I wonder how long it took him to get the puke off of his shoes?

The public's access to the station was a square of worn, scuffed linoleum far too small for such a pretentious word as lobby. Jenny cut across this diminutive wasteland — no one, coppers or civilians, hung out in the lobby for long — with the half flight of stairs to the outside on her right and the front desk to her left.

"Alton, what's that on your face?" Sergeant Rose was at the front desk, a concerned scowl on her face.

"Nothing major, Sarge. He missed the eye." Jenny leaned on the counter to let Rose take a closer look.

The sergeant tilted Jenny's head to catch the light. For a big, solid woman, she had a surprisingly gentle touch. Beneath her spiky black hair, her scowl deepened.

"I don't care if this happened on the job or off," she growled, "the fucker better be suffering payback."

"I think he learned his lesson," Jenny ventured. "And he's sitting in a cell right now."

"That the one you brought in from Regent Park? I didn't hear you call for an ambulance," Rose criticized. "And aren't you two supposed to be doing a sweep with MCU?"

"Yeah, but they were tied up on something."

"Hm." Rose eyed Jenny. "Watch your ass, Alton. We've got some asshole out there beating up the working girls."

Jenny nodded sombrely then smiled as she tapped her injury. "My shit quota's full for the day. What else could go wrong?"

What more could go wrong with our marriage?

Karen stood on the sidewalk staring hatefully at 51 Station. This wasn't her first visit to the station; she'd picked up Jack a few times when his Taurus had been in the shop, had even taken a tour of the place with Jack once, an experience she had no desire to repeat. The building was old and decrepit, dirty and confining, and even the brilliant summer sunlight could not detract from the aura of gloom that hung about it. Instead of brightening the brick surface, the light threw all the disfiguring scars and flaws into harsh clarity, like a dying cancer patient stripped of concealing makeup.

A cancer. That's what this place is. A cancer and it's eating us alive.

But how to cut it out before it killed them? That the cancer, this division and ultimately policing entirely, had to go was brutally clear to everyone except Jack. He had to get out before he was killed doing a job no one cared about. Or worse, in Karen's opinion, before the man he was inside, the man she had fallen in love with and married, died.

That man was already dead in her father's eyes and today when she had met her parents for lunch, he had openly urged Karen to divorce Jack. Her mother, who had always encouraged her to stay committed to the marriage, who had convinced Karen that Jack could be changed — for his own good, of course — with the proper guidance and support, had remained quiet, and her silence had spoken copiously.

But Karen had inherited her father's unflagging fortitude and her mother's sheer stubbornness. She would not give up on Jack, on them, until she had no other choice. She would fight for her marriage and nothing, not this godforsaken station or Jack's new slut of a partner, was going to overwhelm her. If the marriage died, it would be when Karen said so and not a moment sooner.

So she was here to see her husband, would even apologize if that's what was needed to open his eyes. Drawing a deep, fortifying breath, she headed up the short walk to the front doors. She was momentarily lost after stepping from the intense sunlight into the station's fluorescent dimness. Once her eyes adjusted, Karen mounted the few stairs leading up to the lobby.

Lobby? Mom's shoe closet is bigger than this.

There was a large female officer — *PW, I think they're called* — behind the counter and judging from the disapproving look on her face, she was not happy with the tramp she was talking to. The tramp was leaning on the counter, her butt sticking out behind her impertinently. Karen had never seen a prostitute but she was sure she was seeing one now.

The woman's overly long hair was swept to the side to bare her midriff, a look that was no doubt meant to be luring and exotic but came across as cheap. Karen was surprised there was no tattoo on the tramp's lower back — *she could put her price list there* — but the prostitute had the sides of her thong underwear tugged above the waist of her jeans.

I suppose that passes for sexy down here. God, Jack, you want to work in this place? I just got here and already feel like I need a shower.

Karen approached the counter and waited. The tramp was showing the officer her bruised eye and Karen felt a brief pang of sympathy for the woman then abruptly squashed it. If she wasn't giving herself to every man with a fistful of change, then things like that wouldn't happen.

"Hang on a sec, Jenny." The officer turned from the tramp and focused her scowling visage on Karen. "Help you?" she said, rather rudely in Karen's opinion.

"I'm here to see Jack Warren." Out of the corner of her eye, Karen noticed the tramp look at her at the mention of Jack's name. *Probably some hooker he's arrested, that's all.*

"He's busy with a body right now. And you are?" the officer asked brusquely.

"I'm his wife, Karen Warren," Karen gave back, just as icily.

The officer's features softened a bit. "Oh. Like I said, he's busy with an arrest right now." She cocked her head at the tramp. "But Jenny might be able to help you."

The tramp was holding out her hand to Karen and for the first time, Karen noticed the gun on her hip.

Jenny? Jennifer? Please, God, no.

But it was true.

"Hello," the tramp was saying, a smug smile on her whorish face. "I'm Jennifer Alton, Jack's partner. I'm so happy to finally meet you."

Finally? But you've only been his partner for a few days. So how long have you two been . . . together?

It was all so clear now, all of Jack's lies. An icy pit opened in Karen's stomach and her legs trembled, threatening to dump her on the filthy floor. But deep inside, Karen was an iron core born of her mother's stubbornness and, as the truth crashed over her, that stubbornness refused to yield, refused to let Karen fall.

She drew herself erect and stared the tramp in the eye. "I can see why Jack likes working here." The tramp's smile faltered. Karen wanted to smash it from her face but would not stoop to violence. Violence was Jack's way, his answer to troubles, and she was better than that. Ignoring the outstretched hand, she faced the uniformed officer whose scowl had become an angry thunderhead. Karen didn't give a shit.

"You needn't bother Jack," Karen said, her voice cool and controlled. "But please tell him he needn't bother coming home." With that, she strode from the police station and back into the light.

The sun was slipping behind the city when George Hawthorn left his office at the University of Toronto. The lengthening shadows did little to dispel the heat and he could feel his shirt clinging to him beneath his suit coat. He took the offending coat off and folded it carefully over the BMW's passenger seat before easing in behind the wheel. The powerful engine started without complaint and Hawthorn flicked the air conditioning to high, luxuriating in the icy cold as it chilled his sweat-damp body.

Another late evening at work, and he was going to have to commit to many more of them if he was to finish his next book in time for the publisher's deadline. He could write at home, he knew, but lately Evelyn had been stalking about the house like an agitated feline and concentrating with that much palpable tension in the air was currently beyond his abilities. His wife was infuriated with their daughter's husband and what she interpreted as a flagrant offence to Evelyn herself.

Hawthorn slowly shook his head. Evelyn refused to see the truth. She believed Jack could be moulded and guided, developed like one of her social projects, but she was wrong. Jack could not be improved simply because he had reached the limits of his potential. And by working in that division, he was, in effect, devolving. His primal instincts were rising to the foreground and Hawthorn, for one, was ecstatic that those genes would not be mingling with his family's.

That was another source of friction between him and Evelyn these days: the ploy she and Karen had fashioned to control Jack with an unexpected pregnancy. Hawthorn had not known of this plan until after Jack had confronted Karen about it, had, in effect, been the last one to know of it. No doubt Evelyn had presumed her husband would have abandoned his hopes for Karen divorcing Jack once he learned he was to be a grandfather.

Hawthorn nearly felt a twinge of sympathy for his brutish son-in-law. Had the women's plan succeeded, Jack's destiny would have been written, his future plotted out for him. No matter how he detested the man, Hawthorn would not have wished that fate upon him. It would be equivalent to caging a proud, feral beast. In an extremely small cage.

Hawthorn was not so naïve as to believe society did not need its lower echelon of human resources; someone had to maintain the machinery of civilization, keep the body alive in order for the brain to function. He appreciated how a career in policing would be appealing to someone like his son-in-law. The physical challenge, the rush of adrenalin. The simple hands-on approach to solving problems. Alone with his thoughts, Hawthorn could even admit to himself a touch of . . . envy? Surely not.

Curiosity. That's all it is.

There had been a time, a brief time long ago, before he had learned that to change the world one had to change the future leaders and thinkers — the brain cells, in other words — that he had toyed with the idea of becoming a police officer. He had envisioned himself as an immaculate role model to his fellow officers, an unblemished example of intelligence and professionalism. He would alter how the police operated by his mere presence as he ascended through the ranks. A realistic superhero, unlike the costumed crime fighters in the comic books he had so rightfully scorned as a child.

Foolish dreams of a foolish young man.

The young Hawthorn had recognized his fanciful dreams for what they were and had moved on. Now it was Karen's turn to face reality. Over lunch today he had presented his argument for divorce: Jack would never leave his division, let alone policing; he was a man drawn to violence. How many more people would he have to kill for Karen to see that? Did she really want to raise a child with a man immersed in a life of blood? How long before he personally brought that violence home?

Miraculously, Evelyn had not voiced a single objection and Karen had allowed him to finish before raising her counter-arguments and even then, her defiance had sounded habitual and without conviction. Perhaps she was finally allowing herself to see the truth.

Scott Goss and his wife, Lillian, crossed the faculty parking lot, waving politely as they spotted Hawthorn in his car. Hawthorn waved back. Scott and Lillian were dressed for an evening out. The young professor had changed into a fresh suit from the one he had worn during the day, but it was Lillian who captivated Hawthorn's attention and imagination.

Her silky black gown clung intimately to the curves of her figure and the plunging back left no doubt she was braless beneath the fabric's caress. The gown's slit revealed the full length of her right leg and hip and Hawthorn wondered pleasantly if the panties matched the bra. Thoughts flowed to fantasy and Hawthorn grew hard picturing Lillian sitting on his desk, the gown twitched open to reveal that she was indeed naked beneath it.

Did Lillian visit Scott in his office? Had they fucked on his desk as the student body passed his door? Hawthorn had no doubt; a woman who exuded such raw sexuality would not be dissuaded from taking what she wanted, where and when she wanted it.

Hawthorn sighed remorsefully. Evelyn had once burned with such a passion. How shocked would Karen and her husband be if they learned that the prim and proper Evelyn had once muffled her screams of ecstasy by biting and drawing blood from Hawthorn's shoulder as she rode him beneath the stands at a political rally?

But no more. They had aged and their sex life had aged with them, but poorly. For Evelyn, sex was now a need like eating or sleeping. An itch to be scratched as quickly and efficiently as possible. Hawthorn could not remember the last time he had seen his wife nude outside of the bedroom.

Hawthorn put the memories and regrets aside. It was time to go home. A sultry evening; the downtown sidewalks and patios were crowded and he watched the people disinterestedly from behind the barrier of the car window. The traffic on Dundas Street was moving briskly and he wondered how many people were heading home and how many were bound elsewhere.

Stopped at the red light at Jarvis Street, Hawthorn realized he was about to cross into Jack's division. Back when there had been some form of civil discourse between them, Jack had joked with Hawthorn that once you went east of Jarvis the buildings and people got uglier.

Hawthorn had been driving this road for years but had never thought of it as anything but a route connecting his office to the highway. Now, as the cars began to flow again, he studied what lay beyond the front of his car. On his left loomed a neon sign proclaiming the finest nude dancers were inside Filmore's.

A strip club. Had that always been there?

He swung into the curb lane so as not to impede the drivers

behind him as he reduced his speed, captivated by the sights around him. Jack may have been joking but there was a certain . . . dinginess to the area and people, as if life here was not quite as bright. The pedestrians moved slower, at times seemingly without a purpose or destination, and the buildings appeared tired, resigned to a dreary fate.

Hawthorn chuckled softly, imagining what his editor would say if he used such descriptions in his new book.

Stopped at Sherbourne Street, he watched as a group of young men sitting on the steps of a church passed a bottle among themselves. To his immediate right, in a small parking lot, two men suddenly pounced on a third, throwing him to the ground, pummelling him with their feet.

Hawthorn quickly looked around, sure someone would come to the man's aid or at least be reaching for a phone to call police, but no one exhibited anything but mild interest. A few members of the drinking group shifted for a better view of the fight. People walking by either gave the ruckus a cursory glance or kept their eyes purposely averted.

Hawthorn jumped when someone rapped on the passenger window. He turned and found a black man leaning down and grinning a gap-toothed smile at him. The man tapped again, his other hand held palm up, displaying three small pieces of some off-white substance. The man pointed at the pea-sized chunks, nodding encouragingly.

It dawned on Hawthorn that the man was offering to sell him some crack cocaine. Out in the open at a busy intersection. Abruptly, the man walked away, the hand holding the narcotic vanishing into a pocket as a police car, its roof lights flashing, sped silently down Sherbourne Street. Hawthorn thought the police car would pull into the parking lot for the fight but it passed by without even a flash of brake lights. Trouble elsewhere.

A horn sounded behind him and on impulse Hawthorn turned south on Sherbourne, following in the wake of the police car. He glanced at the parking lot as he passed. The two assailants were gone. Their victim was staggering upright, blood, vividly bright in the lot's overhead lights, masking half his face. Then Hawthorn was beyond the lot and the bloodied man was lost to sight.

For the next ten minutes Hawthorn aimlessly cruised the streets of this strange, alien landscape. Twice more, in the span of a few minutes, police cars roared past him, both times sirens accompanying the emergency lights.

Distanced as he was from the conflicts, Hawthorn still felt his heart thumping strongly in his chest in response to the sirens' urgent wailing. Is this what attracted Jack to this place, kept him locked here? The excitement?

Hawthorn turned off the main street. He was travelling onto a side street, residential in nature and an unexpected oasis of tranquility. Ahead of him, a car pulled quickly away from the curb, forcing him to brake suddenly. Hawthorn stared after the car as the driver, obviously unmindful of the possibility of children, sped past the cars parked on the narrow street.

Puzzled as to what could have spurred the driver to such reckless action, Hawthorn looked to his right and found himself staring at a young woman who blatantly returned his gaze. Blatantly but with no hostility. Invitingly, even.

She had on a brief shirt that left her lean, alluring stomach bare to his eyes. Her worn jeans rode low on her hips and Hawthorn wondered what it would feel like to run his hands over those hips, to pull them back against his groin. Smiling, the woman hooked her thumbs under the thin straps of her panties and tugged at them suggestively. She cocked her eyebrow at him, half question, half challenge.

For the second time that evening, he was startled out of a senseless daze by a horn honking impatiently. Embarrassed, Hawthorn drove off, positive the occupants of the car behind him believed he was in search of a prostitute. He turned onto the next major street, not sure where he was until he saw Filmore's again, but from the opposite direction.

Traffic was backed up from the lights ahead and Hawthorn slowed to a stop directly out front of the strip club. A poster hung next to the club's front doors. Behind glass was a picture of a woman wearing a small pair of panties and pulling her shirt off over her head, revealing the bottom swell of her breasts.

In his mind's eye, Hawthorn pictured the prostitute he had stared at stripping off her shirt in a similar manner, giving to him her small, firm breasts. He knew if he desired to, he could go back to her and have her peel off her shirt for him, bare the rest of her body to him. He could take her any way he wanted, could sink his fingers into the depths of her long, dark hair as he thrust inside her. Whatever he wanted was his for the asking. And the paying.

I've never been with a prostitute and I'm not about to start now.

But as the traffic tide bore him to Jarvis Street he turned north with no conscious thought.

I'm just going to take Gerrard to the Don Valley, that's all, he reassured himself. *She won't be there anyways. Someone will have picked her up.*

But as he wheeled onto the side street, again with no conscious thought, she was there as though she was waiting for no one but him. He slowed the BMW and as he crept past her, she shrugged as if to say *Do you want me or not?*

He coasted to a stop by the curb and watched in the mirror, his stomach churning with anxiety, as she sauntered toward the car. Her hips swayed hypnotically. He wetted dry lips. Sudden panic took him. How much money did he have? Would it be enough? Fear of the embarrassment he would suffer if she laughed at his offer dropped his hand to the gearshift.

And then she was there, leaning on the passenger door. She tapped softly, teasingly, on the window, each click of her nails icing Hawthorn's spine down to his balls.

He was reaching for the window control when his cell phone rang.

The unexpected electronic purr shattered the silence inside the car. Hawthorn started, then frantically searched his pockets, consumed by an overwhelming need to answer the phone.

The woman was still at the window. Tapping, tapping.

He couldn't find his phone and it seemed with every ring it grew louder, more impatient with his ineptness. His jacket! He pulled it into his lap and pawed through the pockets.

Tap, tap, tap.

His hand finally snagged the phone and he snapped it open. "Hello?" he said breathlessly.

It was Evelyn. "Are you all right, George? You sound peculiar."

Tap, tap, tap.

"No, no, I'm fine. *No.*" He waved his free hand at the woman, shooing her away.

"No? George, what's wrong? Is everything all right?"

"I'm fine, Evelyn. It's just . . . it's just one of those squeegee people. She wants money."

"Oh, I hate how they pester you. Just drive away, George."

The woman was still there. She stepped back from the car and spun a slow circle for him, showing him what could be his. She leaned down once more, her head tilted questioningly. Hawthorn shook his head emphatically. *No.* The woman shot her middle finger up at him then stalked off.

Hawthorn twisted in his seat to watch her walk away. Her hips no longer swayed seductively. Instead of relief, he experienced an odd sense of loss.

"George, are you there?"

"Sorry, Evelyn. She's gone now. She was rather . . . persistent." Hawthorn dropped the car into gear. "I'm on my way home now."

Jenny was on her own, no backup. She was in this by herself.

First the prick in the Beemer stiffs me, now this.

"C'mon, baby. Jes a li'l suck 'n fuck."

She stepped back as the john reached for her yet again, his electric wheelchair grinding painfully as it lurched after her. *I bet we look like we're dancing.*

The john looked old enough to have fought in the Civil War and smelled like he hadn't showered since. Jenny was almost convinced she could see the reek rising from him in wavering lines like the heat off of asphalt. Faint wisps of blue smoke drifted up from the chair's labouring motor to mingle unpleasantly with the john's vapours.

"C'mon, baby," he crooned. "Ah got muh cheque t'day. Le's party."

"I said no," Jenny snapped, her patience and amusement long since eroded by the john's persistence. He'd chased her up and down and across the street, too horny or stupid to take the hint. She could have arrested him a dozen times over but Kris and Tank had made it abundantly clear with their laughter that they had no intention of coming to her rescue.

"Don' be like that, baby girl." He gummed her a toothless smile. "Ah jes wanna —"

"You just wanna take a hike," Jack said, walking up.

The ancient john twisted in his chair to look at Jack. "Who're you?" he rasped, his eyes scrunched up suspiciously.

"Who the fuck do you think I am?" Jack growled as he tucked his cell phone away. "Get lost."

"Ah'm goin', ah'm goin'," the old man muttered as he steered his wheelchair down Pembroke. "Damn pimps."

"Thanks. He just wouldn't take no for an answer. And those two —" she shot Kris and Tank the finger "— thought it was just hilarious. And where were you?" she asked, turning some of her frustration on Jack.

"On the phone with Mason," he said. "Hope you don't have any plans for the weekend."

"Just a date with Brian. Why?"

Jack sighed. "Then you better hope we catch the asshole who's tuning up the hookers before your date 'cause until we do, you and I are officially on loan to the MCU."

"Great. So much for a social life." She blew hair out of her eyes. "Do we have a choice?"

Jack just looked at her.

"Damn it," she swore. "How about you? What's Karen going to say?" Jenny had filled Jack in on her unexpected and unpleasant meeting with his wife and she had no doubts the news would not sit well with Karen.

Her partner grinned but it was utterly without humour. "Who knows?" he said, fingering the raw flesh of his knuckles. "But after the last couple of nights at home, even this shithole is starting to look good."

Jack cut the engine and the weary old car sputtered before dying. *I hope that's not an omen as to how the night is going to go.* He glanced at the empty spot in the driveway next to his Ford. *Karen's probably at her parents'.*

He opened the front door and after greeting Justice called out hopefully yet pointlessly. "Karen? You home?"

The house answered him silently. Jack paused in the front hall and listened to the silence. The house felt different — not just unoccupied, as in waiting for the owners to come home, but empty.

Jack let Justice out the kitchen door and as he waited for the dog he surveyed the room. The counters were clean; no dirty dishes sat in the sink awaiting scrubbing. He checked the magnet clip on the refrigerator where he and Karen posted notes for each other. Empty.

Justice tagged along as Jack wandered through the dining and living rooms. Again, everything was in its place, as it should be. But then why did the tidiness scare him so much?

He mounted the stairs and with every step his dread grew.

"Karen, you here?" Though his words had been barely above a whisper, they sounded far too loud to his ears.

He checked the office and guest room — what was meant to be, in time, the baby's room — and found both neat and tidy. But empty. He stood outside the office staring down the hall at the master bedroom. Justice trotted along the carpeted hall then stopped and looked back at Jack, as if to ask, *Are you coming?*

"Yeah, yeah."

Jack approached the closed double doors — Karen had started closing them with Justice's arrival, claiming she didn't want the dog on the bed even though the shepherd had never shown any inclination to sleep there — and rapped softly. "Karen?" His stomach clenched at the stillness from the room.

He nudged open the door and followed Justice into the bedroom. Like the rest of the house, the room was neat and tidy. The bed was made and the floor was, as always, clear of clothes. Jack stood at the foot of the bed and slowly turned in place, looking. Looking for what, he had no clue.

"She's probably with her parents," he told Justice. "She'll be h —"

One of the dresser's drawers was ajar, a corner jutting out like a broken tooth. *It got wedged when Karen was putting away laundry. That's all*, he told himself and even he knew it for a lie.

He tugged open the drawer, settling it back on its track. It was Karen's underwear drawer and like the rest of the house it was neat, tidy.

Empty.

Thursday, 26 July
1012 hours

"But why hasn't he called?"

"I couldn't say for certain, dear." Evelyn sat beside her daughter on the guest bed, stroking her hair soothingly. "Perhaps he's still asleep. After all, you just woke up and you weren't working last night."

"I . . . I guess that's possible." Karen sniffed back tears as she clutched an old childhood teddy bear to her chest.

Evelyn frowned at the stuffed animal but kept her expression from Karen's sight. She was secretly pleased that her daughter had come home last night but in no way approved of this childish behaviour. She would tolerate it for a day at most and then it would be time for Karen to begin fighting.

Karen had shown up on their doorstep last evening with a suitcase in hand and a determined yet frightened set to her face. She had blurted out a troubling story involving going to the police station to apologize to Jack — that did not sit well with Evelyn — running into his tramp of a partner — disappointing to Evelyn; she had thought somewhat better of her son-in-law — then storming out of the station and ending up at her parents' home — both actions meeting Evelyn's approval. Karen had stumbled to bed, emotionally exhausted, and Evelyn had spent the rest of the evening expecting a visit, or at least a call, from her son-in-law. Neither had occurred.

"Or he could be waiting for you to call him," Evelyn suggested offhandedly. No need for Karen to be giving Jack the benefit of the doubt.

Karen stared at her mother. "Why would *I* call *him*?"

"I'm not saying you should, dear." Evelyn kept her voice soft, comforting, but silently she rejoiced at the steel in Karen's words. "It's just possible that he's expecting you to call him since you were the one who walked out."

"But I had no choice," Karen defended herself righteously. "I knew he'd come home. Not for me," she added, laughing bitterly. "But to look after that damn dog. There was no way I could be in the same house as him, not after seeing the *good person* —" her voice was mocking "— his partner is."

"I hate to suggest this, dear, but is it possible he came home but didn't stay there?"

Karen stared at her mother in shock, then her eyes widened. In fear or outrage? Either would work but Evelyn preferred outrage. Jack would soon learn the consequences of defying Evelyn Hawthorn and the plans she had for him. No one walked away from her.

"Mom?"

Evelyn focused on her daughter. "I'm sorry, dear, what were you saying?"

"I asked if you really think Jack could have spent the night with . . . with *her*."

"I have no idea," she responded vaguely. "But, as we all know, he's no longer the man we used to know."

Tears welled up in Karen's eyes. "Oh, Jack."

"Would you like to come down for some breakfast, dear?"

Karen shook her head. "No thanks, Mom. I think I'll just sleep for a little while longer, if that's okay."

"Of course, dear." Evelyn patted her daughter's hand. "You've been through a traumatic event. You need your rest."

Her husband joined Evelyn in the kitchen while she was brewing herself a mug of Earl Grey tea. George raised an eyebrow at the mug. Evelyn never strayed from her china cups unless she was particularly upset about something.

"How is she?" he asked.

"She's sleeping right now. Would you like a cup?" George waved off her offer. Evelyn stirred a healthy dollop of honey into her tea then settled at the kitchen table. She raised the blinds on the bay window and sighed contentedly as the heat from the summer sun warmed her shoulders and neck.

George drew a chair close and took his wife's free hand in his. "Does she know what she's going to do? Does she see now that she has only one option?"

Evelyn frowned around the lip of her mug. "Don't push

her, George. I believe she knows what she has to do but hasn't accepted the fact yet. She still hopes he'll call or show up here and beg her to come home."

George scowled. "Do you think he will?"

Evelyn shrugged daintily. "I can't tell with that man any more, but you know our daughter. She wants her white knight to ride to her rescue and sweep her off her feet."

"White knight, ha," George scoffed. "That man is barely civilized, at best." Evelyn smiled sadly but said nothing. George squeezed her hand. "I know you had hopes for him, Evie."

Hopes? With my guidance, he could have become a man you would have been proud to call your son-in-law. And he all but spat in my face.

Again she shrugged, a mere lifting of her shoulders. "I saw the potential in him, that's all."

"We should be thankful it happened now and not later, after Karen had invested too much time with him. The sooner she distances herself from him, the better."

"So we just jump straight to divorce?"

"Of course," George said, sounding surprised Evelyn had to ask. "There are more than enough grounds: his growing tendency — no, passion — for violence, the infidelity —"

"That hasn't been proven," Evelyn pointed out.

George waved her words away as easily as he had the offer of tea. "Irreconcilable differences, Evie, and that's more than enough."

Evelyn sipped her tea to hide the loathing on her face. *That's far from enough. It'll never be enough.*

"Do you think he'll call?" George asked again, almost sounding eager for a fight.

Evelyn stared at the phone sitting innocently on the counter. "I hope he doesn't but . . ." She winced as she lifted her shoulders and set her mug down.

George got up and stood behind her, gently kneading her shoulders. She rested her head against her husband's stomach and let herself surrender to his touch. She was almost dozing when she felt his hands slide from her shoulders to the buttons of her blouse.

"What are you doing?" she asked, pointedly.

"Helping you relax," he replied huskily. His hands parted her blouse and slipped over her breasts.

"Our daughter is upstairs," she told him.

"Sleeping," George countered, massaging her nipples through the thin material of her bra. "You know, we've never had sex in the kitchen."

"And we're not about to," she said, shrugging free of his hands.

"But . . ." he started, sounding like a petulant child.

"But nothing, George." Evelyn buttoned her blouse. "Our daughter is upstairs and her husband could arrive or call at any moment. You certainly did choose an inappropriate time and place to make your advances."

George moved to stand by the counter, blocking her view of the phone. She willed him to move. "I just thought . . ."

"You just thought what?" she inquired, once more holding her tea mug.

Her husband paused then shook his head. "Nothing, Evelyn. You're right, it was a bad time. If you or Karen need me, I'll be in my office."

Alone once again, Evelyn sipped her tea and stared at the phone, willing it not to ring.

Jack stared at the phone, praying for it to ring, but silence reigned in the yard, broken only by his rough breathing and Justice's occasional soft whine. The shepherd was curled up against Jack's leg but not resting easily; his master was filled with too much pain for him to rest.

Jack sat on the deck steps, the kitchen's cordless phone lying impotently in his hands.

Call her, you idiot. You know you have to call her, right?

"Yeah, I know," he muttered miserably. Justice whined in sympathy and rested his head on Jack's thigh. Jack stroked the soft fur unconsciously.

"What if she doesn't want me to call?" Jack's voice was rasping, beaten. "What if . . ." He swallowed, hesitant, afraid saying the words aloud, the words she had thrown at him, would endow them with substance, make them true. "What if . . . what if she *is* better off without me?"

Justice didn't have an answer and Jack sat on the deck with the phone in his lap for a long time.

The Major Crime office was quiet. The shades were drawn, filtering the sunlight and dimming the room in grey shadows. Detective Rick Mason sat at his desk, elbows propped on the cluttered top as he massaged his temples.

Bloody fucking headache. And on the heels of that, *I'm getting too old for this shit.*

Sighing, he dropped his forearms to the desktop with a leaden thump, fluttering papers in the brief breeze. He wearily scanned the files littered in front of him. Homicide at Sherbourne and Dundas. Beaten hookers. Dealers he had his eye on and, on top of everything, that mess over in 52 Division. Just what he didn't need: a pedophile's dead brother.

Crap, he really fucked up on that one.

He felt like a juggler with a few too many balls in the air. He chuckled morosely. *More like knives.* Not for the first time, he wondered if it was all worth it. The stress, the tightrope he was constantly walking. As if in answer, his stomach gurgled uncomfortably. He placed a hand on his belly and as always was shocked and disgusted at how fat he'd gotten.

Marcie would kick your lard ass for getting so fat, old man.

He reached past the clutter on his desk for the silver-framed picture where it sat in the corner, untouched by the sea of shit that was his job. He drew the photograph to him, tracing the woman's features with his fingers. Lovingly, tenderly. Painfully.

"I miss you, Marcie," he whispered.

The door opened and harsh, unnatural light stabbed into Mason's eyes as Tank flicked on the lights.

"Whatcha doing sitting in the dark, boss?"

"I was trying to get rid of a headache," Mason growled as he set the picture back in its customary location.

"Oops, sorry, boss," the big man said. "You want me to turn them off?"

"Fuck it. I've taken a long enough break."

Tank frowned at the detective. "Somehow I doubt that, boss."

Mason scowled. "I'll sleep when I'm dead. Did you and Kris get anything at the hospital?"

Tank eased down into his chair, not relaxing until it had ceased groaning and squealing beneath him. "Nothing," he reported sadly. "The victim couldn't add anything to the description."

"Could he ID the suspect in a photo? If we ever find one, that is," Mason added glumly. Definitely, too many knives.

"I doubt it," Tank reasoned, shaking his head. "We hung around for most of the morning, hoping his head would clear some, but he's pretty fucked up from the beating."

"Wonderful." Mason really didn't care if a few streetwalkers got tuned up — they were just disease-ridden parasites as far as he was concerned — but what pissed him off was that it was happening in his division, on *his* streets, and that would not be tolerated. He didn't care if the suspect was some self-appointed guardian vigilante or a fucked-up pervert getting his jollies from beating on women. Or men, in the last incident. The last of five.

Five since the beginning of the year and who knows how many more if we keep digging?

Kris and Tank had spent the morning, prior to attending the hospital, searching through old reports and had come up with three other serious assaults on prostitutes that could belong to their suspect. Two in 51 and a third just over the border into 52. The suspect description in each was similar in its vagueness: male, white, young, big build. The only connecting details were the victims' profession and the suspect's muscularity and viciousness. All the attacks had left the victims in hospital in serious condition.

Frustratingly, there was no pattern to the attacks. One in February, two in April and now the two this month. The victims, all hookers, came in varying shapes, sizes and colours. Nothing to connect them beyond their working status.

Only one of the assaults involved a car. The rest of the time the suspect was on foot. This, plus the close proximity of the attacks — all five had occurred within an area four city blocks square — told Mason their man was a local. A local with serious issues that sometimes got to be too much to handle.

Despite involving sex workers, none of the attacks were sexual in nature, at least not in the usual sense. All the victims were badly beaten about the head and torso but their breasts and vaginas — and the tranny's genitals — appeared to be specifically targeted. *Is this guy making a statement?* Mason believed the suspect was targeting hookers primarily because of their availability. That, plus prostitutes' usual reluctance to speak with police.

So, we have a local who occasionally gets mad. Mad? Try fucking berserk. He has so much rage that he practically beats people to death but he can hold on to it long enough to find an appropriate time and place. What does that mean? He's been dealing with this problem — whatever the fuck it is — for a long time?

"I should ask the nurse on the nut squad," Mason told himself.

"What was that, boss?"

"Nothing, Tank. Just talking to myself. What time are Jack and Jenny getting in?"

"Four. You told them we should stay out later in case our suspect is wandering around."

"Right. So I did." Mason squeezed his temples between

the heels of his hands. If this headache was anything like the migraines Jack suffered then Jack had Mason's full sympathy. *Crap, I'd consider eating my gun if I got too many like this.*

A shadow fell across his desk. "I'm heading downstairs. You want anything?" Tank offered.

"Yeah. Grab me a Coke and something chocolate, would you? Jack says sugar and caffeine help when he's getting a headache," Mason reasoned through a strained smile.

"I think that's just for migraines, boss. Yours sounds like stress to me. I don't think they'll help all that much."

"Maybe not," Mason conceded. "But it'll give me something to do other than smacking you around."

"One Coke and chocolate bar coming up," Tank announced and backed warily away from his boss's desk. He even turned the lights off when he left.

Tank was a good man, a solid, reliable officer. He and Mason had waded through some shit together, along with Kris and Taft. Good people, good coppers, all of them. Mason knew he could trust them, even trust them with the truth sometimes. But never the whole truth. Never that.

Kris and Tank were comfortable where they were right now — getting more than comfortable with each other by the looks of it — but Taftmore was looking ahead, wanting to further his career. He had his eye on either Hold Up or Intelligence and Mason wasn't about to stand in his way. That meant there would be an opening in the MCU soon and Mason figured Jack was the man to fill it.

That he could trust Jack was beyond doubt; Jack hadn't hesitated when Mason, sitting at this very desk, had presented him with a picture of Anthony Charles in order for Jack to positively identify the fucker in a photo lineup for Homicide.

Crap, what a fuck-up that had become. First, the Crown attorney had withdrawn the charges against Charles, then the little cocksucker had threatened Jack and his wife. And to add to the problems, Charles's little retard brother had his head removed with a shotgun. Another mess Mason could lay at Silva's feet.

But it had all worked out in the end: Charles dead, Jack a hero and no one the wiser. Not even the SIU, that cop-hating civilian watchdog agency, had been able to find anything out of place. Mason wondered sometimes about the shooting, the three bullets Jack had put into Charles. One in the belly and two in the chest. He wondered in what order they had been fired. Not that it mattered.

If only Sy hadn't died.

"Fuck, what a mess." Mason scrubbed his face. Time to pull his head out of the past and his ass. "What's done is done."

Mason, feeling tired and alone, began sifting through the paperwork one more time.

Jack trudged across the station's parking lot. The humidity pressed down on him as heavily as his thoughts. Even the sight of Jenny hurrying between cars to catch up to him did little to lighten his mood.

"Hey, partner," Jenny called out then stopped when she saw Jack's face. "Are you all right, Jack? You look like you didn't sleep at all last night."

Jack snorted a bitter laugh. "I didn't, really. Karen was gone when I got home."

"Gone? What do you mean, gone?"

"Gone. Her and a bag of clothes. I imagine she's at her parents'."

"Oh, Jack, I'm so sorry." Jenny laid a comforting hand on his arm. "Did you call her?"

Jack shook his head, defeated. "Naw. I was going to a couple of times but . . ."

"But what?"

Instead of answering, Jack motioned to the back door. "Let's get inside. It's too fucking hot out here."

Her comforting hand locked on his arm and pulled him back. "You're not sidestepping the question that easily, Jack. Why didn't you call Karen?"

"It doesn't matter, Jenny. Come on, we'll be late."

But his partner stood her ground. "Why didn't you call?" she demanded, not releasing his arm.

Jack sighed and his shoulders slumped resignedly. "I did a lot of thinking last night and maybe they're right," he said, talking to the pavement. "Karen and her parents, I mean. Maybe she does deserve better than me."

Jenny was momentarily wordless as the shock at Jack's statement faded from her face. "That's bullshit and you know it. Karen couldn't ask for a better man."

Jack finally met Jenny's eyes. "Really? I'm not so sure." He shrugged. "I have changed, I know that. But for good or bad? I don't know, but I do know I'm not the man Karen married. Maybe she'd be better off with someone else."

"Sounds like you're giving up," Jenny accused.

"I've *not been* giving up since Sy died," Jack countered. He shrugged again, lost and confused. "Maybe I'm just tired of fighting." He tilted his head, looking Jenny in the eye. "Did you know that when I threw Kayne off the bridge —"

"Don't say it that way," she cut in. "You didn't throw him off. The wood broke and he fell. You didn't do it intentionally."

"Whatever," Jack said, dismissing her argument. "Did you know my biggest concern that day was that I was probably going to miss my workout the next day because of all the overtime I was going to have to do?"

"So?" she asked, not seeing his point.

"Would a normal person think that way? Would I have thought that way a year ago? I didn't care that I had just killed someone, Jenny. Asshole or not, I just didn't care and the man Karen married would have never felt that way. Come on, we'll be late." Jack headed for the door.

Jenny stared after her partner for a moment before following, a worried expression clouding her face.

"Whoa, hey, guys." Tank nearly ran over Jack and Jenny as he pounded down the stairs.

"What's the rush, Tank? The guys' john not working up there?"

"Ha. Very funny, Jenny." The plainclothes copper eyed Jack. "You look like shit, Jack."

"So I've been told."

"Good thing I ran into you guys," Tank said as he herded them down the stairs. "You may as well hang out in the lunch-room for a few minutes."

"Mason got something going on in the office?"

"Nope," Tank told Jenny with a smile. "The boss just needs some time to himself, that's all."

Jenny looked at Jack and they shrugged in unison before following the big man into the lunchroom. Tank headed for the vending machines and while he perused the chocolate bars, Jack got himself a Diet Coke. He held it out to Jenny and when she shook her head he plopped into a chair, popping the tab. Jenny perched on the table next to him before slipping her sunglasses off.

Tank whistled appreciatively. "That's one nice shiner you got there, girl."

Jack paused with the pop can halfway to his mouth. Tank was right, Jenny's black eye was a beaut. The skin around her right eye was a nauseating smear of purple and yellow, but at least the swelling had gone down.

Jack rocked forward in his chair. "Are you okay? Headache or anything?" he asked. God, he felt like such an ass. He'd been moaning about his marital problems and had completely forgotten that Jenny had been hurt.

Way to support your partner, fuckhead, he chided himself.

"I'm fine," she assured him with a little grin. "Besides, maybe Brian will want to examine it for me."

"Brian? Oh, right. The date with the doctor this weekend."

"A doctor?" Tank asked, sitting down next to Jack. "I'm impressed. Way to go, Jenny."

"Thank you." Jenny took a small bow from where she was sitting. "How long do we need to give the boss?"

"Few minutes," Tank mumbled around a mouthful of chocolate.

Kris wandered into the lunchroom in time to hear Tank's comment. "Rick in one of his funks?"

Tank nodded, swallowing. "Like the pink, babe."

"Thanks, Tanky. I did it for you." She fluffed her dyed spiky hair — her biceps bulging with the simple movement — then leaned down to give Tank's bald pate a loud smack. Tank saw Jack and Jenny watching and blushed a deep scarlet.

"What's with Mason?" Jenny asked, taking pity on Tank.

Kris fielded the question after looking at Tank for confirmation. "Every once in a while, usually when the stress is getting to him, Rick gets kind of low. We just give him some space and he comes out of it in a little while."

I know the feeling. "Is he okay?"

"Oh, sure." Tank swigged back his Coke. "He just sits and talks to his wife."

"Tank," Kris hissed and the big man flinched as if he expected to be hit, and judging from the dark look in the bodybuilder's eyes, it wouldn't have been a simple love tap.

"I didn't know he was married." Jenny looked at her partner and Jack lifted his hands to say, *Me neither.*

Tank, embarrassed by his slip, turned to Kris. "You started it," she told him.

The big man sighed and set down his Coke. "He was married, a long time ago." Tank sighed again and rubbed a hand over his scalp. He looked from Jack to Jenny, silently debating with himself. At length, he made his decision.

"Not many people know this and it has to stay that way. Don't even bring it up with Rick, all right?" He waited until both officers had agreed. "Rick got married to his first wife right before he got hired."

"That was what, twenty-five years ago?" Jack asked.

"Twenty-seven," Kris said. She nodded for Tank to carry on.

Tank leaned past Jenny to check the hallway before continuing. "Yeah, a long time ago. Anyway, it didn't work out and she left him. The divorce was pretty messy from what I gather and after that, Rick had a jaded view of marriage."

I know that feeling, too. Jenny glanced at Jack as if she had read his thoughts. Jack pretended not to notice. Instead, he interrupted again. "Did Rick tell you this?"

Kris emphatically shook her head as Tank breathed, "God, no. Sy told me. He and Rick were partners here in 51 back then."

Jack was surprised. "I didn't know they were partners. I knew Sy worked in the MCU with him but he never mentioned being partners."

Tank nodded. "They were paired up for nearly seven years, I think." He waggled his fingers in the direction of the front desk. "If Rick hadn't been transferred out when he got his stripes, he'd be on the quarter-century plaque. He came back to take over Major Crime. Anyway, he was working with Sy before he got cranked. Now, about four years before he got promoted, Rick met Marcie and bam!"

"Bam?" Jack asked dubiously.

"Bam," Kris confirmed. "Sy said he'd never seen Rick so happy, not even with his first wife. He said if he didn't hold Rick down, he would have floated away."

Tank chuckled. "Like Mary Poppins."

Jack smiled at the movie reference. *That's Sy, all right.* He paused, trying to picture the burly slab of a detective bouncing around on his toes, madly in love. *Would he have looked like Manny?*

"A year after they met, Rick and Marcie," Kris picked up,

clearly unable to resist telling this part of the story; her smile was joyful yet terribly sad as she gazed fondly at Tank. "A year later, they were married. Sy was Rick's best man."

Jack cocked an eyebrow. Sy had never mentioned anything remotely resembling a friendship with Mason, let alone standing up for him at his wedding. If anything, Sy had given the impression that he really hadn't trusted the Major Crime boss.

Jenny tapped Jack's leg with her foot and looked a question at him. *Later*, he mouthed and she nodded.

"They were trying to get pregnant," Kris said, her smile subdued yet whimsical. "They were beginning to think one of them might not be, you know, functioning right and then, about two years later, Marcie tells him she's pregnant."

"Was Rick happy?" Jenny piped up, catching Kris's enthusiasm.

"Ecstatic. Sy said he was like a kid with Christmas, Halloween and his birthday all rolled into one." Tank checked his watch. "Better make this quick. One day shift, Sy and Rick ended up with overtime. It was nothing major but he and Marcie were supposed to be going to a dinner party or something when he got home so she told him she'd walk over and he could meet her there."

An icy hole began to form in Jack's stomach. *I've got a feeling this is going to get bad quick.*

"She got run over," Tank said simply, sadly. "She never had a chance."

"Impaired?"

Tank nodded at Jenny. "That's what they thought and the driver was done with impaired causing death."

"What they thought?" Jack asked, not liking the sound of it.

"Yeah." Tank was fiddling with the empty Coke can, passing it between his hands on the tabletop. "Apparently, when the cops got there, the guy could barely stand and didn't even know he had just killed someone."

"But?" Jack prompted, but already knowing the outcome.

"Yeah, *but*." Tank caught the can and crushed it. "The guy was diabetic and had an insulin shock or something like that. Made him look and act drunk. The charges got tossed."

Jack and Jenny just stared at Tank. There was nothing to say to that.

After a moment of silence, Tank continued. "That was the beginning of the end for their partnership. After Marcie was killed, Sy said Rick kind of changed —"

"Who fucking wouldn't?" Kris muttered.

"— and they kind of fell apart. Rick got promoted, transferred and they didn't speak until he came back to take over the MCU. They sort of patched things up, but not really."

Tank double-checked his watch. "Time to go," he declared, pushing back from the table. "Remember, not a word. I only told you guys 'cause Rick likes you." He cracked a big smile. "Now let's go peddle Jenny's ass."

The Jarvis Street Baptist Church lorded over the intersection of Gerrard and Jarvis streets, a Gothic remnant from the late 1800s. Salvation and redemption were promised within the confines of its heavy stone and painted glass. And before the imposing, brooding house of God, Jenny strutted her stuff, her bejewelled belly bared to the sun, her ass wrapped in jeans snugger than a lover's embrace. Or a john's.

The intersection was common ground for the cleaner — and therefore, higher-priced — prostitutes. The girls were protective of their turf and crack whores were definitely prohibited. Undercover police officers were another matter and the hookers had willingly ceded the sidewalk to Jenny after she had explained who she was fishing for. They may have been prostitutes but that didn't mean the women were stupid; they knew it was to their collective benefit and health to get a predator off the streets.

Rush hour was long since done but traffic was still heavy and the three northbound lanes of Jarvis were packed. Gerrard wasn't the major artery Jarvis was but it, too, was jammed bumper to bumper, from red light to red light. The slow-moving traffic gave Jenny plenty of opportunity to study the drivers as they crawled past her. So far, some interested-looking men and a couple of women, but no one matching the description of their boy.

A scout car, its white paint scarred and battered like all its fellow 51 cars, pulled to the curb on Gerrard. The passenger window slid down as Jenny strolled over, moving her hips in a pronounced sway. Coppers were always disrupting sweeps as they cruised by to check out the PWs in hooker dress. It seemed Paul and Connor were no exception.

"Aw, I was enjoying the view," Connor complained when Jenny squatted by his door.

"Don't whine," she admonished. "It doesn't become you. No offense, guys, but let's make this quick; the heat from your engine is damn well killing me."

"That's not the engine. It's my desire for you," Connor told her with a sincere smile.

Jenny glared accusingly at Paul. "Are you encouraging him?"

Paul shook his head. "Nope. You know me, Jenny. I'm much more subtle and chivalric in my flirtations."

"Chivalric? Flirtations?" Connor stared at his escort in disbelief. "Have you been reading the dictionary again?"

Jenny reached through the window and angled the vent up to her face. Paul obligingly cranked the AC. "Thanks," she murmured, luxuriating in the cold air. "What are you guys doing here? You know B platoon is off today."

"Doing a call back," Paul explained. "There's four of us in and we were supposed to concentrate on the dealers at Queen and Sherbourne but A platoon is so short manpower that the sergeant dumped us in a car to answer the radio."

"Thanks again," she said as Paul passed her a bottle of water. She rubbed the plastic against her forehead, enjoying the icy touch of the condensation on her hot skin.

"Better be careful doing that, Jenny," Paul cautioned her. "You might give Pest here a stroke."

"He couldn't afford a stroke from me," she joked. "And neither could you," she added when the big cop opened his mouth.

"You wound me," Paul declared, pressing a hand to his massive chest. "I was going to ask if the rumours were true. Are you and Jack paired up?"

"Sorry, big fella. We are."

Paul's face fell. "You didn't even tell me you were available," he moaned. "Well, if you ever tire of the little white boy, you come calling on Hot Chocolate, baby."

"And that's why you're riding with Connor." Jenny cracked the bottle and drank deeply. She pretended not to notice the stares. "Is this a social visit, guys? I ask because Tank and Kris will be finished with the last john in a few minutes and I'll need to get back to work."

Paul turned serious. "You're doing johns? I thought you were out here for the asshole beating up the girls."

"We are. We're just laying paper on the persistent johns."

Connor twisted in his seat, scanning the area. "Where are they?"

Jenny nodded up Jarvis. "The parking lot on the north side of the church. It's out of sight but close enough if our boy shows up."

It was Paul's turn to look around. "I don't see Jack."

Again, Jenny gestured behind her with a bob of her head. "The front doors to the church. He's just inside."

Connor whistled appreciatively. "Nice. With the shadows, you can't see him at all."

"We cruised Allan Gardens on our way over and didn't see anyone like your guy," Paul advised her. The church sat in the southwest corner of the green oasis, almost connected to the greenhouse.

"Shouldn't you be set up on one of the side streets?" Connor asked. "This seems too busy."

Jenny shook her head. "Only one of the attacks was off the main streets. Three of them were along Gerrard from here to Church." A horn sounded impatiently. "That's my cue, guys."

"Stay safe," Paul counselled. "In between calls, we'll be in the area. Not too close to spook your guy but close enough in case you need us."

"I appreciate it, guys." Jenny blew them both a kiss.

As the scout car pulled away, Connor leaned out his window and, for the sake of the pedestrians, shouted, "Are you sure you won't take a cheque?"

Taylor met Rico in the parking lot down and across from Filmore's. The big bodybuilder leaned against his car, his black dress pants and snug T-shirt complementing the Corvette's glossy exterior. Rico uncrossed his muscular arms to hold out a hand and a greasy smile for Taylor.

"No hard feelings about last time, man? Hope it don't muck up our business relationship."

Taylor studied the outstretched hand for a moment then took it in his own. "No," he conceded. "No hard feelings."

Rico's smile widened into a pleased grin. "That's my man." He gestured to the back of the sports car. "C'mon. I got the stuff you wanted." He led Taylor around the car. "You working tonight, man?"

"Yeah. I'm on break now."

"That's cool."

The Corvette's rear was draped in shadows and in the privacy the inky darkness provided Rico dug into his pocket. He pulled out two small baggies and dropped them on the trunk.

"As ordered, my man. I think your friend is going to be real happy with that." Rico stepped back and waved Taylor forward to inspect the merchandise.

Each baggie contained a generous quantity of white powder. For all Taylor knew about cocaine, it could be baking soda, but

Rico had never wronged him before. At least, not about product he was selling.

"Looks good. Listen, Rico, I told you I couldn't pay you up front but I'll get the money to you tomorrow, day after the latest." Taylor straightened up and something cold and hard jammed the back of his head. He froze.

"I trust you on the money, man. You ain't stiffed me yet." Rico chuckled and Taylor knew it was a gun barrel pressing on his skull. "But this is business, man," Rico went on. "So I think I should get some kinda down payment. You know?"

In the hot, muggy air, Taylor's skin suddenly chilled. Never again. "Forget it, Rico. I'm not doing that again."

Rico snickered and bore down on the gun. "Don't worry, man. I don't want your mouth." He leaned in and whispered in Taylor's ear. "This time I want your ass."

The chill on Taylor's skin sank in to freeze his bones. "Fuck you, Rico," he spat, his voice cold with anger. "Never again." As he spoke, he palmed a small folding knife from behind his belt.

Rico gripped the nape of Taylor's neck and dug the barrel in deeper. "I wasn't asking, man," he snarled. "Drop your fucking pants, motherfucker."

"Taylor?"

Taylor and Rico turned in unison at the tiny, scared voice. Sandra stood in the parking lot, a light jacket thrown over her scant outfit. Her fingers twisted over themselves as she peered hesitantly at the two men.

"Fuck off, bitch," Rico ordered, his words raspy with excitement. "Taylor and me got some business to take care of."

"What's going on, Taylor?" Sandra took an indecisive step back.

Rico shifted to point the gun at Sandra. "I said, fuck off, bitch."

Taylor struck. He twisted, broke free of Rico's hold and with all his rage and strength behind it, thrust the knife for Rico's chest. But the big man's arms were awkwardly crossed before his chest and the knife slammed home into Rico's forearm. Rico grunted and tried to throw Taylor off but Taylor twisted and dragged at the knife, eliciting a drawn-out gasp of pain.

Before Rico could recover, Taylor wrapped his arms around the drug dealer's gun arm and forced it down. Too late Rico realized what Taylor was doing. Taylor slapped a hand over Rico's and squeezed the trigger. The gun went off inches from Rico's knee and this time the big man screamed.

As Rico fell, Taylor ripped the gun from his hand. Rico hit the ground, both hands clutching his shattered knee.

"You shot me, you bitch! You motherfucking —"

Rico's words gagged on the hot barrel of the gun as Taylor jammed it into his mouth. "I told you, never again." He cocked the gun and in the sudden silence, it was a cannon shot. "Never. Again."

"Taylor? Don't do it, Taylor. Please." Sandra inched cautiously forward, her hand held out beseechingly. "Don't do it, please. You'll go to jail, Taylor. I can't lose you. Not like that."

Taylor knelt over Rico, the hand grasping the gun quivering, quivering with hate, loathing, rage. He pushed on the gun, forced Rico's head back. The big man stared defiantly at Taylor over the steel of the revolver.

"Please, Taylor. Don't kill him." Sandra was close enough to lay gentle fingers on Taylor's shoulder. "Please."

Taylor tore his eyes away from Rico's hateful gaze. Sandra's eyes were soft and shiny with tears. She smiled and tears spilled down her cheeks. Taylor could feel her concern, her fear. Her weakness.

But she was right. Killing Rico was not the answer. It would rob Taylor of his freedom, rip open the wounds he had burned closed and expose his shame to the world. He eased the gun from Rico's mouth.

"You bitch!" Rico spat at him. "You're nothing but a little

fucking bitch. I'll fucking kill you for this, man. I'll kill you."

Taylor drew his arm back, then swept the gun down at Rico's head. The steel slammed into Rico's skull, the front sights tearing open a gash over his eyes. Taylor brought the gun across again and this time teeth flew with the blood.

He rammed the gun under Rico's chin, forcing the man's mouth shut. "If you ever come near me again —" he dug at the tender skin with the barrel "— I'll blow your fucking balls off."

Taylor slowly stood up and when Rico rolled to his side, Taylor smashed the heavy heel of his boot into Rico's face. The big man flopped limply onto his back and moved no more.

Sandra watched as Taylor straightened up. His shoulders slumped as he stared at the man on the ground. She had no idea what was going on. Had the other man, a grotesquely huge bodybuilder bigger than any of the bouncers in the club, been trying to rape Taylor? That's what it had looked like but it didn't make sense. Taylor wasn't gay. He was a good man, one Sandra felt could take care of her, and the relief she was feeling was overwhelming.

"Oh, thank God, Taylor," she sobbed. "Thank God, you didn't kill —"

Suddenly, Taylor grabbed her by the throat and shoved her against the chain-link fence. "You're useless," he snarled an inch from her face. Spittle hit her cheek and she could feel — actually *feel* — the hate radiating off of Taylor's skin. "If you weren't so fucking weak and useless, this never would have happened."

"What?" she gasped, forcing the word out past the clamp on her throat. "I don't under —"

He pulled her to him then slammed her back against the fence. "Shut up, bitch. You're weak. Weak and useless. Just like the rest of them. Sara's dead because of you, you useless cunt."

Taylor's hand squeezed tighter and the last of her air whistled shut. Darkness bulged and grew at the edge of her vision. She stared into Taylor's fevered eyes and she knew, as unconsciousness crept closer, he wasn't talking about her. With the last of her strength, she tried to say *I love you* but if the words came out, she couldn't hear them over the roaring of blood in her ears.

She sagged in his grip then suddenly was falling. She hit the ground and rolled to her hands and knees, coughing painfully between harsh, wheezing breaths. She raised her head to see Taylor striding from the parking lot. She tried to call out to him, to tell him it was all right, but a wave of dizzying blackness washed over her.

She never felt the pavement as it slapped her in the face.

Business had been steadily picking up since rush hour ended and now that full darkness — or as dark as it ever got in a city — was upon the streets, the drivers were practically queuing to proposition Jenny.

Am I the only hooker working tonight? she asked herself, sauntering over to the most recent hopeful client. *Please, don't let it be another weirdo. I'll give anything to be asked for straight sex.* Toe sucking, golden showers, spanking — both giving and receiving — had all paraded by her tonight. One john actually wanted her to take a dump on his chest while he masturbated.

It must be a full moon.

The car idling at the north curb of Gerrard was small and dark in colour — black or navy blue; it was hard to tell under the streetlights — fitting the description of the suspect's vehicle that the girl in St. Mike's had given them.

Relax, Jenny. How many thousands of small, dark cars are there in the city?

But when she leaned down to chat with the john, her heart rate jumped. He was young, mid-twenties, tops, with a crop of short black hair. While he wasn't exactly what Jenny would consider muscular, he had a thickness to his upper body. Jenny knew everyone's perception of body types was as broad as the range of sex acts she'd been propositioned with over the last few days. A suspect with an "average build" could turn out to be a toothpick or the Pillsbury Doughboy. Yeah, this guy could be considered muscular, especially if he was whaling the hell out of you.

Jenny squatted and brushed her hair back, alerting her backup that she had a potential suspect.

She hit him up with her opening line and come-fuck-me smile. "You looking for some company, honey?"

"Only if you think you can handle it, sugar lips."

Sugar lips? What a sweet talker.

The john leaned across the seat, resting his elbow on the centre console. He kept his left hand hooked casually over the steering wheel and Jenny noticed he hadn't taken the car out of gear.

And the john wasn't finished sweeping Jenny off her feet. "You've got a fucking amazing ass, you know that?" He grinned, a charming, ear-wide smile. The smile was no doubt meant to be open and friendly but it fell short of his eyes. He watched Jenny intently. Hungrily. Jenny was uncomfortably reminded of Red Riding Hood's big bad wolf and what that wolf's awfully big teeth were for.

But being hungry or horny didn't make him their man. "You like my ass, huh?"

"You bet. I've had my eye on you for a while." He leered a smile at her. "Now why don't you get your sweet ass in the car."

Jenny smiled. "Sorry, hon, but business first. Why don't you tell me what you want?"

The man's face turned mean. "You don't tell me what to do," he hissed at her. "Now, get your ass in the car or you'll get what's coming to you. Just like those other bitches."

Jenny signalled with a hand run through her hair again. *This one needs to be checked out. Now.*

"What did you want to do with my ass, honey?" she asked, burning time and keeping the john's attention on her while her team moved up.

The john's eyes darted over Jenny's shoulder and his brow

furrowed in puzzlement. He looked at Jenny then past her again and this time his eyes widened in shock.

And that's when Jenny knew things were about to go bad.

As the sun set and darkness claimed the face of the church, Jack had crept from the vestibule like some vampiric creature stealing forth from a crypt. Crouching on the top step, he easily kept Jenny in view. And he wasn't the only one watching her. Car after car stopped, the drivers obviously interested in hiring her services. The majority of the wannabe johns drove off alone — horny and frustrated, Jack figured — never knowing how lucky they were.

Jenny occasionally signalled for a takedown but not often. The aim tonight was the Basher, as Kris called him, and not the run of the mill johns, but every once in a while some john just wouldn't take no for an answer. That's when Tank and Kris introduced themselves and took the poor slob into the parking lot for processing.

Jack checked the time. Not quite eleven. Prime time for the Basher; all of the attacks had occurred between ten and three in the morning.

Watching Jenny play the hooker provided him with time to think. Too much time. Did Karen want him to call or not? Jenny seemed to think he should just swallow his pride and call, ask Karen to come home. But it wasn't his pride that kept him from dialling her number; he couldn't get the notion that she might be better off without him out of his head. It was mired there like a car sunk up to its axle in mud.

I don't want her to leave me. He knew he wasn't bullshitting himself because the mere thought of life without Karen ripped a cold hole in his guts.

Then call her, you idiot.

But what . . . he began in his head then whispered, wondering if it would sound silly spoken aloud. "But what if she *is* better off without me? Maybe she's right, maybe she does deserve more than me."

She's the only one who can —

Jenny was on Gerrard, squatting by a small dark four-door, when she ran her fingers through her hair.

Jack shifted back into the deeper shadows and brought his mitre up. "Did you guys see that? Jenny just signalled a possible."

"Got it," Tank came back. They were using a tactical band on the radios so as not to have to contend with the division's usual air traffic. "We'll head around the church and come on him from the rear."

"Got it." Jack lowered the mitre into his lap and waited, never letting his eyes stray from his partner or the car. He couldn't see anything of the john — *I guess it'd be too much to ask for him to turn on the interior light* — so he stayed intent on Jenny, in case she —

"She just signalled again," Jack snapped into the radio. "We gotta take him down."

Jack didn't wait for Tank's reply. He stood up and stuffed the mitre into his back pocket while reaching under his shirt for his Glock. One hand through the hair meant, *Hey, we should grab this guy's info.* A second hair fluff said, *Holy shit, this could be the guy.* And if it was their guy, a man who had already put five people in the hospital, then they weren't taking any chances.

Jack leapt down the short flight of stairs and angled for the front of the car. His task was to convince the driver it would be bad for his health if he tried to drive off. He was halfway to the car when Jenny lunged, or was pulled, into the car and Jack realized things had gone bad in a fucking big way.

The Basher — it had to be their man, it had to be — bolted upright, his hand flashing for the gearshift. Jenny knew it was dangerous, knew it was monumentally stupid, would be the first one to give shit to any copper considering it. She did it anyway. She lunged through the open window, clutching the john's hair with one hand and his shirt with the other. Keeping her knees braced on the outside of the car door, she yanked as hard as she could.

"Police!" she screamed. "You're under arrest, asshole!"

"Get off me, you fucking cop bitch!" The john swung his fist backhanded but it was a clumsy, awkward blow and he did little more than cuff Jenny upside the head.

She bore down and heaved with all she had and something *twanged* painfully in her abdomen. But it wasn't enough. The john's hand slapped the gearshift down and the car lurched forward.

Jenny realized she was in a horrible situation that could only get worse. She could either pull herself completely into the car, unarmed, or let go and throw herself from the car, hoping to avoid falling under the wheels or slamming into a light pole or something else equally unyielding.

She let go of the john's shirt and was reaching for his face when she heard Jack roar, "Police! Stop the car or die!"

The car jerked to a halt, tossing Jenny against the window frame. Grunting in pain, she sank both hands into the john's hair, wrenching his head sideways. Out of the corner of her eye, she spotted Jack standing in front of the car, his gun trained lethally on the john.

"Put the car in park," she ordered. "Do it now."

"You fucking bitch," he snarled. "I'm gonna —"

"What you're going to do," Kris said as she leaned in the open driver's window and nuzzled her Glock against the john's temple, "is put the car in park like she said, turn the engine off and put your fucking hands up. Or I'll splatter your brains all over the inside of your shitty little car."

Jenny sat on a park bench in Allan Gardens, just a stone's throw from the church. She rubbed her hands together, happy that they had finally stopped shaking.

Just leftover adrenalin, Jack says, and I guess he should know.

As if thinking his name had summoned him, Jack sat down beside her. "You okay?" He placed a hand on her shoulder, lightly at first, tentatively even, as if he was unsure about touching her. The feel of his hand on her was comforting and when she didn't pull away, the hand became an arm and she leaned into his solidness, all the while telling herself they were partners and this was allowable.

"I'm good," she reassured him. "I was fine until I started thinking about what could have happened, how he could have scraped me off against another car or something." She sat up and Jack pulled his arm back, rather reluctantly she liked to think. "Guess it was pretty stupid, jumping into the car like that." She laughed, embarrassed.

"We all do stupid things and trust me, you've got a long way to go before catching up to me. What matters is that you didn't get hurt and fuckhead over there is heading to the station."

Jenny looked over at the parking lot beside the church. Tank was loading their suspect — soon to be accused — into the back of a marked car for transportation to the station.

"Is he the one?"

It was Jack's turn to laugh. "You won't believe this. You remember the guy Connor and I grabbed the other night doing the tranny in the stairwell?"

Jenny looked at Jack in astonishment. "It's the same guy?"

"Yup," Jack said, nodding to show he wasn't joking. "One and the same."

"But he isn't . . . ?" Jenny shook her head.

Jack frowned. "Unfortunately, no. The night I got him, he picked up his hooker *after* the Basher grabbed his. Even so, Mason and Taft talked with him just to make sure."

"But what about all that shit he was saying?"

Jack shook his head. "Who knows. He's a fucking idiot."

"Fuck," Jenny swore. "Some asshole playing at being a serial criminal."

"Never underestimate the stupidity of the general public," Jack quoted. "Something Sy used to say," he explained when Jenny looked quizzically at him.

"Very stupid — and the idiot almost died because of his stupidity." She sat up and twisted, cracking her back. "What's the plan now?"

"Lunch," Jack told her with a smile. "Fuckhead's gone to the station where Mason has plans to chat with him again just to double-check he has nothing to do with the attacks." Jack chuckled. "I imagine after Mason's finished with him, we'll never see that idiot back down here. Tank and Kris are grabbing something to eat then heading in to do the paperwork. They suggest we do the same."

"Sounds good. I'm glad we brought two cars tonight; Tank always wants to eat pizza." She stood up slowly, grimacing at the throb of pain in her right hip.

"Yeah. Any idea — what's wrong?"

"When the idiot hit the brakes, I slid into the window frame. Guess I whacked my hip harder than I thought." She unzipped her jeans to bare her right hip. "See?" Even with the park's poor lighting, the bruise was a colourful ink blot on her tanned skin.

Jack peered at the exposed flesh intently. "Nice tan lines," he commented.

"You're supposed to be looking at the bruise, buddy," she said, a mocking seriousness to her words. "Not trying to figure out how small my bikini is."

Jack snorted. "Yeah, right." He sighed unhappily as she did her pants up. "You have a seat and I'll get the car."

"No argument here." She sank carefully back onto the bench.

Taylor stood within the blackness beneath the spreading branches of the old tree. His face was hatred chiselled in stone. Right out in the open, the slut was showing the man what he could have — what was his for the taking — if he desired it.

That fucking slut. Taylor clenched his teeth in rage, his body quivering in response. All women were useless sluts, parading their weakness for all to see. If not for that weakness, his sister would be alive today and his father wouldn't have —

"No!" Taylor snarled quietly and thumped his fist painfully against the tree's unyielding trunk. He would not go there. "You're dead, old man," he whispered, chanted protectively in the dark. "You're dead. You can't hurt me anymore."

The man was gone and the slut was sitting down. Alone. Alone and his for the taking. Taylor stepped from the shadows.

Jenny was gingerly massaging her hip, hoping to ease some of the stiffness from it, when the man approached her. He moved so quietly she didn't know he was beside her until a dim shadow fell across her. She looked up at him, trying to see a face, but he was silhouetted by the weak light behind him. A skittering unease crept down her spine and she slowly stood up.

"I'm not working right now, honey," she said as she casually shifted to her right.

The man turned with her, bringing half his face into the light and Jenny knew she was in trouble.

His lean face was heavy in the brow and jaw, giving him an animalistic look that mirrored exactly what she saw in the eye that wasn't hidden in shadow. In her heels, Jenny was a few inches taller than him but she figured even flat-footed she would top his height by an inch or two. He may have been short but Jenny figured even Jack would think twice before scrapping with him; his arms were thick with corded muscle and his black golf shirt hugged a powerful chest and shoulders.

Although he had yet to speak, the man radiated violence, lethal anger, and Jenny knew who she was facing. In her jeans and tied-off shirt, bereft of her weapons and armour, she had never felt so naked.

"Let's go," he snarled.

Stall for time, Jenny. Jack will be back any minute and we'll take this guy down together.

Ignoring her pounding heart, she tossed her hair and smiled. "Okay, hon, but we don't go anywhere until we settle on a price."

His hand shot out, a striking snake, clamping onto her throat. Jenny's hand flew to the man's wrist as his fingers and thumb dug in beneath her jaw. He forced her head back and with one arm raised her onto her toes. Jenny gagged, barely able to draw a breath. She had to free herself or she'd pass out.

She swung her left arm over his outstretched arm and twisted her body simultaneously, hoping, praying, to break his grip. She might as well have tried to push over one of the park's trees. All she accomplished was adding to his anger.

"Useless bitch." The words were barely more than a growl. His fist lashed out and pain, sharp, excruciating, exploded in Jenny's right eye. An idle, dazed thought — *at least he hit me in the eye that's already bruised* — wandered across her mind as she reeled from the devastating punch. If not for the hand on her throat, she would have fallen.

But Jenny had been hit before and she was not about to give up, especially not to this fucker. She flailed weakly, harmlessly, at the man's tree trunk of an arm until her hands were close to his face, then jabbed for his eyes with both hands.

"Bitch!" he bellowed. Jenny felt her nails scour flesh, but he had twisted his head away, saving his eyes.

"Bitch," he repeated.

Jenny watched through darkening vision as he drew his arm back. She barely saw the punch that knocked her into a depthless hole.

Jack gunned the plainclothes car over the curb and into the park. The wheels gripped for traction, spitting chunks of sod and dirt. The headlights illuminated a horrific scene: Jenny hanging limply in some asshole's grip, his arm cocked back to pummel

Jack's unconscious partner. Jack howled his rage, a wordless roar blending with the shriek of the engine.

The Basher — it was him, of course it was him — whirled to face the onrushing car, his face a snarling mix of frustrated anger and surprise. As the car slewed to a stop, he tossed Jenny aside and sprinted away. Jenny hit the park bench then slid bonelessly to the ground, discarded and broken.

"No!" Jack screamed as he leapt from the car.

The Basher was disappearing into the gardens and every muscle, every fibre, in Jack's body burned to give chase. He dropped to the ground next to his partner. The Basher could have another hundred women; Jenny was all that mattered to Jack. To his terrified eyes, she looked lifeless sprawled among the dead grass and cigarette butts —

Sy on the ground, his blood hot and thick on Jack's hands, staining the asphalt red

— but as he pressed his fingers to her throat, she moaned and her left eye fluttered open. Her right was already swollen shut.

"Get . . . him," she croaked. "Get . . . that bastard."

Even as she spoke, Jack was reaching for his mitre. When his hand slapped his empty back pocket, he remembered it was sitting on the seat in the car.

"Be right back," he said gently then sprinted to the car. He flung open the door and snatched up the portable radio. "Major Crime 51 with a priority!"

Silence.

Fuck. Still on the tactical band.

He dialled over to 51's band and the usual police crap squawked out of the mitre.

"— neighbour was smearing feces on his car. Don't know if they're human or —"

"Major Crime 51 with a priority," Jack interrupted. "Major Crime with a priority."

The dispatcher took control immediately. *"Units stay off the air,"* she ordered. *"Unit with the priority, go ahead."*

"It's MK 51," Jack said as he knelt beside Jenny again. "Suspect for assault police last seen running northbound through Allan Gardens." He scanned the area around him. Just because fuckhead had run off didn't mean he wasn't coming back. "Male, white, muscular build. Wearing a black shirt and blue jeans. Units be advised, this male is possibly the suspect for the assaults on prostitutes and should be considered extremely violent."

"MK 51, are you in foot pursuit of the suspect?"

"Negative, dispatch. We're at Gerrard and Horticultural Lane."

"10-4, MK 51. Units to respond. Suspect last seen northbound through Allan Gardens." She repeated the description then came back to Jack. *"I have units heading to the area, MK 51. Do you need an ambulance?"*

Jack looked at Jenny as she struggled to sit up. He slipped an arm under her shoulders as he keyed the mike. "10-4, dispatch. I need an am —"

Jenny's fingers weakly gripped his wrist. "No," she managed.

"You're hurt," Jack explained. "You need to go to the hospital. Dispatch, get —"

"No," Jenny said, stronger this time and her grip tightened on his wrist. "No time."

"I have an ambulance attending your location, MK 51. Can you advise of injuries?"

Jack watched as Jenny dragged herself up onto the bench. Her hair had pulled free of its ponytail and draped over her face. Shreds of grass and tiny bits of litter clung offensively to her black tresses.

"Jenny," he beseeched but she would have none of it.

"No," she said, her voice stronger. Stronger and harder. "We don't have time. I'll go later."

Jack studied her for a moment, seeing past the battered flesh to the steel beneath. She met his eyes defiantly, challenging him, and he felt a rush of pride for his partner.

"Cancel the ambulance, dispatch. We don't need it." He pocketed the radio and helped Jenny to her feet. "What's the rush?"

Jenny swayed on her feet then steadied as the dizziness passed. "His shirt had a crest," she said, twirling her finger over her left breast. "Filmore's. The bastard works at Filmore's."

The chubby man scratched his chin. "That sounds like Taylor. Always thought he was a little off centre. Something not quite right upstairs."

"How so?" Jack asked.

"Can't really say," the manager of Filmore's tried to explain. "Always had this look on his face like he was hiding something. Gave some of the girls the creeps, the way he looked at them."

"Looked at them how?" Jenny asked from where she stood by the open office door, keeping an eye on the hallway leading from the club's main room.

"Like he had a problem with them. Hated them, I guess. Sorry this is taking so long. This piece of shit runs slower than I do." He drummed stubby fingers on the computer's keyboard. A chunky gold ring that matched the chunky gold necklace and even chunkier gold watch glinted in the fluorescent light.

Jack ate his impatience. "Was he at work tonight?"

"Yeah, he was. Supposed to still be here but he never came back from his break." He slapped the computer. "Come on, you bloody thing. Probably got a virus or something. You know anything about a gunshot earlier? Some customers said they heard one but I can't hear shit back here."

"No, but we've been busy with other things." Jack checked his watch. Kris and Tank would be finished searching the building soon and Jack wanted an address to hit when they were done. "How much longer?"

"Shouldn't be much longer," Filmore's head man promised.

"Unless this thing crashes again. Last week I was doing payroll and just before I finished, the bloody screen went blank. Poof! Just like that. Took me hours to do it all over again."

"That sucks," Jenny commiserated absently. Jack ground his teeth.

"Here it is," the boss said at last. "Taylor Furlington."

Now we've got you, asshole. Jack pulled out his memo book and jotted the name and birthday down. "You got an address for him?"

"Sure thing. It's —" The boss man paused, his fingers hovering over the keys. "He ain't gonna be able to sue me over this, is he? Breach of privacy or some shit like that? Maybe I shouldn't be giving you this stuff until you get a warrant or something. What did he do, anyway?"

Jenny strode over to the desk and leaned across it. She brushed the hair from her face so the boss wouldn't miss any of the swollen and bruised flesh. "This," she snarled.

The boss's face blanched and his fingers dropped to the keys. "Here's his address."

They cut through the dark club, past tables. For a Thursday night, the strip club was quite busy but the patrons, alone or in groups, avoided looking around at their neighbours. Jenny and Jack roused some attention with their purposeful strides but again, no one showed much interest. Eyes would flicker to them then quickly avert back to the stage and the woman dancing in the hot lights.

Not that I consider that dancing, Jenny mused as she spared a look toward the stage, although the woman currently on stage was doing some impressive moves and holds on the brass pole. *Good upper body strength.*

Jenny figured she'd be getting more looks if her shirt was still tied off beneath her breasts, but the shirt was down and her Glock, baton and handcuffs were a comforting weight riding on

her hips. They had an address for their suspect and she was looking forward to payback time. She touched the hammered flesh
of her face and winced.

So much for looking good for my date on Saturday.

Tank and Kris were waiting by the front doors, the two
bouncers near them trying not to look unsettled by the presence
of two pissed-off cops. Jack broke free of the tables with Jenny
right behind and they headed for the doors. A dancer slipped up
to Jack, reaching out with a tentative hand.

"Excuse me." She was almost shouting but Jenny barely heard
her over the thumping music. The blonde woman — *probably
closer to girl* — had a diaphanous red scarf ingeniously wound
around her hips and small breasts. Jenny glanced at her partner
and was pleased, somewhat childishly and possessively, to see that
his eyes never left the woman's face.

"Is Taylor in trouble?" the dancer asked, shifting her look
between the partners.

"Why do you think we're looking for Taylor?" Jenny asked.

"I . . . I heard . . ." she stammered, gesturing at the doormen.
She took a deep, steadying breath, then rushed ahead. "I heard a
couple of them talking. He isn't in trouble, is he?"

"He is in trouble and he knows it," Jenny told her, none too
softly. "If you know where he is or how to get hold of him, tell
us now before he makes it worse."

"What did he do?" The woman was wringing her hands.

*This girl is a stripper? I thought strippers were supposed to be tough.
She should be back in high school.* "What's your name?" Jenny asked,
easing up.

"Sandra," she said timidly.

"Well, Sandra, this is what Taylor did." She pointed at her
face. With her hair tied back, the darkening bruises and scabbing
cuts were painfully visible.

Sandra's hand fluttered to her mouth. "Oh, my God. Taylor
could never . . ."

"Yes, he could. And did," Jenny said harshly. "Do you know where he is?"

Sandra shook her head. "He didn't come back after . . . after his break." She latched onto Jenny's arm. "You don't understand," she implored. "He's only been here a little while. He isn't used to the city."

"He's from someplace where men are allowed to beat on women?" Jenny snorted as she disengaged her arm from Sandra's fingers.

"No," Sandra answered, a confused look on her face. "He's from Sudbury. This isn't . . . it can't be his fault."

"Well, it is, Sandra, and if we find out someone called him to warn him," Jenny cautioned, "we'll be back for you."

They left the naïve stripper alone with her worry and Jenny muttered, "Stupid bitch. I wonder how many times this asshole has beaten on her."

"You got a name?" Tank asked as Jenny and Jack joined the two MCU coppers by the doors.

"And an address," Jack told them with a nasty smile. "200 Wellesley," he said, once they were all outside.

"Cool." Tank flipped open his cell phone. "Thomas, it's Tank. I need you to meet us at 200 Wellesley with a pass-key." A pause. "About five minutes ago, that's when." He tucked his phone away. "I've got a buddy on Housing security. He'll meet us there with the key."

The two MCU cops led the way in their car, Jack and Jenny close behind. "How you feeling?" Jack asked as he eased the car to a stop at Dundas and Sherbourne.

"Okay," Jenny said, nodding. "Sore as hell but okay."

"Good thing you've got a date with a doctor this weekend," Jack joked.

Jenny laughed, then grimaced in pain. "Ow, don't make me laugh." She rubbed the side of her jaw gingerly. "Yeah, I'd already thought of that. Glad to see my love life is a concern of yours.

Now, what about yours? Did you call Karen tonight?"

Jack shot Jenny a look as the light greened. "When would I have had time to call?"

Jenny stared at her partner, her disbelief clear. "Come on, Jack. You were sitting in a church for about five hours."

"I was supposed to be watching you," he pointed out. "Not calling my wife."

Jenny laid a hand on Jack's shoulder to remove any bite from her words. "If you don't call her, how much longer will she be your wife?"

Jack stared ahead, not answering, but his hands clenched the steering wheel, bunching the muscles in his forearms with the strain. In a whisper, he said, "Not now, Jenny. Let's get this asshole. Then I'll worry about Karen."

Jenny heard the pain in his words, no matter how hard he tried to hide it, but honoured his request and let the short trip ride out in silence.

200 Wellesley Street was an apartment building in St. James Town, the division's northern hot spot. The housing complex comprised a dozen or so high-rises and on a hot summer night like this the playgrounds and walkways between the towers would be crawling with human vermin. But they were after one specific vermin tonight and hopefully he had run home, thinking he was safe. He was about to be proven wrong.

Jack parked behind Tank's car and the four of them approached the front doors together. Surprisingly, the lobby door was locked —like Regent Park, locks didn't stay intact long in St. James Town — and Tank's friend Thomas was waiting for them by the elevators. Clad in the drab uniform of Toronto Community Housing Security, he looked big enough to play linebacker without the shoulder pads.

Looking at the three men and Kris, Jenny felt immensely undersized. *Is it something in the water down here?*

Tank and Thomas shared a quick hug with lots of manly

backslapping then exchanged rapid-fire Chinese — Mandarin or Cantonese, Jenny couldn't tell. She looked at Tank with new respect.

"I didn't know you spoke Chinese," she said.

The big copper shrugged and actually blushed a bit. "Thomas taught me some," he confessed. "Just enough to get laid."

"Of course."

"It's near the elevators," Thomas told them, handing Tank a key. "Pretty much right next to the elevators."

"Cool." Tank bounced the key in his palm. "Okay, we'll each take a stairwell and meet at the apartment. Thomas, you taking off?"

Thomas looked shocked at the suggestion. "And trust a 51 copper to return the key to me? Are you nuts?" Only the barest of smiles said he was joking.

Jack and Jenny headed up the east stairwell while the three behemoths took the opposite end. They made it to the second floor without running into any crackheads and ghosted down the hallway, rendezvousing with the others at the apartment. Jack and Jenny were on the key side so Tank tossed Jack the key.

Jack listened at the door then raised his hands palms up. All quiet. Tank twirled his finger impatiently. *Let's go.*

Jack slipped the key into the lock and gently, quietly, turned the knob. The door cracked open and gunfire erupted from inside the apartment. Three bullets hit the door, punching through it in small splintery explosions, slamming the door shut. Jack slapped himself against the wall and tugged his Glock free at the same time.

With the gunshots still echoing in the concrete hallway, Jack grasped the knob and flung the door open. Moving as if choreographed, Jack and Tank took the doorway, Jack high on his side and Tank kneeling across from him. Jack stayed tucked in behind the wall as best he could, very aware he wasn't wearing his vest.

The living room was sparsely furnished — an old couch and a TV — with their man, Furlington, standing by the balcony door. He was still wearing his black Filmore's shirt and had a knapsack slung over his back. His face was fixed in a snarl of rage. He held a silver revolver firmly in his hand as he contemplated the two cops training their guns on him.

"Police!" Jack yelled. "Drop the gun!"

Furlington glared at them then darted out the balcony door. He never paused before vaulting over the railing.

"Fuck!" Jack swore, remembering they were only on the second floor. He bolted into the apartment and across the living room. The glass in the balcony sliding door shattered as he shouldered it open. He pulled up at the railing, scanning the darkness beyond the haloed light thrown by the building's apartments. Part of him, the sane part, realized he was silhouetted against the bright windows, a perfect target if Furlington decided against running. The emotional side of him, the animal that craved vengeance, wanted Furlington to take a shot, to reveal himself so Jack could unload a magazine of bullets at him.

No shots came and in the distance, fading swiftly, the slap of running feet on concrete.

"Fuck." Quieter this time, frustrated and mad.

"Damn it," Jenny echoed him from the other end of the balcony. She had silhouetted herself as well but at least she'd had the brains to keep away from Jack, presenting two targets instead of one.

Jack pulled out his mitre but knew it was too late. By the time cars arrived to throw up a containing perimeter, Furlington would be blocks away. Even farther if he had a car.

"Fuck," he repeated and keyed the radio.

The atmosphere in the Major Crime Unit was subdued, gloomy and irritated. Furlington had gotten away from them twice. But at least they had a face for their suspect and a name for the face.

Even Tank, with the remains of an extra-large pizza in front of him, wasn't his usual bubbly self.

"I don't fucking believe it." Jack shoved away from the computer. "Not a damn fucking thing on him. Not so much as a ticket."

"Where's his DL registered to? Maybe he has history somewhere else." Mason was slumped behind his desk. God, he was tired. He imagined the dark circles under his eyes were sagging down his cheeks like wet mascara.

"Hang on," Jack muttered as he clicked over to check Furlington's driver's licence. "Sudbury. Guess he never got around to changing that."

"Sudbury, huh? I'll give them a call." Mason pulled out a directory from his desk drawer. Over the course of his career the detective had attended police conferences all over Canada and the States. As far as he was concerned, the training and exchange of information at the gatherings was secondary to establishing contacts in other law enforcement agencies. He had business cards from officers in police departments with less than a dozen guys right up to cards stamped CIA and DEA. He was sure he knew someone in Sudbury.

While he thumbed through his collection of contacts — *I have to put these on a computer someday* — he saw Jack rubbing the heel of his hand into his right eye. "Have you eaten anything, Jack?"

"Nah." Jack scrubbed at his face. "I'm too pissed off to eat."

"Go get something from downstairs," Mason ordered. "We can't afford you getting one of your bloody migraines. And since Tank didn't order enough pizza for everyone . . ." The grouchy detective glared at his officer.

"Hey, I asked," Tank protested. Grumbling under his breath, he added, "It's not my fault getting shot at makes me hungry."

"Anybody else want anything?" Jack canvassed the office. Kris shook her head as she stole a slice of Tank's pizza then smacked his bald head as he raised his hand.

"I guess not," Tank mumbled, glowering at Kris. She blew him a kiss.

Mason shook the can of Coke sitting on his desk. Faint sloshing sounds echoed out of the tin can. "I could use another Coke."

Jack nodded. "Jenny?"

Jack's partner looked up from where she was catching up on her notes and Mason noted the way she looked at Jack. *Lucky bastard. What I would give to have a woman like that look at me that way.*

Were they sleeping together? Mason doubted it; there was too much sexual tension between them. It hadn't been tapped yet, but Mason figured it was only a matter of time.

"See if you can dig up some ice somewhere, Jenny," Mason suggested. "Let's see if we can get some of that swelling down."

"Duh." She lightly rapped the heel of her hand off her forehead. "I should have thought of that."

"You've been busy. Now both of you get going; I'm thirsty."

Mason eased back in his chair, idly tapping a pen against his knuckles. He wondered if Jenny would be a good addition to the unit. She was a smart cop and after the beating she took tonight, her toughness was carved in stone. Was she a team player? Mason knew Jack was solid; the whole mess with Charles stood testament to that.

How much about that have you told her, Jack? Something worth considering, but not tonight. He had enough on his plate as it was.

Fuck. He sat up, shaking his head. He was supposed to be looking up his contact in Sudbury. *I am getting old. Fucking senile.*

He flipped through the cards, found the one he wanted. He punched the number, hoping the detective was at work. *Won't do me any good if he isn't in the office.*

The phone rang three times before it was picked up; a harried voice coughed, "Detective Garrelson."

Finally, a bit of luck. "That's not a very pleasant way to answer your phone, you grouchy old prick."

"Yeah?" rumbled the Sudbury detective. "Depends on who the fuck you are."

Mason laughed. "It's Rick Mason from Toronto, you miserable son of a bitch."

"Mason!" Garrelson chuckled, brightening up. "How the fuck are you? You still got that rat's nest on your chin?"

"Damn straight. Gonna start braiding it soon."

"Wouldn't fucking doubt it." Garrelson's tone sobered. "Now what can a jerkwater-berg police force do for the high and mighty Toronto police? I'm assuming this isn't a personal call, that is."

"It isn't, Garry, and yeah, I need your help."

"Then talk to — hang on." There was some commotion in the background and Garrelson barked, "Drag his ass down to the cells if he's gonna be like that. Sorry about that, Rick."

"I catch you at a bad time, Garry?"

"Naw, not really. We got a guy in for fighting with his neighbour over a fence." Garrelson chuckled. "You wouldn't believe this shit. These two morons have been pissing in each other's pants over this stupid fence for the last year. Well, today, one of them decided to finish the argument with a chainsaw."

"He cut down the fence?"

Garrelson laughed out loud. "Hell, no."

"Ouch," Mason sympathized. "Homicide?"

"Not yet," Garrelson admitted. "But my money says we have one by morning."

"Well, good luck. I think." Mason wasn't sure if Garry was using a turn of phrase or had actually bet on his victim dying. When it came to humour and gambling, cops were kind of fucked up.

"Ah, peace and quiet. Now what can I do for you?"

"Need to see if you have anything in your files on a suspect of ours." Mason slouched back in his chair, the phone tucked under his chin. "We've got a guy down here who's putting the boots to the hookers. Sent a couple of them to the hospital and tonight he laid a beating on one of my officers doing a sweep."

"What do you need?" Garrelson asked and Mason could hear the northern detective straightening up.

"We've got a name on the guy," Mason told him, "but there's nothing on him in our files. His DL has him at an address in Sudbury so I was hoping he'd have some history with you guys."

Garrelson snorted. "You'd think we'd be able to access other police records. Like the assholes don't move around. What a fucked-up system."

"Would have saved me from talking to some grouchy old fart, that's for sure."

"Yeah, fuck you, too. Go with the info."

Mason passed on Furlington's name and DOB. *Come on, give me something I can use.*

"Hang on." The phone clunked down and while he waited, Mason twined a rubber band through his fingers. Garrelson was back in less than a minute. "I've got one hit on him but you ain't gonna like it."

Of course not. Mason sighed. "Give it to me."

"He's dead," Garrelson said.

"Dead? What do you mean, dead?"

"Dead. As in not living anymore."

"Fuuuuck," Mason breathed out. The rubber band snapped. "Let's have it."

"Taylor Edward Furlington, date of birth January sixth, nineteen seventy-seven. That's your boy, right? Well, he was killed in a car accident eight years ago."

"Shit," was all that Mason could say to that.

"Somebody using this dead guy's ID?"

"Looks like it. Fuck." *Back to square one.* "Just out of morbid curiosity, what are the details?"

"Let's see." Garrelson muttered to himself as he scrolled

through the report. "I remember this one now. Thought the name was familiar. Pretty sad case. Taylor was a decent kid, real good athlete. Had a chance to make something of himself but he had a drunk for a father."

A chair creaked over the phone line and Mason could see his friend leaning back, getting ready to tell a story. Garrelson didn't disappoint.

"It was after the kid's hockey practice, I think. His mom usually picked him up, I know, because the dad, more often than not, was too pissed to drive. But that night, Mom couldn't go. Something to do with Taylor's sister, I think. Anyway, Dad picked him up, drunker than a priest after a day of confessions. Sure enough, they got into an accident on the way home. The kid was killed and the dad walked away without so much as a fucking scratch."

"God looks after drunks and fools, they say," Mason judged. "Don't fucking know why, though. Dad get done with impaired?"

"He did." Garrelson sighed and Mason didn't have to be told there was no happy jail-time ending. "He walked. The arresting officer messed up the breathalyzer demand and the case got tossed. So much for justice, eh?"

"It's a wonderful world. Anything else?"

"Not much." Garrelson paused as a pop can fizzed open in Mason's ear. "Ah, that's better." The detective belched, not bothering to cover the mouthpiece. What's a long-distance burp between professional colleagues? "After the accident, the mother started medicating herself pretty heavily and about six months later ended up dead, as well."

"Suicide?"

"Your guess is as good as mine. Suicide, homicide or that old standby, death by misadventure. Take your pick."

"Homicide? The dad?" Mason mused.

"That would be my pick," Garrelson agreed. "Story around town is that besides being a drunk, the dad was also a mean son of a bitch and beat his family whenever he was into the sauce. Which made the beatings an everyday occurrence, I'd guess."

"He ever get done for it?"

"Nope," Garrelson said disgustedly. "None of them ever complained and no witnesses ever came forward. The kids were into sports big time — the sister was almost as good an athlete as the boy — so bruises were easily explained. And the wife, well, she hardly ever came out of the house."

"So what happened?"

"Well." Garrelson slurped and belched again. "After the wife kicked off, the old man's drinking hit high gear and he lost his job at the mine. Don't know if he really felt guilty about killing his kid or just saw him as a future meal ticket. Either way, a few months later, he and the daughter moved out of town. Ain't seen or heard of them since."

"Any idea where they went?"

"Not a clue. Hang on a sec." This time Garrelson covered the phone but Mason could still hear him bellow, "Gus! Hey, butt-head! You know where old man Furlington and his kid moved to? Where? Okay, thanks. Gus thinks they went to the Sault," Garrelson told Mason.

"The where?" Mason's ears were still ringing from the detective's hollering.

Garrelson scoffed. "Sault Ste. Marie, moron. You're Canadian, right?"

"Yeah, sorry, Garry. It's been a long day. Could you do me a favour?"

"You want me to call over to the Sault and see if they have anything, right? You're thinking your man got the kid's ID from the sister, right? You find her, you find your man."

"Something like that, yeah."

Garrelson chortled. "See? You don't have to be a big-city detective to have any brains. You'll be at this number for awhile?"

"I never fucking leave," Mason bitched.

"I know the feeling. Give you a shout in a few minutes." That was Garrelson's version of goodbye and he hung up.

"Bad news, Rick?" Jack asked, coming into the office and handing Mason his drink. Jack dropped into his seat, his lunch — a Diet Coke and a package of oversized oatmeal cookies — cradled in his lap. Jenny sat next to him with her own Diet Coke and a bag of what looked like snow pressed against her face.

"You found some ice?" Mason guessed.

Jenny nodded. "Scraped it off the inside of the freezer."

"You talked to Sudbury?" Jack prompted.

"Yeah." Mason popped his Coke and guzzled half the can. "And it ain't good news." He summed up what he had learned and finished with, "I'm waiting to hear back after Garry talks to the police in Sault Ste. Marie."

And as if cued, the phone on Mason's desk rang. "Mason," he answered.

"And you say my phone etiquette sucks," Garrelson contended. "You owe me, my friend."

"Good news?" Mason refused to get his hopes up.

"Don't quite know if it's good, but it sure is interesting." Paper rustled as if Garrelson was checking his notes. "Here goes. Furlington and his kid didn't move to the Sault proper but a little town close by. Anyway, the kid hit the sports big time. The old man was always at the games, practices too, and always pissed. People learned to keep clear of him while his kid was playing. He'd pick a fight with anybody.

"And he was hard on the kid, too. People said he'd always be giving the kid shit after the games, screaming at him. If the kid had played well, Furlington would say he could do better. If the kid messed up or the team lost, well . . . The police got called a few times but Furlington was careful never to hit the kid in public."

Garrelson flipped a page. "Here's where it gets juicy. About four years ago, old man Furlington ends up with his shotgun in his mouth and the top of his head all over the living room ceiling."

"This is one fucked-up family," Mason said. "Suicide or homicide?"

Garrelson laughed. "Well, it certainly wasn't an accident. Not unless Furlington had a strange way of holding his shotgun while he was cleaning it. The official ruling was suicide but not everyone was convinced, and since the kid disappeared at the same time . . ." Mason could picture the detective shrugging as if to say, *Who knows?*

"Disappeared? You mean, took off?"

"Or Furlington killed him and dumped the body somewhere before offing himself. But from the way the old man treated him, the kid could've helped the old man with his suicide then buggered off. If you find the kid, the cops over in the Sault would appreciate a call; they'd like to ask him some questions."

"Wait, wait," Mason urged, confused. "You keep saying 'him.' You mean her, right? The son died in the car accident. Furlington left Sudbury with his daughter, that's what you said."

"Yup, I did," Garrelson said, sounding smugly pleased with himself. "That's what's so fucking weird about this. As far as anyone in the Sault knew, Furlington lived with his son, Taylor."

Mason rocked forward in his chair and thumped his elbows on his desk. "Wait a fucking minute. Are you saying Furlington was passing off his daughter as his son?" Mason caught four startled faces staring at him and he waved them to silence.

"Pretty fucked up, huh?" Garrelson sounded like a soap-opera fanatic gushing over the latest plot twist. "You should have heard the detective over in the Sault when I told him Taylor Furlington was dead. They *really* want to talk to your suspect."

Mason still wasn't convinced. "But how could he do it? How could he pass his daughter off as a boy?"

"Easy, really," Garrelson replied. "He had all his dead boy's ID. Birth certificate, health card, driver's licence, the works. They

240

were new to the Sault, no one knew their history and outside of the sports, the kid kept to himself. I mean, herself."

"Okay, I get he had all the paperwork. Did he change the photo on the DL?"

"Didn't have to," Garrelson stated as if it was obvious.

"What do you mean, didn't have to?"

"Didn't I tell you?" Garrelson asked. "The daughter, Sara, and Taylor were twins."

Taylor dropped his backpack by the old tree and squatted among the roots that ran through the dirt like protruding varicose veins. He leaned his head back against the rough bark, savouring the first rest he had allowed himself since jumping off the balcony. He scrubbed crusted blood from his brow. He searched for the night sky but it was hidden from him by the leafy canopy of intertwining branches.

He had expected the cops to show up at his door — he couldn't take the chance the bitch hadn't noticed his shirt — but not so fucking soon. He'd barely had enough time to grab some clothes and the cash he had hidden away in the kitchen before those bastards threw open his door. Ever since his feet had hit the concrete, he'd been running.

At first, he had fled in blind panic, buildings and people passing by unseen. The screech of tires and a blaring car horn had finally snapped his mindless flight; he had run onto the road. Only then did he stop, gathering his thoughts. He was on Howard Street, in the north end of St. James Town. He staggered to the sidewalk, was about to raise his hand in apology to the driver when he realized he was still holding Rico's gun. He hurriedly tucked it behind his belt, making sure his shirt kept it hidden.

Sirens, but in the distance. Were they coming for him? Since moving to the city, he had learned that sirens of all sorts — police, fire truck and ambulances — were a constant background, but never had he been so aware, so attuned, to their presence. Best to get off the streets, but where to go? Where?

They'll catch you, his dead sister whispered from deep within his mind.

"Fuck off, bitch," he growled softly. A woman pushing a stroller scampered past him, keeping a leery eye on the muscular, violent-looking man.

They'll catch you. They know you killed Father. They know everything.

"I didn't kill him, you useless cunt." Taylor looked around him, still mindful enough to see if anyone had heard him. He couldn't afford anyone calling the police about some nut talking to himself. "He killed himself, bitch. And he deserved it. After what he did . . ."

Memories, dark and terrible, swarmed through Taylor's mind, slashing and tearing. Memories, fragments of pain and humiliation, sliced at Taylor's eyes. Memories of his father . . .

a heavy leather belt, clasped in his father's hand, lashing out . . .

his drunken father screaming at him, "You're all useless. I'll show you what you're good for . . ."

Rico, snarling, "This time I want your ass . . . "

the gun going off, blood erupting from Rico's knee, Father's head . . .

the feel of wood against his cheek, Father's hand pinning his head, fumbling at Taylor's belt . . .

Father, spitting, crying, "I'll show you . . . useless . . . you're good for . . . useless, all useless . . ."

"Useless, all useless." Taylor muttered the words over and over as he huddled, cowering from the onslaught. Rocking, he moaned, "Stop, please stop. Please, Daddy, stop!"

Then Sherry was there, holding him, soothing his fears, chasing away the horrors as she had done so many times before. Sherry, he was safe with Sherry, loved. But Sherry was dead. She fell.

If you leave me, I'll tell!

Sherry falling, falling. His father crying, pleading. The shotgun kicking in his hands.

"*No!*" Taylor surged to his feet, slammed into concrete. He stumbled, pawing at the blood running into his eye, hit concrete again. Where was he? He couldn't see and the air felt stale, closed around him. He was trapped. Panic, horrifying and comforting in its mindlessness, clawed at him, gripping him tighter.

"Hey, man, you okay?"

The words, softly spoken in a gravelly voice, pierced the panic and Taylor latched onto them desperately. He kept his back pressed to the concrete behind him, splayed a hand across its rough surface. Solid. Real. Slowly, controlled, he wiped his eyes, clearing them of the obscuring blood.

Carefully, he looked about himself, but the dead were dead and not with him. He was in a tunnel, short and tight. Too much like a grave for Taylor's liking.

"You okay, buddy?"

At the tunnel's mouth, a hunched figure regarded him with cautious concern. Feeble light falling from the tunnel's ceiling barely illuminated the man, making deep gorges of the wrinkles in his face.

"Yeah, I'm . . . good. Just banged my head." Taylor backed away, sliding into the shadows hanging in the tunnel. The old man muttered something and shuffled off, leaving Taylor to fend for himself.

Taylor fought with his breathing, forced it and his heart to slow their wild galloping. He recognized where he was. The pedestrian walkway running under Bloor Street. He must have wandered into it while the memories were assaulting him. But the memories were gone, the voices quiet, relegated to their dark prisons.

The tunnel spilled out into Rosedale Valley, high above the road that twisted along its belly. A narrow bridge spanned the distance to the neighbourhood of Rosedale, but he would be too conspicuous walking those affluent streets.

Where to go? There was no going back to his apartment, he knew that, and the realization caused a pang of regret. As shitty as the apartment had been — roach-infested and falling apart — it was home. He had no home now, no safe place to go.

Safe. The word taunted him. The last time he had felt safe had been with Sherry. She had accepted him as he was, understood the scars he carried on his soul. But she was beyond him now, taken from him by some cruel, malicious God. The same God who had allowed a sadistic animal to . . .

"No," he grumbled, shoving those thoughts away. To revisit that night would invite madness and he needed to stay alert, aware of his movements. Unconsciously, he rubbed a hand across his chest, soothing ghostly pain.

He stared down into the valley, watching as the odd car passed by beneath him. The vale was dense with summer foliage, still thick and lush, untouched by the arid days of August to come. The valley snaked north through the city and could take him far from here, safely out of sight from hostile or curious eyes.

But go where? Away from here was still within the city and the city was toxic. Coming here, hoping to hide among its faceless masses, had been a mistake. There was no place safe for him.

But the question remained: where to go?

"Anywhere but here," he concluded and vaulted the railing, vanishing into the undergrowth.

How much time had passed since he had dropped from sight? He didn't know; he had lost his watch sometime, somewhere behind him as he pushed through the woods, scurrying from shadowed tree to shadowed tree. He had followed the contour of the valley, keeping well away from the road, until he had come across a path. Its broad, well-packed surface spoke of regular use but at this time of night its length was untravelled but for himself. He jogged along its empty stretches and despite his apparent solitude, he kept a wary eye ahead and behind.

The forest's peaceful stillness calmed his mind and soothed his fears. And then the trail abruptly ended, butting up against a paved, populated road. His flight had come to a sudden, despairing stop.

He sat with his back to a tree, the road a ribbon of unwanted civilization barely glimpsed through the trees. Everything was unravelling, had been for some time now. It all started with that asshole in the laneway. The asshole and his green-haired whore.

"Fucking whore. If I ever find you, I'll fucking kill you." His voice was soft yet menacing enough to silence the night creatures around him.

Unravelling. The time in the hospital, leaving Sherry. The fight with Sherry, and Sherry . . .

"Falling," he whispered. "She fell."

He waited, expecting his sister to say otherwise, but Sara was mercifully quiet. Maybe even ghosts can get tired of nagging.

All he wanted was a normal life. A life free of violent, drunken fathers, drug-addicted mothers and dead sisters who refused to stay dead. He'd come close with Sherry. The voices had stilled, the memories faded, the shame and anger chained.

But now . . . now it was all gone. Nothing but empty memories and useless hopes. As useless as the women in his life.

What about Sandra? a little voice asked, his own voice. Could he have that normal life with her? Would she accept him as he was?

No, she wouldn't. He remembered the revulsion on her face when she had touched his chest, felt the damning scars beneath his shirt.

A siren blared to life nearby and Taylor dropped to the forest floor, hugging the earth to hide from the police. But no police came and soon the siren faded from hearing.

"A fire truck," he quietly assured himself. "Or an ambulance. They aren't looking for me here. Not here."

But they *were* looking for him. He shot at the cops. Had he hit any of them? He didn't think so, but it didn't matter. Shooting at them was just as bad. They'd never stop chasing him, hunting him. They'd never stop.

"They know," Sara said from beside him.

His sister, his dead sister, was sitting on the roots next to him. Taylor uttered a short shriek of fear and flung himself away from her. He scrambled backward, pawing at the dirt and digging furrows with the heels of his shoes until he slammed hard enough into a tree to snap his head against the bark, shooting flashes of darkness across his eyes.

He clamped his eyes shut until the pain subsided, praying, hoping, that when he opened them, Sara would be gone. Cautiously he slitted his eyes, raising them slowly, fearing what he would see.

Sara was still sitting on the tree roots next to his backpack. Her hair was short, as she had always worn it; long hair had never suited her and she had hated it when it had obstructed her vision, especially in sports. She was wearing her AC/DC shirt and the old pair of jeans she refused to throw out no matter how many patch jobs Mom had done on them.

"They know," she intoned, her voice the hollow din of a broken bell. "When they catch you, everyone will know."

"I'm sorry, Sara." He held a hand out to her, reaching for her and warding her off simultaneously. "I'm sorry you're dead but you had to die. *You had to.*"

Sara sadly shook her head, but who she mourned for, Taylor didn't know. "I didn't have to die. You didn't have to kill me."

"But I did," he sobbed. "Father made me."

"Don't be blaming me, boy." Taylor's father stood off to his left, the distant streetlights shining faintly through him. "You're useless, boy. You're only good for one thing." His father reached for him.

Taylor leapt to his feet, fleeing back along the forest trail. And like any wounded, frightened animal, there was only one place for him to run to.

A woman. Jack just couldn't get his head around the possibility. Granted, Furlington — if that was his name; Jack was still favouring the idea of the sister's boyfriend using the dead brother's ID — was on the short side but the sheer savagery of the attacks said they were done at the hands of a man.

Kris and Jack temporarily had the office to themselves. Jack studied Kris. She was an amateur bodybuilder, nationally ranked, and more muscular than most guys ever dreamed of being. But even without the boob job she still wouldn't be able to pass for a man; her face was too feminine, spiky hair and all.

Kris glanced up from her computer and caught Jack staring. She smirked. "I know what you're thinking, Jack." She stretched and Jack couldn't help thinking that breasts that spectacular should not be paired with arms that freaking big. "You're wondering if I could pass for a man."

"Um, something like that," he admitted. "Okay, I can see a woman posing as a man but not fooling co-workers, people who see her all the time. No disguise is that good."

She shook her head. "Think about it, Jack. Maybe she's a masculine woman to begin with. Add in some steroids, growth hormone, testosterone and you've got one muscular woman. And if she was taking enough testosterone, it could make the bones of her face grow."

"Really?"

"Yup. You can see it with the real hardcore women bodybuilders. Their jaw and brow will thicken. Some go for surgery to have the bones shaved down."

"That's gross, but . . ."

"But you're thinking about boobs, aren't you? Typical cop." She laughed quietly. "Not every female athlete goes out and buys herself a set of jugs and you said our suspect looked pretty lean."

Jack nodded. "Not quite as lean as you get when you're competing but close. He, I mean she, whatever, wasn't carrying around much excess body fat."

"And that could take care of the boob problem. Some of the women I compete against are so flat when they diet down, if their posing suits weren't padded, they'd have no breasts at all. Or maybe our girl tapes them down."

"So you think we're looking for the sister?"

Kris shrugged. "Who knows. We could be chasing the sister or a friend of hers or someone who just happened to pick up the dead kid's ID one day. We'll know when we catch him. Or her." She smiled. "Whoever."

"Fucked up, whoever it is." Jack spun his chair to his computer. He pulled up the person-query screen and typed in the surname Furlington, searching under female this time. *Let's see what that gets us.* Jack drummed his fingers, waiting for the computer to spit out whatever information it had, but all it did was spin the hourglass icon moronically.

Wonderful. Great time for the computer to freeze up.

His cell phone chirped and it was his turn to freeze when he saw Karen's name in the display. An elated thrill squeezed his stomach but it was laced with fingers of cold dread.

He flipped the phone open. "Karen?"

"Hello, Jack."

Okay, not a warm hello but definitely not cold. I can live with that. "I'm . . ." He swallowed nervously. "I'm glad you called."

Karen paused, then said, "I don't know why *I'm* calling. Shouldn't you be the one calling me?"

"I . . ." He drew a deep breath and plunged in. "I didn't know if you wanted me to."

Another pause but what it meant — did she agree with him or not? — he didn't have a clue. "Why wouldn't I want you to call?"

"Hang on a sec." Jack left the office, seeking whatever privacy he could find in the hallway. "I'm back. Why wouldn't you want me to call?" He repeated her question, knowing he was stalling for time. But there would never be enough time. Again, he steeled himself and simply spat it out. "I've been thinking about what you said, that you deserve better, and maybe . . . maybe you're right."

"You think you're not good enough for me? Is that what you're saying?"

Sy dead, Jenny almost shot then brutalized. Karen taken hostage in their own home, pistol-whipped. Despair and guilt draped across his shoulders like a wet, heavy blanket.

"I don't know," he whispered. "Maybe."

"I can't believe what you're saying," Karen said and now her voice was cold. "I spent most of today arguing with my parents. They both think I should leave you. And every hour you didn't call or show up at their house gave more weight to their argument, proved to them I could do better. They said if you truly loved me, you'd come after me. I told them you would but you didn't. You didn't."

The hurt in Karen's voice was palpable and it hit Jack in the guts like a cold knife. *I caused that*, he thought wretchedly. *I'm so sorry, Karen.* "I wanted to, but . . ." *But maybe you'd be better off without me.*

"But what, Jack? What?" Karen's pain was frosting over, icing into a cold anger. "I waited for you to call and you didn't. So I need to know, Jack, what's more important to you. Me or the job and that tramp you work with?"

"That's not fair, Karen. We were doing a hooker sweep and she had to dress like that." Jack felt his anger stirring.

"Just tell me, Jack," Karen demanded venomously. "How long have you been fucking her?"

"What?" Jack couldn't believe what he heard. "I'm not —" He looked up and down the hall furtively. "I'm not fucking her," he said in a forced hush.

"Then why are you whispering, Jack? Don't want your girl-friend to hear?"

"I'm at work, Karen," Jack defended hotly. "It's not exactly the most private place for this kind of talk."

"Then come home, Jack," she said simply.

"You're home? At our house?" Hope fluttered excitedly in Jack's stomach. If she had come back to the house . . .

"Yes, Jack. I'm home. So come home and we'll talk."

"I . . . I can't," he said miserably, Jenny's battered face stared at him accusingly from within his thoughts.

"Can't or won't?" Karen challenged.

"Don't you think I want to? But I can't, Karen. We're —"

"Goodbye, Jack." Karen hung up.

Jack stared at the silent phone in his hand. He punched in Karen's number. He had to make her understand. He couldn't go home, not with that maniac out there. If Jack left now and someone else got hurt — another woman or a cop trying to arrest that asshole — he would feel responsible. Fuck, what if a copper got shot? The asshole had already fired at cops. Jack had to make Karen understand. They could talk tomorrow, all day. They could go to counselling if she wanted to. They could —

Her phone went straight to voicemail.

"Fuck!"

Jack's anger ripped through the bog of guilt and bleakness he was wading in and he threw his cell phone at the wall. It exploded in a brief shower of plastic and electronics.

Kris stepped out of the office. "You okay?" she asked, eying the demolished phone.

"Yeah," he said wearily. God, he was tired. Tired of all the shit with Karen and her parents. Tired of being forced to choose. Just tired. He forced a sickly smile. "Just a bit of a domestic, that's all."

"Ohhhh-kay," Kris said uncertainly. "Do you need to go home?"

Jack shook his head. "I doubt there's anything there for me now." He scooped up the remains of his phone and dumped them in the trash next to his desk, then sank into his chair. *Fuck, what a mess.*

I'll fix it later, he promised himself. *I'll fix it tomorrow, Karen. I swear.*

But could he? Could it be fixed? Something had broken between him and Karen just now and he would have to admit that it might be beyond fixing.

He turned to his computer. *Might as well finish up —*

His search request had finally come back and he stared at it in disbelief.

"Kris," he said slowly. "Get Mason in here. I know who Furlington really is."

Friday, 27 July
0107 hours

"Stand by for the hotshot." The dispatcher paused as details were relayed to her. *"5111's area. Large fight at the Guvernment nightclub, 132 Queens Quay. Ten to twelve people fighting, unknown weapons at this time. Units to respond."*

"Don't bother," Jenny reproached, slapping at Jack's hand as he reached for the radio. "Mason wants us to talk to that stripper and there's plenty of cars going. Besides, I doubt we'd be that much help, anyways. You with a broken rib and me with a busted-up face."

"Yeah, guess you're right," Jack reluctantly admitted. He stopped at the red light at Parliament and watched wistfully as two scout cars flew through the intersection, lights and sirens blazing.

"Are you sure?" Jenny asked. "About Furlington, I mean."

"Absolutely. I was there, remember? Fuck, what a bloody

mess that was. I've never seen so much blood."

"More than the machete killing Manny's working?"

Jack nodded. "Buckets." The light turned green and Jack checked the time. "Just after one. The stripper should still be there."

"Unless she's already bailed to hook up with her boyfriend." She paused then looked purposefully at her partner. "I hear your cell phone had a little mishap earlier."

"What? Oh, yeah," Jack confessed, chagrined. "Just a little disagreement with Karen."

"About?"

Jack sighed. "About why I didn't call, why I wasn't at home, why I put the job ahead of her all the time. And when I said I couldn't come home, she hung up on me."

Jenny winced. "That doesn't sound good."

"Nope," Jack agreed, shaking his head. "Sounded pretty final to me."

Jenny touched his shoulder in support. "You could go home, Jack. You don't have to stay."

He shook his head again. "This guy tunes you up, takes a couple of shots at us and you think I should go home? No way. Not while there's still a chance of catching him. If you or anyone else got hurt . . . No way. I'm staying."

"I understand why you're staying, but Karen may not."

"It wouldn't matter, Jenny. Whether I go or stay tonight won't break or fix us. Karen and I, I mean," he said as he pulled the unmarked car to the curb out front of Filmore's.

"Any unit to respond to a possible entry in progress. 285 Shuter, apartment 712. The complainant says a male is entering an apartment that is supposed to be vacant. Apparently, there was a suicide or suspicious death there last week. Any unit?"

Jack froze with one foot out of the car when the dispatcher announced the address. "Get in the car," he told Jenny. "Get in right now."

She jumped back in and Jack wheeled away from the curb, pulling a tight U-turn on Dundas and heading for Sherbourne Street.

"What is it?" she asked as she buckled her seat belt.

"It's him. Furlington. That's where he used to live."

"Damn," Jenny breathed. She hoisted the mike. "MK 51, put us on that call on Shuter."

"10-4, Major Crime. I have no one to back you up at this time."

"10-4, dispatch. We'll advise."

Traffic was all but non-existent and Jack flew down Sherbourne. He didn't slow enough for the left onto Shuter and the Taurus's rear end slewed sideways. Jack fought the skid, righted the car and tromped the gas.

"Guess the suspicious death is a little more suspicious now that our friend is involved."

"I'll put my money on homicide," Jack said as he pulled into the parking lot. 285 Shuter was the middle of three high-rises in Moss Park and Jack screeched the car to a halt by the front doors. They ran for the front door, Glocks already in hand, passing a group of residents drinking on the minuscule lawn attached to one of the ground-floor units.

"Somebody's gonna get their ass kicked," one of the drinkers commented as the two cops sprinted by.

Jack punched the elevator button but Jenny ran past him. "Stairs are faster." She tugged open the stairwell door and darted inside. Jack followed her up the stairs, pulling on the metal railing with his left hand to haul himself up the flights faster.

Without needing to say anything, they both stopped the sprint at the fifth floor and proceeded the rest of the way cautiously, ears and eyes keyed to the floors above them. They paused by the seventh-floor door and Jenny slowly eased it open. The building was shaped like a wide V and Jack hated the layout. They were in the middle stairwell and would have to step out into the hall to see down either branch of the V.

They slid into the hall, back to back, each taking a different arm of the floor. "This way," Jack whispered, recalling the apartment's location from his last visit. That time he'd been with Manny and they had no idea what they were about to step into.

The door to 712 was closed. Neither the frame nor the door showed any signs of forced entry.

Guess the fucker still has a key.

Jack checked with his partner across the door and she nodded. Jack reached for the doorknob.

Moonlight blended with the artificial glare from the streets below to cast a meagre light through the balcony windows. Taylor sat in the shadowed apartment, feeling for the first time in days safe and secure. He knew he couldn't stay here for long; it was only a matter of time before the police learned of his connection to Sherry's old home, but for now, for tonight, he could stop running.

He sank his head into the armchair's cushy back and closed his eyes. When he had moved in with Sherry, the only furniture she'd had in the living room was a three-legged sofa and a TV. A mattress on the floor in the bedroom had passed for a bed. Even the dining nook off the living room by the balcony door had been bare.

Taylor ran his hands lovingly along the chair's overstuffed arms. It was the first piece of furniture they had purchased as a couple.

Home. This had been his home and would probably be the closest he ever came to having a normal life. If he managed to stay alive. Rico and the police both had reason to want him dead.

The room was hot and stuffy, the air baked lifeless from the week's heat. He was surprised the apartment hadn't been rented out yet, but maybe even Housing had some respect for the dead. All that remained to give silent testimony to the tragedy that had occurred here were a few latex gloves scattered on the floor, their blue colour muted and sad in the dimness.

Taylor wiped wetness from his face. Tears or sweat, he didn't know. He'd run to the apartment, keeping to the woods, then laneways among the concrete forest. He hadn't even considered what he would do if his key no longer worked, but it had and once he was inside the familiar walls, the voices — Sherry's, his father's, but mostly Sara's — had fallen silent. And silent, thank God, they stayed.

Taylor's eyes snapped open, focusing on the door across the room. Had he locked it behind himself? He couldn't remember.

He pushed himself up and quietly crept across the floor, careful not to wake the ghosts. After locking up, he would go to the bedroom and wrap himself in the sheets he and Sherry used to sleep in, love in, live in. He wondered if they would still have her smell on them. He hoped so.

He reached for the doorknob just as it began to slowly turn.

Jack faced Jenny across the width of the door and nodded, *one, two . . .*

Three!

Jack flung open the door, yelling, "Police! Don't move!"

After the bright lights in the hallway, the dim apartment was almost pitch black. Directly ahead was the little walk-through kitchen with the living room off to the right. Jack cut right, sweeping the living room with his gun. Jenny's responsibility was the hallway on the left, leading to the bedroom. She scanned the kitchen — empty — as she swung to her left.

And that's when things went bad, fast.

A shadow lunged out at her and smashed the gun from her hands. The force of the impact across her wrists threw her off balance and she was helpless as an arm, the muscles as rigid as iron, snaked around her throat. She was pulled tight against a body and what could only be the barrel of a gun was pressed to her temple.

"Move and you're dead, bitch," a hard voice rasped in her ear.

"Drop the gun and let her go. Do it now!" Jack was not ten feet away, his Glock thrust in front of him, rock steady and aimed somewhere to the right of her head.

Furlington just chuckled and inched to his right. Jenny balked, refusing to co-operate, but the arm encircling her throat squeezed threateningly and she was forced to shuffle-step sideways.

"Let's keep this private." Furlington toed the door shut. "Lock it, bitch," he ordered. He dug the gun in when she failed to move. "I said, lock the fucking door, bitch."

Ever so slightly, Jack nodded, so Jenny reached out to her side, groping blindly until she found the deadbolt. A flick of her fingers locked the three of them in the apartment.

"It's over, Furlington," Jack said, speaking slowly and clearly. "We know who you really are."

Furlington flinched as if Jack's words had physically struck him.

"Just open your hand and drop the gun," Jack coaxed. "You drop the gun and let her go and we all walk away from this. It's over."

"Bullshit," Furlington snarled. "Nothing's over. You know my name. Big fucking deal. That don't mean shit."

"Let her go," Jack ordered from behind the sights of his gun. "Let her go, Sara."

Furlington moaned at the sound of the name. "That's not my name," he groaned. "That useless bitch is dead."

"No, she isn't. She isn't dead. You're Sara."

Furlington moaned again, a deep, wounded sound. Jenny began to slowly inch her hands up to Furlington's arm.

"No, no, no." Jenny could feel Furlington's head shaking in denial, in refusal of the truth. "I'm not Sara. Sara's dead. I'm Taylor." He thrust the gun at Jack. "My name is Taylor!"

As soon as Furlington's arm straightened out, Jenny reached for it. If she could pull the gun away from Jack —

Roaring in anger, Furlington shoved Jenny at Jack, driving her forward with a hand on her back. Jack couldn't get out of the way — Jenny's face slammed into something hard and her world exploded in darkness.

Not again. Not again. Not again.

The words echoed in Jack's head like a funeral bell tolling endlessly. Another standoff, another partner taken hostage. Jack's vision wavered and suddenly an image of Sy, a knife to his neck, ghosted in front of Jenny. Jack's hands were slick with Sy's hot blood.

No! Not now!

He violently shoved the memory away. He had to concentrate. Jenny's life depended on it.

Furlington had a thick arm wrapped around Jenny's neck and a snub-nosed revolver, its silver skin gleaming deadly in the dim light, pressed to her temple. His face was hidden behind the gun and Jenny's hair. The target was too small; Jack dared not risk a shot, even as close as he was.

All he could do was talk, reason with Furlington, get her to drop the gun. He couldn't even reach for the mitre in his back pocket; he needed both hands on his gun in case an opportunity arose. If this was a movie, he'd know the words to say to gain Furlington's trust, to work past the anger, but how could he reason with a woman who's been masquerading as her dead brother since she was sixteen?

Reason and orders weren't working. The only thing that elicited a reaction was confronting her with the truth about herself.

If I can get her mad enough to point the gun at me, it might give Jenny the chance she needs. He noticed Jenny's hands slowly creeping upwards.

"No, she isn't," Jack said. "She isn't dead. You're Sara."

"My name is Taylor!" Furlington screamed, shoving the gun toward Jack.

Jenny lunged for Furlington's arm as it straightened out, then suddenly she was flying at Jack, the crazed woman driving her forward. Jack had time to pull his gun up out of the way before Jenny crashed into him but that was all. Jenny's injured face whacked into his elbow as the three of them tumbled to the floor.

Furlington shoved Jenny's limp form aside and pounced on Jack. Her knees drove into his broken rib and pain, nauseatingly sharp and exquisite, exploded in him. He couldn't hold back a scream. Furlington pinned Jack's gun hand then swiped her gun at his head. The barrel cracked off his skull and his vision flared with spots of darkness.

Furlington's voice came out of the inky blackness. "Got a problem with your ribs, fucker?"

Furlington stretched a leg back then drove it forward. Jack tried to curl protectively around his rib, bracing himself for the blow, but nothing he did could have prepared him for the white-hot lance of agony that ripped through his guts. His gun was wrenched from his hand and he dimly heard it clatter onto the floor.

Fucked. I'm fucked.

Cold steel kissed Jack on the forehead. His eyes refused to focus; Furlington was a large blur as she held her gun to Jack's head.

"What's my name, fucker?" When he didn't answer, she nudged him in the ribs and his stomach clenched against the burst of pain. "What's my name?"

"Doesn't . . . matter." Jack forced the words out through gritted teeth.

"I'm Taylor, you fucker. Taylor." She leaned on the gun and Jack concentrated on the precise circle of pressure, using it to block out the pain in his rib and the throbbing in his skull.

"It doesn't matter what you call yourself," Jack said once he could speak without gagging. "If you kill a cop, you'll go to prison for the rest of your life. A *women's* prison." The weight behind the gun eased up and Jack pushed harder. "You'll be forced to live as Sara. There'll be no hiding who you are. You'll be Sara and your brother will be dead for good."

Jack could feel the gun quivering where it touched his sweat-soaked skin. Quivering in uncertainty? Or rage?

"Give up now and Taylor will live. Kill me and you kill Taylor."

"Fuck you." Furlington's hand lashed out again and struck Jack in the jaw with the butt of the gun. More pain and blood flooded his mouth.

Strong hands gripped his shirt and smoothly pulled him to his feet. Jack tried to use the momentum to land an elbow but Furlington brushed his arm away contemptuously.

"My name is Taylor," she whispered hoarsely in his ear before driving a fist into his stomach. Jack doubled over and caught her knee in his face. Something cracked and new daggers of pain sliced through the agonized cloud already clogging his head.

Furlington seized his shirt with one hand and grabbed a handful of hair with the other. She spun once, Jack's feet tripping across the floor as she twirled him around like a child, then flung him away. He had an instant of freedom before he crashed through the glass door and out onto the balcony. He slammed into the railing and his head snapped back as if the metal barrier had just rear-ended him.

He collapsed to his knees, only one hand desperately gripping the railing holding him upright.

Glass crunched as Furlington followed him onto the balcony.

Jack slowly lifted his head. The pain from his rib, mouth and skull had massed into one throbbing, pounding entity. His vision wavered. Furlington blurred, became two, three, then back to one person. Jack's baton was tucked into his back pocket and his hand ineffectively twitched toward it as Furlington dragged him upright again.

Leaning in close to Jack, close enough to kiss, she told him, "Time to die, fucker."

"The same way . . . you killed your girlfriend?" Jack managed.

Furlington jerked back. "What?"

Jack's mouth didn't want to work; it was wadded up with pain. He spat a mouthful of blood, dimly aware that most of it ran down his chin.

"Like you killed Sherry?" Talking hurt. He sucked in a ragged breath. Breathing hurt more. "Throw me over, too?"

Furlington flinched as if Jack had physically struck her. "Sherry jumped. I didn't push her. She jumped."

Furlington let go of Jack and he slowly toppled to the side, fetching up in the balcony's corner. His rib issued another bark as he thumped into the railing. He wrapped his arms around the railing to keep from collapsing.

"She jumped," Furlington was muttering. "She said if I left her she'd tell. She jumped, I didn't push her." Her head came up, eyes suddenly, firmly, fixating on Jack. "I didn't push her but I'm gonna push you." One hand gripped Jack's throat, the other his belt. "Say goodbye, fucker."

The pain in Jack's head was gradually ebbing, receding to a level where he could think. *Time, I need time.*

"You . . . owe me . . . your life," he wheezed.

"What are you shitting about?" She laughed uncertainly.

"Four months ago." He forced the words out between clenched teeth; the hand on his throat was jamming his jaws together. "In the bathroom down the hall."

"No! Shut up!" Furlington dropped Jack. His heels struck the concrete floor with a jarring thump, rippling a shockwave of pain up through his body. He threw out his hands to the sides, desperately gripping the railing to keep from falling.

Furlington moaned and Jack could hear her pain, could almost share it; he knew how agonizing memories could be. He had her shocked, stunned, but to live he was going to have to do more than that. His hand fell to the butt of his baton. He was only going to get one swing at her and it would have to count.

"I saved your life," he pushed. He slid the baton free of his pocket, held it closed, gripped it like an ice pick. "The night Randall Kayne raped you." *One shot to the temple and pray it's enough.* "The night you cut your breasts off."

"No, no, no." Furlington chanted the word as she shook her head. Her hands went to her chest, clutching at the ragged scars Jack was sure lay beneath her shirt. "I'm not Sara. Sara's dead."

Jack took an unsteady step toward her, within arm's reach. Furlington was lost in her own world, oblivious.

"I'm not Sara. I'm Taylor." Furlington's head snapped up. She screamed, "My name is Taylor!"

Now! Jack fought through the pain, ate it and spat it back out. Roaring his defiance, he swung his steel ice pick with everything he had.

Furlington casually leaned back and the tip of the baton passed harmlessly by her eyes.

Jack had twisted when he swung. His broken rib was an open target and Furlington drove a fist into it. Jack screamed again, sheer agony this time, and fell to his knees. The baton clanged free from his suddenly useless hand.

Furlington sank both hands into Jack's hair and once more, for the final time, pulled him to his feet. "Pathetic," she sneered. "You're as weak as she is."

A shadow moved behind Furlington. The shadow lashed out and there was a cracking thud. Furlington grunted and her knees buckled. She fell forward into Jack's arms and the sudden weight almost pulled him over. He locked his knees and Furlington clung to him, posed like a pleading lover.

"Hit her again!" Jack cried.

Jenny swung her baton again, driving the butt solidly against Furlington's skull. This time, delivered from above, the blow carried tremendous force and Furlington's eyes rolled up as if she had suddenly found all the answers in the night sky. Her hands slipped free of Jack's shirt and she slowly toppled to the side, then crashed to the floor.

Jenny stepped from the shadows, her baton held at the ready in case Furlington twitched. "You okay?"

Jack nodded. "Fucking sore but I'll live."

"Good." She knelt and quickly snapped handcuffs on an unresisting Furlington. With the last metal click, she sagged in relief. She laughed, then fixed Jack with a serious stare. "Can we have one night when we don't get into a fight with someone?"

Jack started to laugh then winced and pressed a hand to his head. "I'm going to have a fucking hell of a headache. And yes, no more fights. I think we've had our quota for the year."

"Good," Jenny repeated. She looked into the apartment. "Now help me find my damn gun."

Jack pulled into his empty driveway in front of what he was sure was his empty house. The Honda was still absent from the driveway's left side. Jack had taken to parking in the same spot to minimize the oil stains from the slightly incontinent old Ford.

Old car, old cop.

Jack turned off the engine and simply sat still. It felt like he hadn't stopped moving since . . . well, since forever. Even at the hospital, in between X-rays and concerned doctors, he was busy. Busy apprising Mason, busy checking on Jenny, busy answering questions, busy doing his notes.

Now, finally, blessed peace.

He was amazed he was home this early. If the doctors had had their way, he'd still be in St. Mike's, but Jack had insisted on gathering up his collection of injuries and heading home. And it was an impressive collection: a broken rib — not just cracked anymore — a slight concussion, a stitched-up lip, a few loose teeth and a broken nose.

He felt like how Jesse Polan had looked.

He fingered the splint holding his nose in line. *Guess I deserved it; I've busted a few over the last year or so. Welcome to the crooked nose club, Jack.*

Jenny's doctor friend had poked and prodded Jack, all the while poking and prodding for info on Jenny. He had also seen to Jenny and even though her injuries were a lot less severe than Jack's — nothing broken, nothing stitched, just one big-ass black eye, thankfully — Brian had spent much more time with her. Jack figured their weekend date had gotten off to an early start.

Well, at least someone's love life is going well.

Jack stared at his house and wondered how much of a home it would feel like without Karen.

Not much, I'm guessing.

He eased himself out of the car. The heavy air settled around him like a wet blanket, matching his feelings perfectly. It was good that Karen wasn't home. And she was right, she didn't deserve this. She didn't deserve to suffer a husband who came home all too often with troubling injuries and who today had come far too close to not coming home ever again.

I had my ass handed to me by a woman and if not for Jenny, I'd be nothing but a stain on the parking lot.

"You're right, Kare. You can do better than me." He had failed the people most important to him. Karen should get as far away from him as possible before he did it again. That thought hurt him deep inside and it was a hurt no amount of painkillers could erase.

Thank God for Justice. A slight smile twitched Jack's swollen lips as he shuffled across his neighbour's front yard.

"Holy shit, Jack. Are you okay?" His neighbour stared at him in shock.

"I'll live," Jack assured him. "Just had a run-in with someone. I'll tell you the whole story some other time, Mick. Right now I just want to grab Justice and drug myself to sleep."

"I guess." Mick hooked a thumb over his shoulder. "Justice is out back playing with the kids. I'll go get him. He may be a bit wet; the kids were playing with the sprinkler."

Jack smiled. Or tried to. "That's okay. Thanks for looking after him."

"Any time, Jack. I'll be right back."

Jack leaned against the wall and gently closed his eyes. *A run-in with someone?* That was one way of putting it. One fucked-up, juiced-up crazy lady.

Furlington had escaped the fight with the fewest injuries. Her skull was thicker than her delusions. She was facing a slew of charges, starting with attempted murder and going from there. Mason had still been typing when Jack had left and probably wouldn't stop until Furlington was hauled off to Show Cause court tomorrow morning. Not that Jack figured she'd ever face any of her charges in court. It was a safe bet she'd be declared mentally unfit for trial and end up in a padded room somewhere.

And once the current charges were all typed up, Mason would be digging through four years' worth of old occurrences to see how many could be laid at Furlington's feet, starting with her girlfriend's death. Jack remembered the distraught, frail girl from the night Furlington had mutilated herself after being raped by that savage Kayne. She'd been hysterical and had obviously cared for Furlington deeply. And she was dead.

Did Furlington kill her or did Sherry jump off the balcony? Only Furlington knew the truth and Jack had serious doubts about her memory. Anyone who could convince herself she was her dead brother could easily recall a homicide as a suicide. And in the end, it really didn't matter. Sherry was dead and nothing would change that.

It was the same with Furlington's father. The Sault Ste. Marie police could question her all they wanted, lay as many charges as they deemed appropriate, but it wouldn't matter. Dead was dead.

The frenzied skittering of nails on tile brought Jack out of his thoughts. Justice bounded onto the porch, turning circles and barking excitedly. All the shit and darkness weighing Jack down sloughed off his shoulders with Justice's animated greeting.

Slowly, carefully, Jack knelt. The shepherd — and yes, he was indeed wet but Jack didn't give a damn — calmed almost immediately and gently nosed the bandages on Jack's face. He tenderly licked the stitches holding Jack's lip together and whined softly as if to say he understood Jack's pain.

Jack smiled — fuck the stitches — and felt his eyes tearing up. It was good to have someone who loved him waiting for him to come home.